THE COMPROMISED LADY

RITA BOUCHER

OLIVER
HEBER
BOOKS

Published by Oliver-Heber Books

0 9 8 7 6 5 4 3 2 1

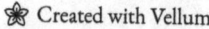 Created with Vellum

To Amy, Binnie, Chassie, Connie, Katherine, Linda, Nancy, Randi, Ruth and Toby, for the decades of encouragement, advice, and support and keeping the group zooming in these troubled times.

ONE

PORTUGAL, 1808

"Scots, wha hae wi Wallace bled,
Scots, wham Bruce has aften led,
Welcome to your gory bed,
Or to victorie."

— ROBERT BURNS, "SCOTS
WHA HAE"

T he sun had just set over the river, and Captain
Stephan Aubrey leaned back in his chair, his
hands steepled, as he waited for his host, Alec,
Lord Denby, to make his move on the chess board.
Now, with the dark setting in, the comfortable room
appeared much like any London library, with well-
stuffed chairs and a hearth to warm the chill from
winter nights.

Only the books on the shelves gave a hint that this
was not England. Both original volumes of *Don Quixote*
sat side by side upon shelves full of other works in Spanish, Portuguese, Latin, and Greek. A few English tomes
sat in ironic proximity to those in French. No doubt the
villa was the property of an educated man, likely one of
the aristocrats who had fled with the Portuguese royal
court in the face of Napoleon's invasion.

During the day, however, one had only to glance out a window to know this was not England. The spectacular views from the hillside were of the red tile roofs and sere landscapes of Portugal. Far too close for comfort, Napoleon's troops were ravaging the Iberian Peninsula. Despite the influx of hordes of civilians fleeing the clashing French, British, Spanish, and Portuguese armies, Alec had managed to procure prime lodgings. The villa was superior by far to the housing secured by the rest of the English diplomatic legation, providing yet another sore point between Alec and his newly appointed superior, Stephan's cousin, Lord Camford.

The absentee owner of the villa had also left behind an excellent cellar, and Alec never travelled without his own stock of fine liquors. After a superb dinner, Stephan and his host were enjoying a dram and a hard-fought game of chess. Alec moved up his pawn and Stephan pounced, taking it with his knight and catching the baron in a fork that would either cost him a bishop or a rook.

Lord Denby groaned. "Might as well have gone off to attend your cousin's congratulatory dinner if I had wished to be humiliated tonight."

"I'm grateful that you didn't, although somewhat surprised, I admit," Stephan ventured, his curiosity getting the better of him. "I know why *I* am not in attendance. General Wellesley and his brother, the Foreign Secretary, are well aware that George can't stomach the sight of me."

Predictably, Alec elected to save his rook. "You would do far better for the title than either George or his son," he commented.

"Not a situation I desire, in any case," Stephan said, taking the bishop. "However, I do know that you were the best candidate for the post George is filling. Tonight's fete should be in *your* honor."

"These things happen all the time in the world of diplomacy," Alec said, with a wry twist of his lip.

"Curious about that." Stephan picked up his whisky and stared at the fractured glitter of candlelight through the crystal. "I would have thought that you might put a good face upon it and raise your glass of hypocrisy along with the rest of those who heartily detest George and wish him to purgatory."

"You are sorry that I am not out toasting George's success?" Alec lifted a hoary brow.

"Quite the contrary," Stephan admitted with a laugh. "Otherwise I would be eating questionable vittles with the other poor unfortunates who are not attending the celebration. I fully agree that George is an idiot, wholly unsuited to any office requiring any measure of brains."

"An idiot with a great deal of influence, unfortunately." The baron rose, trying to put his weight on his foot yet again. Stephan caught Alec before he fell, and eased him back onto the divan.

"If you keep on doing that, I will begin to doubt *your* intelligence," the Captain chided. "When I said that nothing is broken, it is only battlefield experience speaking. I am no doctor. Nonetheless, I can tell you of a certainty that you must keep your weight off of that ankle or else you may do yourself further injury."

"What if I bind it?" Alec suggested. "Use a walking stick of some kind?"

"Why on earth are you so determined to be up and about?" Stephan asked. "You must have tried to step upon it at least half a dozen times since you tripped down the stairs? And you look at the clock every few minutes as if you are expecting it to explode at the next tick."

"I suppose there is no help for it." Lord Denby muttered a curse. "This leg of mine will not serve. I was supposed to meet tonight with a man known as the Bruce.

He has some critical information that he was supposed to pass on to me. It should be no more difficult than picking up a parcel from a tradesman."

. . .

It should be no more difficult than...

As he made his way through the city, Stephan shook his head, castigating himself for his own gullibility. As a military man, he should have known better from the moment he heard that phrase. All too many orders from superiors were variations upon that theme. In Stephan's experience, most estimations of simplicity usually meant ignorance of the difficulty involved.

The night seemed particularly fraught with ill portent. Although he could not yet see the river, a mist rose up, sending fog fingers into the town's twisted alleyways. The moon was obscured by scudding clouds, giving occasional light, and imbuing shadows with the semblance of motion. He shivered, not with cold. The instincts that had warned him to watch his back on the battlefield had him reaching for his pistol, only to let it slide back into its concealment with a snort of amused acknowledgement at himself for entertaining useless fears.

He had often come this way by day, when the plaza was filled with shouting children and quarrelsome housewives, haggling fishmongers, baskets balanced atop their heads as they loudly proclaimed the quality of their wares.

But by night, this part of the town had undergone a seemingly sinister transformation. Stalls were shuttered. The only open doors were those of the *tavernas*. The smell of grilling sardines reminded him that it had been long hours since his meal. A guitar strummed the opening strains of a *despedida*, but the words of pain and loss faded into unintelligible echoes.

Stephan drew up the hood of the black cloak that Alec had provided. Moving parallel to the winding water and scanning to search for the landmarks that would guide him to the rendezvous point; he skirted the wavering puddles of moonlight.

Finally, he found the narrow flight of steps that led to the appointed square. It was a long climb and he paused in the dim illumination to check his father's timepiece. Even with the river as his guide, it was difficult to find identifying features in the streets transformed by night.

It was not yet the hour, and the Bruce was due at the half.

Too early.

So Stephan located a lookout in the lee of a doorway and kept his eye on the possible points of entry. He was beginning to mourn the fact that he had forfeited a night of dreaming on a good featherbed, when a shrouded figure was momentarily limned by the moon. A glimmer reflected briefly in the well-polished sheen of boots. What little could be seen of the unknown's garb seemed to be in keeping with an English gentleman, but before Stephan could move, the shadow slipped back into the pool of cover.

Was this the Bruce then? A domino had shielded the man's face from view. Stephan waited to hear the pass phrase that Alec had given him, but the figure remained curiously silent. Just as the Captain was about to reveal his presence, an urchin made a cautious foray into the square. Due to his dark clothing, the child had been nigh on invisible until he stepped into the open.

The shadow blocked the boy's path back to the stairs. "I know you have it."

The urchin halted.

Although Stephan could make out the words, the man's voice was strangely distorted by the accoustics of the empty plaza and the sounds of the nearby river.

"I will let you live if you give it to me, *now*." The man's echoing reply was punctuated by a gale of contemptuous laughter, magnified into a macabre flood of sound that ended abruptly as a stone flew and hit the shadow's shoulder. With a roar, he ran at the youngling, who fled into one of the archways that led to a multiplicity of paths tangling into the warren of streets and alleyways. Strangely, instead of following the boy, the dark figure stood, watching and waiting.

Though Stephan did not understand the drama that had taken place before him, there seemed no more need for hesitation. The use of English left little doubt in his mind that the watcher was the Bruce, anticipating contact. Once again, the Captain was about to step into the open when, unexplainably, the ragamuffin returned.

This time, his well-aimed rock knocked the Englishman off his feet. As the boy's gaze swept the small plaza, a blade glinted in his hand, silvered in a thread of light as the clouds passed to reveal the full moon. The ragamuffin assumed a stance that announced readiness to defend or fight. Once again, he scanned the surroundings as if expecting...

Someone.

He was stalling for time. Was an ambush about to unfold?

Stephan pulled his pistol and stepped into the open. He noticed the metal flash of the barrel, even as the boy's shout of warning echoed.

"'Ware the gun!"

The ball that would likely have left Stephan gut-shot dislodged a chip of stone instead, hitting his hand and spoiling his aim as he returned fire and ducked back into cover.

A second report echoed. Scrambling to his feet, the attacker retreated, scanning the square in confusion, but the waif had used the distraction to disappear. With both pistols spent, the would-be killer apparently decided to do the same. He turned and ran.

Stephan searched for signs of the boy, but he had chosen his lookout well. Half a dozen bolt holes led to the stews of the city.

"*Scots wha hae, wi Wallace bled,*" a reedy voice echoed in a faint whisper.

"*Welcome to your gory bed, or to victorie.*" Stephan swiveled toward the sound as he supplied the requisite response.

"Left, guv'ner."

In the corner of a filthy alleyway, curled upon himself so tightly that he was nigh onto invisible in his dark clothes, the urchin waited, wicked blade at the ready.

"You can put that by, now" Stephan said.

"Makin' sure you ain't been followed." The pup's voice was pitched low, the words barely discernable. The knife disappeared and with a gasp, he rose.

"You're hurt."

"Been worse." The boy beckoned him back to the place where he had first appeared and pointed to a midden pile in the corner of the blind alley. "Dig at th' left bottom, near th' wall."

Even in the dark, his revulsion must have been evident, because the urchin gave a quietly mocking laugh. "Afeared t'get yer 'ands dirty, boyo?"

"A clever hiding place." Stephan tried to mask his reluctance as he dug an oilcloth-wrapped packet out of the heap filled with muck and feces.

"Lookin' forward t'see 'is lordship diggin' it out, I was. But you ain't Denby." The cub turned and staggered, putting a hand on the wall for support as he slowly made his way back towards the square. "Bruce says better t'ditch th' goods lest wrong 'uns gettin' mitts on't."

"Wisdom, indeed." Stephan moved forward to help

the lad, but the child held up a hand that bade him to come no closer.

"You can barely stand," the Captain observed. "Best come with me."

"No worry of yours. Time t'be gone." Slumping shoulders conveyed a world of weariness despite the display of bravado.

"Where are you going?"

"T'find that bastard and finish him." Although softly spoken, the words were no less than an oath. The Cockney accent was fading, steps becoming stumbles. "As for you, get the cursed dispatches to the Wellesley brothers and bid them to better manage the family business that they have made of the Peninsula!"

Stephan reached out to hold the urchin upright, but when he clasped him by the arm, the boy gasped and pulled away.

As Stephan stared at his now bloody fingers, the waif's cap slipped to the ground. A fall of dark hair tumbled down the child's back.

The—*girl* took another step in retreat, then fell to her knees, tracks of tears glistening on her cheeks as she took a deep breath.

"Tell them that the Bruce is dead and likely Hendricks as well!" Abandoning her attempt to disguise her voice entirely, she commanded him with the diction and icy hauteur that would have done credit to a duchess. "Tell them that my father is dead, and that he will haunt them on their way to Hell. As will I."

Her eyes rolled upward as she crumpled to the ground.

The darkness of the chit's shirt had hidden the stain spreading on her arm. Clearly a ball had met its mark. It was a marvel indeed that she had remained upright, given the severity of the wound.

With the possibility that their assailant might return with assistance, there was no time to waste. Stephan staunched the bleeding as best he could before wrapping her in his cloak and hoisting her over his shoulder. To his surprise, the girl was not as slight as she appeared, and he could feel the ripe, lush curves of a woman grown. Beneath the smells of the street, he caught her scent, notes of jasmine and cinnamon.

Castigating himself for his wayward thoughts, the Captain prayed for strength as he concentrated on the tasks of staying on his feet and keeping them both alive. It would be shameful indeed if he failed to deliver the package that had seemingly cost England one of its agents, and might yet take the life of the woman who claimed to be his daughter.

. . .

Stephan had left the gate to the hillside terrace unlatched, and he carried his burden directly into the library.

"There you are at last! I was beginning to think that--" Alec winced as he hoisted himself up from his chair. His annoyed expression changed to one of consternation as he turned to see the crimson stains coating his protégé's neck and hands.

"She's bleeding." Stephan gently placed the wounded woman on the divan "Damnation, it's started again," he observed, as he peeled away the cloak.

"Fiona!"

"You know her?" Stephan asked.

"The Bruce's daughter."

"He's dead, she says, the Bruce and one other. Hendricks I think. She's been shot."

Alec took a sharp breath. "And the package?"

"She may be dying." Stephan was too weary to conceal his incredulity. "We need doctoring. You ask about the package?"

"I do." There was sorrow in his gaze as he met Stephan's glare of condemnation.

Mutely, the younger man pulled the packet from his shirt and put it into Alec's trembling hands.

"It is doubtful that we could find a physician before morning." Alec unwrapped the protective covering and regarded the wax imprints sealed with Napoleon's imperial eagles. "You will have to do what you can. Given the quality of medicine available hereabouts, you will likely serve better than any quack we might find at this hour." He limped toward his desk and pulled out a sheet of paper, letting the filthy rag flutter to the floor unheeded.

Stephan picked up the soiled oilcloth and saw that it held the drying imprint of the girl's—Fiona's—bloody fingers. He folded it away in his pocket.

The servants had been dismissed for the evening. Ruthlessly, Stephan stripped the fine linen cloth left on the dining table and tore it into strips. Rather than take the time to seek out and draw fresh water from the well, he raided Alec's cabinet of whisky for liquid.

Once her shirt was cut away, it became clear that Fiona was no child. The cloth that she had used to bind her breasts was soaked in the blood leaking from her arm. Carefully, he removed the fastenings, tried and failed to ignore the beauty beneath.

Alec raised an eyebrow when Stephan broached a bottle of MacLean's Gold and poured it liberally on a piece of cloth. "Tell me what happened while it's fresh in your mind."

As he worked, Stephan gave a narrative of the evening's events. To his relief, he found that the ball had gone in and through the fleshy part of her upper arm, missing the bone entirely. Alec winced as Stephan broached another bottle, using it generously to carefully cleanse the torn flesh of both the exit and entry until he could see no fragments of fabric remaining.

Stephan ran and fetched his bag from the bedroom.

After a moment of rummaging, he found what he was seeking. No officer on General Wellesley's staff wished to be caught with buttons gone or rips in his uniform. Stephan threaded a needle from his sewing kit and stitched the skin at the entry and exit with care. Laving his work with an abundance of whisky, Stephan took perverse pleasure as Alec winced at the waste.

After the flow from the wound was fully staunched and bandaged, he braced himself for what other damage he might find. Her dark clothing made it difficult to determine the nature of the muck upon her, but the smell of blood was seemingly everywhere, including the stained, tattered breeches she wore. Fortunately, after removing her garments, it became clear that most of the gore was not from her body. Once he determined that there were no other serious injuries save the one, he covered her and tried to make her comfortable.

Beneath the ill-fitting boots he found blisters forming at the bottoms of her feet that provided more mute testimony of her desperate flight. He began to bathe those as well. As his father, the Colonel, had been wont to say, many a soldier had met his Maker by being careless of the soles that kept him marching. Taking up another clean cloth, he applied more whisky.

"Owww! Burns like...fires of hell. Waste of a fine dram...ever...there was one."

Hazel eyes flecked with emerald regarded Stephan. Her heart-shaped face was a dirt-smeared picture of confusion.

At the sound of her voice, Alec looked up from his writing. "Thank God!"

"Lord Denby," she breathed a sigh of apparent relief. "Made it...did we?"

"Not quite yet, dear girl." He began to fold the documents away. "Job's not done without a report. Then we shall weep for him."

"Aye," she agreed and winced as she took a deep

breath. "Seems...too many...tears...of late...Hendricks...betrayed...Da said."

Alec nodded. There was an emotion in his gaze that Stephan had never seen before. Cold rage, all the more dreadful for the shell of calm that contained it. "This time, the pieces on the board changed at the last moment. That might have been the saving grace tonight. We still have the packet, because Hades was confused."

Stephan marveled as she fought to gather the shards of her composure

"Didn't...help Da...killed...ambushed...Da..." She choked back a sob. "Sacrificed to...make certain...I got away, but the bastard knew...knew the meeting place. The time... How? Hurts...burns."

"You were shot in the left upper arm," Stephan supplied.

"Worse than...last time...I got shot." she murmured, then met Stephan's horrified look with a wisp of a smile. Fiona inclined her head to the bottle he held. The movement made her grimace. "Could use.. splash or three... I'm thinking."

Stephan felt his lip quirking at the chit's sheer grit. He poured and held the glass to her lips. She drank greedily.

"Aye...much better...tad more," she whispered. Stephan complied and she drained the glass yet again. "Shame on me...drinking your precious...whisky like water. Da would be—he would be—" She gasped, her eyes filled with pain of heart and body, before the lids flickered shut once more.

"Unconscious," Stephan answered Alec's anxious look.

"No...m'not...need more'n few drams...put me...out...for the count," she murmured.

"I will question her further," Alec scribbled a note. He took up a Chinese puzzle box from his desk and worked it rapidly, removing a letter from the hidden compartment within. After binding it with the dispatch from the pouch, he held a beeswax stick to a candle. "This information must be delivered immediately. You can answer any queries Arthur may have," Alec instructed, sealing the lot with a stamp in the puddle of wax. "I trust you fully, but I fear there is treason afoot. These documents will remain confidential for your safety, and for Fiona's as well. This way, there will be no questions. No one can accuse you of revealing that which you do not know. And you will tell no one, save General Wellesley and those whom he deems trustworthy, of tonight's events." He held out the packet. "Your commander needs must see these before morning. We cannot allow tonight's sacrifices to be for naught."

"Da..." Fiona whimpered softly. "Betrayed."

Stephan regarded his friend with a silent question. All thoughts regarding the apparent callousness of his behavior vanished at the stricken look upon the older man's face. Stephan tucked the papers into his waistband beneath the concealment of his shirt, and took up his bag.

"I swore upon my honor to Lord Douglass that if aught were to happen to him, his daughter would be well cared for." Alec's adamant expression emphasized his quietly spoken vow. "You need not worry for her."

"William Douglass, the Pasteboard Laird? I've heard of him." Shock stole the words. "He is...was..."

"A gambler? A wastrel? A ne'er-do-well who dragged his only child all over the Continent in search of the perfect card game?" Alec's voice trembled, his expression, an odd mix of laughter and grief. "All of those, and one of the finest that England had in the field. Can you think of a more impeccable disguise?"

"Halooo the house! Where are you hiding, Uncle? Missed the most boring of parties, you lucky dog! Too many speeches and a paucity of fair *señoritas*," a voice called, followed by brays of laughter. A door slammed closed. "Hope you don't mind, but I brought you some company. Beds are scarce here, unless you wish to rent them by the hour, so I told them that we have room to spare!"

"Nigel!" Alec paled at the sounds of footsteps mounting the stairs. "Go. Quickly. the way you came. My nephew and his friends mustn't find you here."

Stephan hesitated. "A lock?"

"Broken. Get out!"

Stephan took one last look at Fiona, her eyes dazed with whisky and confusion.

"Go to Wellesley!" Alec demanded with furious desperation. "Now!"

Stephan obeyed.

...

Within a day, the news raced through the camp with a speed rivaling the lizards that scurried from the cover of rock to rock. Indeed, the titillating tales proliferated so rapidly that even the London gossips would have marveled at the speed. Lord Denby, long looked upon as the golden model of English integrity, had been found to possess feet cast in clay. The damning circumstances made the disgrace all the more satisfying.

"They say when the lads burst into the room, the Pasteboard Laird's daughter was naked as Eve in the Garden," one of the subalterns was chortling as Stephan entered General Arthur Wellesley's military headquarters. "Smelled like a tavern. Empty bottles all over the room. The old dog had got himself a pretty little bitch, I hear. Blood, too. Didn't know he bent that way."

"Wife told me that the old fool is going to marry the little harlot," another added. "Heard he has no choice in the matter. Seems the *señorita* is the whelp of a noble Spanish family. Smart slut, to get him stuck in the honey trap after all the London mamas have been trying to snag him for years. The man's title goes back to William the Conqueror, and he's rich as Golden Ball. Isn't that so, Aubrey?"

Stephan tried to keep his expression bland, and flexed his fingers to keep his fists from clenching. Alec could protect himself, but to hear them abuse Fiona so after all of her loss and sacrifice was almost beyond bearing.

"Lord Denby is a friend of yours, Aubrey, is he not?" Lionel Holm ventured, making the word *friend* sound like something filthy.

In the normal course of events, General Wellesley had little patience for gossip of this kind, but he had stood silently before his table of maps, seemingly engrossed. Now the entire staff, including Wellesley, appeared to be eyeing Stephan, waiting for his answer. The general's glare could easily be interpreted as censure, but Stephan knew it for a warning to tread with care, and keep to the story they had concocted the previous night.

"Lord Denby served under my father, the colonel, years ago." he replied cautiously.

"Looks like the Denby has got someone serving under *him*, these days," another junior officer observed with a smirk.

"Didn't see you at Camford's celebration yesterday," Holm continued. "Heard you telling Strethan that you were taking dinner with Lord Denby."

Denial would be foolish. "Actually I did join him for dinner," Stephan admitted. He could almost see their necks stretching forward, like a nest full of cobras, poising for the strike. They knew full well that General Wellesley was a stickler when it came to the propriety of his staff, especially their treatment of Spanish allies.

In the aftermath of battle, the havoc wreaked upon innocent civilians by unrestrained British troops could easily turn a victory into as much of a political disaster as a moral tragedy. Any hint of involvement in defilement of the daughter of a prominent family would destroy Stephan's career, as surely as it had ruined Lord Denby.

Doubtlessly, more than one of the captain's comrades hoped that his answer would poison his chances in the administrative game of favor and promotion. Only he and the general knew that the stakes were far higher. "Unfortunately, the poor man injured his leg and had to cry off on our plans for the rest of the evening. It made no sense to stay the night, as I had intended."

"Really!" Holm replied with a snort of disbelief. "From what they tell about town, you missed quite the event then. Or did you? I know that you didn't make it back to quarters that night."

"Do you doubt my word?" It was an effort to keep the steely edge from his voice.

"Don't blame you for denying it." Holm's look was sly. "I know I would have, had I the chance to frolic with Lord Denby and his fancy piece."

"Indeed, I am delighted to have a greater grasp of your supple standards of truth, Captain Holm." Wellesley looked down his prominent nose like a rifleman staring down the sight of his musket. "And I remind you all that none of us, myself included, knows what actually transpired the other night. You are quite fortunate, Holm, that Captain Aubrey is an honorable and prudent man who would not dare violate the prohibition against dueling. He is an excellent shot, and I have no doubt he could end your foolish blather forever."

The general's gaze encompassed the entirety of the suddenly silent room. "One thing I do know of a certainty. At the time of the *event*, as you so call it, Captain Aubrey and I were here in discussion with my brother Richard, Marquess Wellesley, The Foreign Secretary." He pronounced each title and office with the precision of a well-aimed shot in Holm's direction.

"The Captain is to be commended for putting his duty above a tryst with his pillow. Now, *gentlemen!*" General Wellesley's sarcastic inflection and the scowl that accompanied it, encompassed them all. "Might I suggest that we now devote ourselves to more trivial matters, such as the recent movements of our dear friend Marshall Junot and his troops. If you would attend me, Captain Aubrey, I have an assignment for you."

TWO

LONDON, 1810

The best laid schemes o' mice an' men
gang aft agley.

— ROBERT BURNS, ODE TO A
WEE MOUSIE

Sleep had fled beyond recall. Fiona slipped on her wrapper and knelt by the fireplace. Some embers still glowed in the back of the grate, and soon a blaze burned before her. She settled herself in the armchair to watch the dance of flame.

Carlotta would be annoyed, Fiona thought, biting at the nail that she had cracked. Clumsily done, but now turning her hand for anything resembling labor was a seldom thing. Callouses, mute witnesses to the years of scrubbing, washing, and cooking, had given way to the strict regimen of creams and unguents that her friend had imposed. Only the hidden puckers of bullet wounds marred otherwise smooth skin, testimony to her past life.

Now that she was fully awake, her breath slowed from its frantic rasps, her body was finally convincing itself that she was no longer running through the night streets of Portugal. The solid, elegant reality of the fanciful frescoed ceiling, the great velvet-hung bed with its mountain of cushions, and the Axminster carpet, soft beneath her feet, dispelled the last shreds of her chimeras. Yet, despite these material bits of reassurance, Fiona still felt a growing uneasiness.

A coal fell in the grate, clattering into the pool of silence in the vast house on Berkeley Square. From the street came the early predawn clatter of a cart on the way to market. As the clopping faded to a distant echo, Fiona felt the familiar ache of loneliness. *Only the ghosts understand*, she thought. *They are my companions now.*

Slipping on a figured silk wrapper, Fiona went to seek her one sure source of solace. After her son's birth, she had chosen to nurse him herself, defying convention. Even though he had weaned early, she still found that she did not want little Alejo's bedside to be more than a few steps away.

Childhood memories of having to take flight at a moment's notice were still strong. Proximity to basic necessities provided a measure of safety. Her son was one of those needs. So she chose to forgo common practice yet again, refusing to consign him to a nursery in the uppermost reaches of the house.

Alec had gently mocked her habit of maintaining stashes of food, money, and weapons. *You are safe, my dear*, he had assured her, *I will keep you safe*. But the Bruce had taught her well. *Safety is but an illusion* was a truth that had kept her alive. Unfortunately, Alec had not paid proper heed to that creed of survival.

She stood, watching the rhythmic rise and fall of her boy's breath until the racing of her own heart slowed to a normal pace. A hint of scent alerted her to the fact that she was, once again, about to prove her father's axiom.

Abruptly, she snuffed the candle and pivoted to face the towering figure who stood between her and the door. An upraised blade flashed in the firelight. Fiona answered the challenge by pulling her own knife from the sheath at her thigh. Then grabbing the brass candle-stick, she held it at the ready to block and to strike.

Despite the shadows, she could see Carlotta del Castillo's smile of approval at Fiona's rapid response. With a finger to her lips, she inclined her head toward her still-sleeping son and nodded toward the stairs. In silent accord, the two women descended to the library.

"What were the other weapons you had at hand?" Carlotta asked, as she poured them each a generous tot of brandy.

"Testing me, are you?" Fiona raised her glass in a sardonic salute.

"As is my duty." There was no humor in the reply of the woman who had appointed herself Fiona's guardian.

Six feet tall in stockinged feet, Carlotta still managed to present a deceptive appearance of fragile femininity. All the more deadly due to that delicate façade, Carlotta was a mistress of weaponry, from sabers to explosives. Using their connections to the aristocratic houses of Spain, she and her late husband had helped the Bruce to organize and arm the resistance against Napoleon that had come to be known as the *guerillas*.

"Alec and all of your father's Scotsmen promised the Bruce that we would do everything in our power to help keep you safe if he could not. That includes your ability to protect yourself. Now with your Alec and my Benito gone, that task falls to me." Carlotta finished her drink in one gulp and shook her head as if to banish the ghosts that haunted them both. "Tell me what else could you have used in your defense?"

"The poker was within easy reach. I would have grabbed it when you ducked to avoid the candlestick. The tie of my gown is silk, strong enough to make a handy garrote."

"Too difficult." Carlotta dismissed the ploy with a chuckle. "You would have had to climb me like a monkey to get the proper leverage."

Fiona ceded the point with a nod. "I could have screamed to rouse the nursemaid in the adjoining room. Dottie is quite formidable, as you know. Would you like me to go on about the pistol in the wardrobe? The sword on the wall that is sharp and ready?"

"These days, you could not wield a sword to save your life. We must practice this, but it is sufficient unto the day." Carlotta lifted her glass in a gesture of approval. "And how did you detect my presence?"

"You have a heavy hand with attar of roses."

Carlotta sighed and nodded her head, reaching up to remove the combs and release the crown of her long, midnight hair. "I am getting careless. This is not good."

"Did you find out anything of value tonight?" Fiona ventured as she rose to refill her glass.

"Very little information of import to be gotten at Almack's, I fear," Carlotta admitted regretfully, her russet gown swishing gracefully. The dress of figured silk, with its high round shoulders would have overpowered a smaller woman. On Carlotta, it had a curious effect, making her seem fragile and feminine, the deep eggshell flounce drawing the eye down to minimize her height while in no way compromising the dignity of her stature.

"A little is better than nothing." Fiona's laugh was tinged with bitterness. "For all my vows of vengeance, all I may do is sit here and feel useless! I doubt the patronesses will let me in at all, despite my title."

Carlotta seated herself, easing off her slippers and massaging her feet before tucking her long legs under her skirts. "My neck is sore from looking down upon those miniscule men! Even so, it was wonderful to dance again! Pah, I am getting to be an old woman if I ache after only a few turns around the floor."

"Old woman? You look younger than my five-and-twenty, though you have another seven years in your dish," Fiona said, reading her friend's hesitation with growing unease. "What have you learned?"

Carlotta sighed. "Your name is once again being bandied about with all of the accusations."

Fiona took a sip to help her digest the news. "That makes no sense at all. Alec is gone well over a year. When the fires of old gossip burn anew so brightly, there must be a bellows that stokes it."

The older woman nodded agreement. "So we have one more thread that leads us into the maze. With so little to guide us, though, I am beginning to believe that there would be no shame in retreat to Denby Chase. You and Alejo can go back, while your friends investigate."

"No, I have come to London for a purpose. I will find the truth." Fiona rose and set her glass down upon the escritoire. "Thus far, the resurgence of the rumors is one of the few clues we have."

Carlotta frowned. "You know my feelings, Fiona."

"And I appreciate that you are helping me, despite your advice. But I refuse to run back to the country and cower again." Fiona rummaged through the papers and picked up the sheet of gilded vellum, holding it before her with a frown, as if she could somehow induce the paper into a confession. "Besides, this invitation would seem to indicate that we have already stirred up the pot. There are others who apparently want me to return to the fray."

"If you wish to rejoin society, then you hold the ticket in your hand," Carlotta proclaimed, plucking the summons from Fiona's hand and waving it like a banner. "Once you appear at Carlton House, your voucher to Almack's will be approved despite your reputation, and they will eagerly take your ten guineas. No matter how much of the old talk has revived, every hostess in London will be eager for your presence."

"Until then, there is little I can do. I must resign my-

self to wait for Prinny's social benediction, I suppose."
Fiona sighed and lifted her glass in a silent toast. "You
are right, of course. If the *ton* were to deny all the adul-
terers and fornicators, there would not be a ballroom
able to muster the eight couples required to dance the
Roger de Coverly."

Carlotta poured herself another splash of liquor.
"You have no reason to fear them."

Fear.

Fiona finally acknowledged the fact that for over a
year, she had been ruled by dread, and allowed herself to
tremble in hiding. It was time to marshal her courage
and confront reality. She let the liquor's smooth fire slip
down her throat before she spoke. "I was a fool to run
away as I did. The trail will be cold."

"Nonsense! You were only recently widowed and
carrying a child. Inquiry would have made you a target."

"And now we have yet another question to be answered." Fiona stood and stirred the fire, staring into the
flames as she contemplated her course. "Why does the
Prince suddenly choose to acknowledge my existence
once more? Especially if rumors of my infidelities are
circulating once again."

Carlotta played devil's advocate. "Your husband was
one of his most trusted friends and advisors."

"All the more reason to keep his distance from the
woman who supposedly drove Lord Denby to suicide."
Fiona countered. "The Prince cannot afford any more
such broth in his bowl, particularly when rumor has it
that his father is beginning to descend into madness
once more."

"That too, I have confirmed tonight," Carlotta
said. "Those whispers are true. Parliament will be reluctant to name him Regent, but there may be no
choice."

Fiona's sigh was rueful. "I vow, the very thought of
that man on the throne of England is enough to make

me a believer in Francisco de Miranda's delusions of glorious revolutions and republics."

"Heaven help us all," Carlotta murmured.

"Now *there* is a path I can pursue!" Fiona declared, setting her empty glass aside. "If anyone has his finger on the pulse of political intrigues, it is the old weasel."

"I would not bother." Carlotta pursed her lips as she considered. "His failed expedition to Caracas has made him into a tragic laughingstock."

"You underestimate him, Carlotta," Fiona said, considering the possibilities. "The Americans of Britain's former colonies may loathe him now for the Leander affair. It is their citizens, after all, who ended dead or imprisoned due to his failed effort to rouse revolution in Caracas. But here in England? He is received everywhere."

"Of what use can he possibly be to us, Fiona?" Carlotta shook her head. "It would be a mistake, I think."

"The man knows everyone. The Bruce considered him one of his best informants." Fiona speculated, her brow furrowing.

"Wrinkles! I see wrinkles! Remember that wrinkles are the lines upon which your feelings are writ for all to see." Carlotta warned putting a hand upon Fiona's brow to smooth it. "You have forgotten how to hide your thoughts. Become a blank slate that no one may see anything other than what you wish to reveal. And you will keep your youthful complexion besides."

"It bothered Alec no end that he could never read me as easily as he could everyone else."

"Your late husband was no open book either."

"I know," Fiona said sadly. "I wish he had taken me into his confidence. So many 'whys' to ponder."

"Perhaps we will be able to find the answers you seek, *querida*, but not tonight."

"As Papa used to say, 'Sometimes you can't get answers because you fail to ask the right questions.'"

"Aye, one of the Bruce's favorites, that was," Carlotta agreed. "He would also say 'Dinna fash yerself, wee Fee, when there's naught ye can do.' Tomorrow is soon enough to begin our queries."

"It's nearly dawn." Fiona shook her head with a smile. "Why don't you go upstairs? I think I may read for a bit, think this through."

Carlotta kissed her cheek. "Do not think overly much. That, too, causes wrinkles. Tomorrow we shall select our armor for the upcoming battle. You will need an entirely new wardrobe, of course, if you are setting your mourning aside. I wish you a good night."

Fiona perused the shelves, selecting a dog-eared translation of Homer's *Odyssey*, one of Alec's favorites, but the words of the ancient Greek bard seemed to dance across the page.

Taking her mother's battered guitar from a cabinet, Fiona tuned the strings. Alec had gifted her with a fine new Italian instrument with inlays of ivory. He could never understand that the old guitar sang with her mother's voice. Whispering the lyrics, she picked out a lullaby to the moon that asked the full *luna* to send messages to her love. Carlotta was correct, it was time to set mourning aside, but that did not mean that Fiona had the right to forget. As the dawn broke and moon faded with the light, she vowed that she would finally settle the score.

. . .

Stephan Aubrey, the newly minted Earl of Camford, turned his attention to his horses. The fashionable world was abroad, and consequently, the streets were congested with carriages. He drove with care, pretending to himself that his lack of speed was due to the fact that London had somehow changed since his last visit.

As he approached his destination, he remembered the excitement of coming to the city on his own for the very first time. At seventeen, he had been quite the swaggering young sprig, proudly garbed in just-purchased regimentals, buttons shiny as fistful of new sixpence. To a freshly minted officer on the brink of the battlefield, *eat, drink, and be merry, for tomorrow we may die,* seemed an appropriate credo.

A decade and a half of experience, with most of the recent year spent hovering at the brink of Heaven's gate, had given Stephan a different perspective. Lying in bed while recovering from his wounds had provided ample time to contemplate how easily he might have gone wrong, in those heady times after buying his colors.

In hindsight, Stephan realized that his father's letter of introduction to his former subordinate had opened doors to far better places than brothels, gambling dens, and taverns. While his friends were wallowing in the fleshpots, Alec had taken the colonel's son under his wing and connected him with those who could assist in the promotion of a young man's military career. Moreover, Lord Denby had become more than a mentor—he had been a good friend.

Stephan's unexpected return to London made him all the more cognizant of Alec's absence and just how much he owed the man. Although Stephan had never anticipated being elevated to an earldom, the introduction that he had been given to the highest circles of polite society would stand in good stead, especially now that he was being called upon to repay a portion of that debt.

His arrival at the entrance of Camford House recalled him to the present. A servant took the reins, and Stephan limped up the stairs.

His late cousin George, like many of Prinny's set, had contracted a severe fit of architectural fever. However, the Prince's bouts of building fancy were often tempered by talented architects and a flair for elegance, both of which George had decidedly lacked. The building before him bore witness to the previous earl's deficiency of judgement.

Stephan recollected the original house before George's fit of refurbishing. The structure had been a gem of Palladian harmony, classical and elegant in its pure lines. Unfortunately, George had favored the Gothic, and gruesome gargoyles now snarled at the park across the way. Hooded stone figures stared mysteriously from the fascia. It was easy to imagine one of Mrs. Radcliffe's screaming heroines begging for rescue from the crenellated tower above. Indeed, there were times when Stephan felt like screaming to be saved himself. Unfortunately, the interior was almost as dismal and hideous as the exterior.

Stephan was relieved to find the front door open. In a sign of definite progress, piles of boxes lined the stairway. It appeared that George's wife, Lillian, had finally conceded the battle, and was removing the last of her personal possessions from the premises.

Since the deaths of her husband and stepson in a carriage accident, Lady Camford had removed herself to a dower property in a more fashionable part of town. To Stephan's dismay, she still considered Camford House to be an extended suite of personal storage rooms. Moreover, almost every time that Lillian paid a visit, small valuables seemed to disappear. Until Hollins, his former batman, who now served as his butler, had reported seeing the countess slip a bauble into her pocket, the servants had lived in constant fear of being accused of theft.

Stephan too, had his own worries. The woman's annoying presumption that she could pop in and out of the property at will also made for many awkward and increasingly disturbing encounters. With all the subtlety of a smith's hammer upon an anvil, Lillian persisted in her attempts to seduce him so that she might forego the title of Dowager Countess in favor of becoming the present countess. Removal of her possessions would allow him to more easily bar her from adding to his Gothic nightmare.

Although Stephan would gladly have lived more modestly, Richard Wellesley, the Foreign Secretary had been quite clear in his instructions. Camford House was a symbol of Stephan's new consequence. The past days had been filled with a nightmare of needle-wielding tailors, bootmakers, and barbers, hastily grooming him for his role as part of the plan to set a trap for a traitor.

"Stephan!" Lillian shrieked.

Stephan watched in astonishment as his cousin's widow rushed past a footman nearly knocking the poor man and his armful of bundles headlong down the stairway. He had a brief second to brace himself against the wall as she flung herself into his arms, otherwise his bad leg might have given way.

"Dearest Stephan! I decided to come early and save you some trouble." Her long eyelashes fluttered and her eyes sparkled with a hint of tears as she sniffed daintily. "I am so glad that you are here. Taking leave is so much easier when one has one's family about. Friends ease a journey."

"Lillian," Stephan reminded her as he disentangled himself from her grasp. "You have been abiding in Piccadilly for half a year now. Or so say the bills I have been receiving."

"But I am taking my leave of the house that I came to as a bride."

Stephan pulled out his handkerchief in anticipation. Lillian's tears were much like a floodgate. He had not long to wait before she opened it to full flow.

"Only five, or was it six years ago? An innocent girl of nineteen," she dabbed at her limpid blue eyes as she looked up at him like a beseeching ingénue facing the merciless villain in a Drury Lane drama.

Stephan had to admit, she played the part well. Her blonde, cropped hair curled around her face, distracting the casual observer from the fine lines on her forehead and at the corners of her eyelids.

Five or six years? He repressed a snort of disbelief. How foolish of her to fiddle with a notorious history. Closer to ten, actually, since her liaison with George had pre-dated the demise of his wife. No doubt Lillian failed to recall that Stephan had been one of the legion of admirers who were all but invisible in the face of her aspirations. Since *that* Stephan Aubrey was a military man with pockets to let, minimal expectations, and no family influence, he had been beneath her notice.

By all accounts then, Stephan figured that his cousin's widow was closing in on her fortieth year. With beauty as her sole dowry, Lillian had fixed her sights on his cousin, George. The Earl of Camford was already married, but his wife was ill, near her last prayers. Although George's first wife held on to life tenaciously, breathing another year to spite her husband, her gravestone was barely etched when George stood in the family chapel and married Lillian.

"I do so miss dear Lady Melbourne and the lovely view of the park." Lillian sniffed. "Do promise that I can visit whenever I choose, dearest Stephan."

A license to plague him at her whim? He would grant her nothing of the sort.

Her woebegone air was so ridiculous that it was almost amusing until Stephan happened to glance past her to the piles of belongings awaiting transport to her new home. He pried her fingers off his jacket and picked up his fallen cane. Pulling back the covering from the exposed corner of a painting, Stephan revealed a Reubens.

"I believe that used to hang in the library?" Stephan inquired.

"That stupid footman!" Lillian barked, her annoyance at being discovered quite genuine. "Some of the new servants that you have hired are quite incompetent, if you will forgive me for saying so. I distinctly asked your man to fetch the portrait of George, the one with the two hounds."

"I shall have to reprimand him," Stephan agreed with dangerous civility. "I fail to see how anyone could mistake this lovely lady for a spaniel." He nodded at the portrait. "Perhaps I ought to see if any other such errors have been made by my incompetent servants?"

"I will check it myself." Lillian offered, a shade too quickly. "I suppose that some confusion is inevitable. It is so difficult to move one's possessions after all these years. The house in Piccadilly is so small and there are so many dear keepsakes, so many odds and ends that carry fond memories."

"And you shall have all that is *rightfully* yours," Stephan promised. "I am very sorry to discommode you so, Lady Camford."

He did not wish to give George's widow further license to rummage about the house and pilfer. Unless he was mistaken, the canvas peeking out from behind the hatboxes was a Botticelli, and Stephan would wager that there were other family treasures mixed within the mélange of parcels.

It would be interesting to check with his man of business and compare the house's current inventory with the master list that should have been made. The baubles that had disappeared thus far might never be recovered, but he vowed that Camford family treasures would cease to be a source of pocket money for George's widow. Stephan turned and rang for Hollins.

The servant must have been lingering nearby, surveying the looting and sacking. It was but a matter of seconds before he answered the summons. He exchanged a wordless look with his master, and the answer that Stephan read in his retainer's eyes was as close to mirth as he had yet to see in the somber Yorkshireman.

"I insist, Lady Camford, that Hollins assist you." Stephan kept his tones gracious. "He has been with me almost forever, as you know, and will doubtless prevent any further such unfortunate mishaps. Think how inconvenient it would be to arrive at your new home and find that the servants had left behind some of your most cherished possessions, or that they had parceled up something else you would be required to return."

Lillian's fury was poorly concealed behind her pretty show of confusion. "Oh dear!" she exclaimed, her eyes blazing. "George always said that I was the most muddle-headed woman in creation. I fear that he was correct in his estimation."

"George did you an injustice, milady, for I find you a most clear-minded soul. If you require my assistance, I shall be in the library, taking care of some long-neglected business." He bowed and beat a hasty retreat.

Despite his resolution to actually take care of some of the multitude of estate affairs that were heaped upon his desk, Stephan found himself going to the window and remembering the view from another library. Given the true nature of the affairs that had drawn him back to London, it seemed inevitable that the memories of that night in Portugal were much on his mind these past weeks.

Over a year ago, while Stephan had been fighting for his life in his sickbed, Alec had died by his own hand.

Last month, his widow, Fiona, Lady Denby, had left the isolation of Denby Chase and returned to London. According to the Foreign Secretary, Richard Wellesley, her arrival had coincided with the revival of an organization known as Hades. Wellesley did not believe that the timing was a matter not of chance, but of treason.

Stephan had reluctantly agreed to serve as the bait in the snare.

. . .

The salon of Madame Robard seemed small. Its deliberately sparse furnishings provided an ideal showcase for the products of the modiste's talents. Her clients and her fashions were enhanced by the muted simplicity of the setting, the discreet intimacy of the atmosphere. One did not go to meet one's friends at Madame Robard's. The woman catered to her patrons individually, with one-of-a-kind designs. It was said that Robard never made the same gown twice, and as a result, her creations were exclusive and expensive.

According to reputation, Madame herself did not appear until her customers had made some initial decisions. Her staff of able assistants aided the clients in coalescing vague ideas into the substance of Madame's magic. Fiona and Carlotta were ushered into the inner salon, and a girl wheeled in a tray loaded with cakes and pastries. "Madame will be with you in a moment," she said.

Surprisingly, Madame Robard followed almost immediately.

"Ah, Carlotta—so you have finally persuaded her. I have long waited for this day." The birdlike woman rushed to embrace Carlotta, who did not seem the least disturbed by the unusual familiarity. In fact, she hugged the modiste with equal verve.

As she seated herself, Carlotta smiled at Fiona's obvious surprise. "Natalie and I know each other from the old times. Your mother—"

"*Une minute*." Madame Robard exhorted. She closed the door behind her. "Now," she said, "you may say what you will. Even now, some things are not safe to speak of in the open. I still have those I care about who remain under the Corsican's thumb. You can never tell whose ears might be listening."

Carlotta chuckled. "You have always been discreet, Natalie."

"An indiscreet seamstress does not stay long in business. If I were to chatter to both wife and mistress, I would soon have no clients," the modiste declared with a chuckle, before turning to Fiona and inspecting her with an artist's eye.

"The face and figure are Esperanza's. You will be a pleasure to dress."

"You knew my mother?" Fiona asked, turning to Carlotta in surprise.

"*Oui*, but of course. Her loss when you were but a small girl was a great tragedy." Madame Robard pulled a wisp of exquisitely embroidered linen from her bosom and wiped away a tear. "You must forgive me. For me to see once more the daughter of the woman who saved my life, is a great joy."

"You have met me before?" Fiona asked.

Carlotta gave a nod of affirmation in response to Fiona's querying looks.

"It is true!" the modiste verified. "You too, *ma petite*, had a part in rescuing me from Madame la Guillotine. It surprises me that you have not told her, Comtesse?"

"It was not my story to reveal," Carlotta said, pouring a cup of tea. "I know that many of us have no wish to recollect, much less share those terrible times. This is one of the reasons I rarely make use of my title these days. I have no wish to explain what I have lost."

"True enough. The memories that haunt our nights are sometimes all we have left." The older woman sighed and turned to Fiona. "But I shall tell you of your *maman's* bravery, yes? Your father learned that I was among those on the Committee of Public Safety's infamous list for arrest. Few survived the so-called *trial* that followed.

We hired an old farm wagon to take us into the countryside, but your papa received word that they were conscripting all able-bodied men for the army. He would surely have been taken, so your *maman* drove the wagon on that day."

"Just before they stopped us, Esperanza pinched you, and you began to scream loud enough to startle our mule to braying. How the soldiers laughed at the chorus you made! They let us pass without even checking our forged papers. So now, how may I thank you for that moment of pain that you endured for my sake?"

"She needs something fit for Carlton House," Carlotta said, producing the invitation.

The modiste's eyebrows rose as she scanned the date. "You believe I am a sorceress, Carlotta?" Madame Robard wagged a chiding finger. "Luckily for you, I have already woven the spell you require! I have just the dress! Only for the daughter of Esperanza would I take from one customer to give to another," the seamstress added with a sly smile. "It does become an easier choice when the *chienne* commands me to make alterations that are nothing less than sacrilege. Also, she thinks to pay her bills with only promises that she will soon have much money."

"The women of the *ton* would be horrified, wouldn't they?" Fiona laughed. "By how well you have their true measures?"

"Many of my clients are very careless with their talk." The modiste eyed Fiona speculatively. "Carlotta tells me that you have returned to London with a purpose. Tell me the names of those whose information you require, and I will do all in my power to assist you. We can speak while I fit the dress. If you are to have a new and remarkable wardrobe, there is much to do."

THREE

Suspicion is a heavy armor, and with its
weight it impedes more than it
protects.

— Robert Burns

As the hordes of carriages edged toward the entrance of Carlton House, Stephan fingered the carved ebony head of his cane. Briefly, he considered alighting and walking the short remaining distance, but discarded the idea. The dull throb in his leg presaged an evening of pain if he kept pushing the boundaries of his recovery any further.

He leaned back against the velvet squabs of the elegantly appointed carriage, trying in vain to find a position that would relieve the ache. No doubt it was the effect of the unceasing tension of the past weeks, the circumstances that had led to his unwanted return to the circles of the *ton*. Staring ruefully through the glass, he realized that he had been absent from London long enough to appreciate the panorama unfolding outside.

Carlton House was brilliantly illuminated. Somberly clothed men, dressed in the fashion that Brummel had made *de rigeur*, contrasted with the jewel-toned garb of the women, as they mounted the steps like an unwinding strand of gems against dark velvet.

Stephan sighed. He had no cause to complain of his lot. Half the beggars in London were broken men in faded uniforms. Suddenly, the opulent scene before him lost its charm. The innocent days, when the cost of Prinny's pleasure had meant nothing to him, were beyond recapture. Not so long ago, he had been part of the walking waxworks that styled itself the *Beau Monde*, yet it seemed as if another Stephan Aubrey had danced and flirted with the females at Almack's.

The task that faced him robbed him of any joy that he might feel in rejoining so-called *Polite Society*. Tonight Stephan would play his role, costumed in a coat of superfine stretched so taut that he could scarcely shrug his shoulders. His gleaming pumps that smelled of new leather were stiff and uncomfortable with nary a crease of wear. The pristine expanse of starched linen that swathed his neck itched badly, but he scarcely dared to scratch lest he displace his valet's flawless knotting.

Opening night had arrived, but this would be an ad hoc performance without a clear knowledge of the plot, much less a script with set lines.

A footman in the Prince's distinctive livery drew the door of the carriage open. Stephan alit reluctantly, to find that the audience had been well prepared for his debut.

"Cor! It be him!" one of the crowd yelled.

"It be him!" another voice shouted. "The Earl of Camford, hero of Busaca!"

"Put them Frenchies on the run, 'ee did!" Someone else declared. "Huzzah!"

The onlookers who had come to pick a few pockets, or just ogle the toffs and their ladies, were happy enough to join in a cheer for a hero. That most had not heard of him mattered not.

Stephan acknowledged their acclaim with a wave

and a smile, while he tried to quell his rising embarrassment. A man or two had been planted among the crowd, no doubt. Stephan had been warned to expect it by Lord Wellesley—Stephan corrected himself, *Richard* — the Foreign Secretary had demanded the familiarity as part of his scheme. Still, as the former captain limped his way up the stairs, he was conscious of too many eyes upon him.

Richard and his younger brother, who was now both Viscount and General Wellington, had prepared the ground well. Too well it seemed. After over a year biding in the quiet of the country, all of Stephan's senses were subjected to a full-out assault.

Everyone had to shake hands with the hero of Busaca. His fingers were wrung by matrons who had cut him dead in his untitled youth.

New-met acquaintances roared over the hubbub of the crowd, blasting his ears with their convictions that he had always carried the potential for greatness. Past connections elevated themselves to the rank of bosom friends. Mothers of eligible daughters were weaving their webs of marital entrapment as they pushed their darlings forward for introductions. Sweat and heavy perfumes competed for dominion with seldom-washed flesh.

Stephan attempted to scan unobtrusively for the one woman he sought, but the situation seemed hopeless. A mob of well-wishers pressed him, making his progress seem even slower than that of his carriage before. He cursed inwardly as he smiled politely. Just when it seemed that there was no escape from death by felicitation, a familiar voice came bellowing through the crowd.

"Stephan!" A flaming crop of red hair, rising almost a full six inches above the sea of heads, came plowing toward him. As the people parted, it was easy to see why even the most avid of the new Earl of Camford's admirers made way for Percy Strethan. The man's height was well matched by his broad muscular proportions. Little wonder that the voice that emerged from that huge barrel of a chest seemed to boom like a great bass drum. Stephan grasped at Percy's extended paw as a drowning man would grab at a log.

"Percy." Stephan's broad smile was genuine. "I cannot credit it! When did you return? Have you finally decided to take some of the leave that's coming to you?"

"Only leave I've taken is of my senses," Percy informed him. "Uncle Walter, rest his soul, left me a fine estate. I've finally sold out and decided it's time to do my duty to the Strethan name, and provide my mother with hordes of grandchildren."

"Heaven help us all!" Stephan moaned in mock horror. "Especially that poor female you choose as wife. I am imagining hordes of Strethans. The fall of Rome all over again, with masses of Strethans to stand in for the Goths and Vandals."

Percy grinned, and Stephan was reminded of a painting that he had once seen of a great bear about to devour its prey. However, the ursine creature before him was impeccably dressed, garbed in evening clothes that showed the hand of a tailoring genius. Only a master could have contrived to fit Percy's hulking form in the first stare of fashion, making the giant seem a gentleman, not a buffoon. Stephan stayed Percy's hand as he tugged at the neckcloth, nearly ruining the perfect folds.

"Fool thing's too tight," Percy muttered. "Dash it, everything's too tight. These blasted shirt points will cut my throat before the night is out, I vow. It took near an hour for Cobble to help me into this jacket, and if he ain't there to help me out of it, I'll be sleeping in it. I told him I wanted the tailor to put a pocket in it for my books and the man nearly cried."

"Cobble?" Stephan asked, as the two friends walked through the antechamber. With Percy in the lead, frowning at those who dared to stand in their way, the crowd parted before them like a veritable Red Sea.

"Mother made me hire a valet," Percy replied. "Got to cut a dash with the ladies to catch one, Mama said, especially a great ox such as yours truly. Cobble, they say, turned down Brummel when he tried to hire him into his service. Claimed the man came from common stock, Cobble did. Took me on, he said, because I presented a challenge." Percy looked at his friend with a critical eye. "Now you, friend, could do much better by your tailor if you got some meat on them bones of yours."

"You sound like Hollins."

"Still with you?"

Stephan nodded glumly. "He is to blame for my current state of near-suffocation by neck linen. Threatens to find something better at least once a week and after his conspiring with the tailors against me, I am tempted to let him go."

Percy's booming laugh caused the more timid among those who lingered at their periphery to scurry away. Those braver souls who seemed inclined to actually interpose were quickly discouraged by the Strethan Stare. One dandy was heard to declare that Percy's smiling glare made one feel "as if you were being invited to step into the crocodile's jaws." A group of conversing bucks were thus induced to abandon a cozy corner to the two men. Stephan eased himself into a chair with a barely stifled sigh of relief.

"Still pains you?" Percy's look was concerned. "I wonder that you are out and about."

"I hear enough of that from Hollins, Percy. If I seem weary, it is a result of too much arm-pumping, shoulder-thumping, and jaw-boning. All the while, I have to smile and act pleased at being on show. The guest of honor, and it is your fault, Percy."

"How do you figure that?"

"Were it not for you, I would be laughing from Hell at this gathering, and counting myself lucky to be with the Devil. You were the one who kept the doctors from hacking off my leg, Hollins told me."

Percy blushed almost as red as his hair. He quickly turned the subject. "True what they say about you being appointed to the Foreign Secretary's staff?"

Stephan saw a flash of movement in an alcove nearby. "I suppose that I can confirm it, Percy. It will be announced this evening."

"Well, you've had handshaking enough, so I won't do that. I am just glad to see you back among your friends."

Stephan's smile was wry. "I never knew until tonight just how many I have. Unfortunately, Richard tells me that I won't have much time to myself."

"So the General's brother has become *Richard*, has he, now that you have come up an earl? And you out-rank Arthur Wellesley now, since he was only created a Viscount Wellington last year." Percy grinned. "What are you calling 'Old Nosey' these days, eh, now that you no longer have to call him 'Sir'?"

"Though I am no longer his commanding officer, and a mere Viscount, I would hope that he calls me a friend, Strethan," Arthur Wellesley commented, his lip rising in a wry smile as his former subordinate turned a bright crimson. "Still reading Rousseau now that you have mustered out?"

"Gone back to the Greeks, milord," Percy answered. "Socrates."

"Maturity at last." The viscount smiled at Stephan. "My brother Richard informs me that we will be working together closely. I must confess I am looking forward to it."

Only Stephan could see the look of satisfaction on his former superior's face as Lady Whitcomb scuttled from her shadowed listening post to pass on the tidbit of information that she had just gleaned. Stephan was sure that within minutes, the sensitive nature of his position would become common knowledge.

"Now that you've returned to the land of the living, I hope you'll find a little time for your friends." Percy frowned at the General's back as he rejoined the eddying crowd. "Don't let Wellington and his brother work you back into your sick bed."

Stephan sighed inwardly.

He would have no choice but to lie to Percy, and who knew how many other falsehoods would be required before the business was done? "I will keep some time free, if only to see how your bride hunt progresses. Have you chosen your victim?"

Percy laughed. "Willing victims. They were all rushing to my altar. It is my turn to be grateful. Before you came on the scene, oh conquering hero, I was the catch of the season. Couldn't take a turn in the garden without a chaperone, lest some managing mother throw her darling into my arms and cry 'view halloo!' Bombarded, I was. What with my charm, wit, wonderful address—"

"Did they all run screaming back to their mamas?"

Strethan snorted. "You, Earl of Camford, cast me entirely in the shade."

"On the contrary, Percy." Stephan rose slowly from the chair. "It is you who cast the shade. I will merely stand in your ample shadow and depend on you to fend off the more formidable matrons."

Percy handed him his cane. "Craven that you are!"

"My secret is out!" The rest had eased the throb. "Now you know why I was always beside you at the charge, my friend. You afforded so great a target, I was sure that the French would not bother a puny soul like myself."

Percy was still chuckling as he asked, "Care to join

the hunt for a spouse, Stephan? Know the field well, I do. I can point out a few choice fillies."

"Not yet, Percy, not quite yet." For a moment, the crowd ebbed in front of them. Stephan caught a brief glimpse of a young woman in colors of half-mourning, but she was obscured almost instantly.

Somehow, he knew.

After their brief encounter, Stephan had wondered whether he would be able to identify her. Since that night in Portugal, the little news that he had heard about Fiona had been through the grapevine of gossip. When he had seen the woman last, she was smeared with dirt and blood, covered in the remnants of a tablecloth.

After being wounded, Stephan's world had narrowed to the space of a bed. Due to Hollins' care, he was healing, but the past few weeks had seemed like one of his fevered nightmares. His mind kept reeling back to the unpalatable realities.

Denby was dead.

Fiona, his widow, was suspected of being a traitor to the Crown.

As if to emphasize the bizarre nature of this whole charade, Richard played the ghillie on the hunt, casting a significant glance toward a nearby crowd, signaling that Lady Denby was at hand.

Percy noted the direction of Stephan's gaze and his jaw dropped. "Who is the dark-haired beauty?" he gasped.

"Have no idea," Stephan prevaricated. It would complicate matters beyond measure if Percy became infatuated with Alec's widow. "Up against stiff competition there. I see Glengyle, Lord Bradford, and I don't recognize the other. Has the look of a Spanish grandee."

"*Criollo*, a Spaniard born in their American colonies, you know. Related through his late wife to the del Toro family, I'm told," Percy informed him. "Richer than Croesus. Came in with Francisco de Miranda. You know him?"

"If anyone in the Foreign Office were to say that he is unacquainted with Francisco de Miranda, you know instantly he is working his first day or he is a liar," Stephan commented. "Francisco is a—"

Percy's eyebrow raised and he scratched his ear in the signal they had long ago created to silently alert each other of trouble from behind. Stephan instantly amended what he was about to say. "—splendid fellow, I fully agree. A dedicated and eloquent advocate of liberty."

"*Mes amigos*, it would appear that the hero whom we celebrate tonight is a believer in our cause!" As the silver-haired Miranda turned and translated for his companions, Stephan's smile was genuine. The Foreign Secretary had hoped to manufacture a meeting with Miranda later in the evening. This chance encounter was far more spontaneous and conducive to the plan's progress.

Miranda had friends and connections everywhere on the Continent and in the colonies of the Americas. According to Richard, the elderly expatriate from Caracas had the capacity to spread information faster and farther than any penny broadsheet or newspaper. "If you do not mind, *señor*, I shall be delighted to practice your language, if you will be so kind as to forgive my mistakes," Stephan replied in fluent Spanish.

"But of course," Miranda enthusiastically agreed, "This is how I have mastered French, English, Italian, German, and Russian. For my Latin, I thank the Jesuits, and of the Greek, I am still but a student."

"So modest, and he can curse fluently in every one of those languages!" A towering female drifted forward to join them. "You will perform introductions, yes, *Tio* Francisco?

With a courtly bow, Miranda complied. "Allow me

to present the fair *señora,* the Comtesse del Castillo, who is not truly my niece, so I may flirt with impunity."

Percy's dazzled expression faltered as he heard the word *señora.* Stephan felt a pang of pity. A wedded woman might do for dalliance, but not for marriage.

"Impunity?" She tapped the old fox playfully with her fan. "You do recall that I am a friend of Sarah, no? Remember her? The mother of your two sons?"

"Ah, these women, they conspire together against us," Miranda mourned, his hand covering his heart in mock dismay.

Laughter sounded from behind Stephan, and a familiar voice asserted. "We have no choice but to do so, if only for our own protection from the wiles of men like you, Francisco."

Stephan turned to face the woman who had piqued his interest earlier. How had he doubted that he would recognize her? The eyes that regarded him with cool curiosity were an unforgettable shade of hazel, flecks of green glinting in the hidden depths of mystery. But it seemed to him that her gaze held a new, sad wisdom, a knowledge that is sometimes seen in the faces of elders, but was uncommon in one so young.

Lady Denby's features, taken one by one, could be agreed upon as pretty, but as a whole, their effect added to regal elegance that stunned. Certainly it was hard to reconcile this woman with the waif that Stephan had carried over his shoulder. Classical beauty would be a false label, though her figure, as outlined by the flowing muslin, was well-proportioned. Olive-toned skin spoke of her Spanish heritage, contrasting with the peaches-and cream-complexions that surrounded her, to make them seem insipid. The crown of her hair gleamed in candlelight, burnishing its rich chestnut with glints of auburn. Piled high and dressed with jewel-inlaid pins, her coiffure caused them to seem of similar height. Let loose, that curtain of silky brown had fallen past her waist, he recalled.

Dressed with a deceptively simple sophistication that made every other woman in the room appear over-embellished, her gown rippled with the light as if stirred by an unseen zephyr. The play of color reminded him of the fields of lavender he had seen in Provence during the brief Peace of Amiens. She was Persephone emerging to proclaim spring. Somehow, the shades of half-mourning had been fashioned into a banner celebrating rebirth.

As their eyes met and locked, he would swear that there was a spark of something.

A brief span of puzzlement vanished in a second to be replaced by a blank, socially bland slate.

A merry rejoinder from Miranda returned his attention to the company.

"You speak of protection? Is that not the job of men, dear Fiona?" Miranda exclaimed.

"We all know what kind of *protection* you would offer to two defenseless widows!" Fiona retorted, adding a knowing smile to her sardonic reply.

At the word *widows*, Percy's face lit like a beacon.

"Ah, if I were only twenty years younger!" Miranda said, punctuating regret with a sigh.

"If you were twenty years younger, you would be the Liberator of Caracas," the man who had been introduced as Simón Bolívar proclaimed stoutly. "And I would be wielding a sword beside you!"

Another voice piped up from behind Stephan, also in Spanish. "Are you planning to liberate Caracas yet again, Miranda?" Nigel Brewster strolled into the circle to lift his glass of wine in a mock toast, patent sarcasm in his tone. "One go at it was enough, don't you think?"

Bolívar bristled as Miranda's face went stark white. Stephan could see that the older man was fighting to contain himself.

"It is fortunate indeed, we are under the roof of

your prince, or you would be a dead man, insolent dog that you are." He bowed cordially to Stephan. "Excuse me, milord, I see my friend Mr. Wilberforce, and I have promised that I will make some introductions." With a fulminating look at Brewster, he shepherded the delegation away.

"I know. I should never have goaded him so." Brewster looked at Stephan apologetically. "The fool still believes he could rival the Corsican even though there are many still languishing in Spanish prisons because they believed his lies." He looked at Lady Denby apologetically." You must forgive me Aunt Fiona."

"Unfortunately, nothing that you have said is untrue." Still, her tone was gently chiding. "May I introduce my late husband's nephew, Nigel Brewster—"

Brewster, Stephan now had a face for the voice on the stairs.

Lady Denby hesitated politely, looking toward Stephan, waiting for a name. Could it be she did not remember him? Certainly, it would make his mission more difficult.

Percy stepped into the breach.

"May I present Lord Camford, the Prince's honored guest for tonight."

...

Hands reaching for her, the chill of air on her bare skin. Faces mocking... leering...Alec's voice shouting... Defenselessness... Fear... A haze of pain and whisky.

"Lord Camford!" Fiona barely kept herself from spitting out the name like an epithet. George was dead, but his heir, Lucas, had been among Nigel's companions that night.

Alec's nephew had ultimately hauled away his drunken collection of friends, but by then, the damage was done. Lucas was the one to put a name to her, bruited it all over the city, along with a story that grew in its infamous detail with every telling.

Fiona realized that she must have recognized the new earl as one of those blurry phantoms that had haunted her dreams since that ill-fated night. The hero of Busaca indeed! Though she desperately longed to strike the polite social smile from his face, that would not promote her plans.

"I was a friend of Alec's," the Earl said.

"Indeed, were you?" Despite herself, Fiona could not fully erase disbelief from her voice. She felt as brittle as the smile she feigned. "Alec had many friends, I now find."

"I share the same problem," the Earl replied, with a look that would have been charmingly sheepish, had she not known what was hiding behind that affable veneer. "I had no idea that I had so many friends until this evening. Unfortunately, the knowledge may cost me the use of my arm, with all the shaking it has gotten."

Son of a—she tried to cease her internal cursing, knowing that it was interfering with the demeanor she needed to display. "All knowledge has its costs, milord, but surely as George's son, you would know that."

"Oh no, Aunt Fiona, you are quite mistaken," Nigel interjected. "Lucas died in the same accident that killed his father. This is his cousin from the cadet branch of the family."

"Your late husband knew me as Stephan Aubrey," the Earl said.

Fiona paled. Stephan Aubrey! "Stephan Aubrey," she repeated. "Alec and I believed..."

"That I was dead." He finished for her. "I was, nearly. If they had been placing odds at White's and Boodle's upon my survival, I would have demanded chances no less than a hundred to one."

"I must apologize." Fiona belatedly extended her hand. "I am delighted to make your acquaintance at last.

Alec told me so much about you. He was frantic when there was no news of you following the battle. He never gave up, you know." She knew that she was babbling, and to her dismay, she felt her eyes burning and blinked back the tears.

"If any apologies are required, they should be mine." The Earl clasped her fingers in his. "I should have written as soon as I came to myself, but I was ill for a very long time."

There was something unsaid, something critical, Fiona thought. A strange tenor in the timbre of his voice made her feel defensive, as if she ought to be the one to seek penance. *Never ignore your instincts, lassie*, the Bruce had often said. Unfortunately, in the case of Stephan Aubrey, the message of her intuition was extremely strange and contradictory. As his fingers enveloped hers, she felt a curious sense of well-being.

Thus far, her evening had been spent in a state of constant vigilance, noting every nuance, trying to determine friend and foe, with all too many tallied on the antagonist side of the ledger. Yet, while he held her hand, she relaxed as if she had somehow reached a sanctuary within this social battleground.

In some inexplicable way, Fiona felt that she knew those eyes, blue and enigmatic as the Mediterranean. His face was gaunt, almost hollow from his illness, making his regard seem all the more intense. Her reaction to his proximity was more than the mere recognition of someone that she might have encountered briefly in her travels.

It was a homecoming.

Fiona would likely have questioned him further, but they were interrupted by a blowsy blonde woman in a mauve gown.

FOUR

A wanton widow Leezie was,
As canty as a kittlin.

— ROBERT BURNS,
HALLOWEEN

"Stephan!" The woman grabbed the Earl's arm with a force that caused him to wince. "I have been hoping to speak to you regarding my jointure."

"This is neither the time nor the place, Lillian." His discomfort was obvious as she moved closer than common courtesy would allow, clinging like a limpet to a rock.

"One might think that you are avoiding me!" She chided him in a childish baby voice that might have been forgiven in a newly hatched chick, but was ridiculous in a woman of maturity.

So this was Lady Camford. All of Fiona's instincts flared to full alert as the countess eyed Fiona with the territorial look of a cat defending its spot near the hearth. She might have been moved to pity toward any woman unfortunate enough to be George's wife. However, the countess had been among those that Madame

Robard had described in detail, and Fiona had no sympathy for a woman who had brazenly humiliated a dying wife.

The modiste had cited cards as the instruments of Lady Camford's ongoing financial folly, and it was instantly obvious why the woman was coming up a loser at the baize tables. Her expressions were a tableau of vivid tells. With all the subtlety of Mendoza in the ring, the countess's narrowed gaze assessed the quality of her opponent's attire and her rung on the ladder of prominence. It was almost amusing to watch the would-be coquette turn the force of her smile upon the males of the company.

So deep had Fiona sunk in the mire of reproach, that she felt a curious degree of indifference. The knowledge that there was little that this woman might do to cause damage to Fiona's reputation was liberating. Carlotta's warnings of *wrinkles, wrinkles,* came to mind as the woman's brow furrowed with a pout of impatience, an implicit demand for an introduction. It was apparent that the dowager countess wished to more fully evaluate her potential adversary before she made the choice of civility or combat.

Lord Camford finally took the hint. "Lady Denby, may I present my late Cousin George's wife, Lady Camford."

Fiona had stepped back into the crowd at the woman's onslaught. Now, as Fiona moved forward, her gown was no longer obscured, and she saw startled realization on the countess's face. It was clear that she recognized the creation that Madame Robard had refused to ruin. Horror was followed by calculation, as Lady Camford clearly wondered how that knowledge might be used to her advantage.

The gown that she had chosen in its stead substantiated the modiste's assertions about Lady Camford's lack of taste. She wore an abundance of flounces and furbelows in an unfortunate attempt to ape the appearance of a miss just out of the schoolroom. Instead, the surplus of decoration robbed her of the dignity that a gown more in keeping with her years might have bestowed.

Indecision paraded across the woman's face as she looked around her. Fiona could almost hear the murmur of the countess's inner dialogue: *How did this social pariah get an invitation from the Prince? Would it be foolish, then, to give her the cut direct?*

But that would have required her to release her death grip upon Lord Camford's arm and stalk away in righteous indignation. Lady Camford's cat-in-the-cream smile signaled when she arrived at the conclusion of her calculations. *Meoow, hisss, tremble before me because I have decided to unsheathe my claws.*

"Lady Denby, I have heard so much about you during George's posting in Portugal," the countess purred in a tone that clearly implied that nothing good had been said. "I confess myself surprised to see you."

Little did the ill-mannered kitten know that she was facing a lioness.

"Are you indeed?" Fiona asked, with a feline smile of her own that should have been a warning to the wary.

Lady Camford clearly did not possess that instinct for caution.

"I admire your courage, showing your face in public. Such tragedy we share! Poor Lord Denby!" Lady Camford coupled a pregnant pause with a dramatic accusatory look. When Fiona failed to spring at the attempt to lure her into response, Lillian tried another approach. "I know how difficult it must be for you to speak of it. Why, I can barely bring myself to think of George and Lucas, and *that* was an *accident*."

"So sad, and less than a year gone!" Fiona observed, candidly laying out the fact that Lady Camford had violated a cardinal convention in bypassing the full measure of bereavement. Fiona's sweeping gaze was nothing less than a visual condemnation of the deadliest kind. "Half-mourning, I suppose, is better than no acknowledgement at all. What a lovely shade of—is that mauve? Unfortunately, one cannot dress to reflect the full measure of one's grief in the Prince's house."

Lady Camford was clearly startled at the riposte to her dig. The countess chose another weapon for her next strike. "I must say that I cannot even put a name to the hues of your gown. I believe I saw something of the kind, discarded on the rack of a modiste I was used to frequent. A tatterdemalion costume for a masquerade, I thought it."

"We were quite fortunate," Carlotta said, coming to Fiona's side. Their eyes met and with a nod, Fiona invited her to join the hunt. "I have been long trying to convince Fiona that Lord Denby would not have wanted her to mourn forever."

Carlotta paused significantly. "She accepts tonight's invitation, but insists that nothing but half-mourning will she wear on her first foray back into society." She paused dramatically, drawing her listeners into the narrative. "But Fate intervenes. The fool for whom Fiona's gown was fashioned has grown beyond her corset's ability to contain her. She demands the seams be let out. Then—this is beyond belief!" Putting a palm to her mouth, Carlotta muffled a snicker. "The woman wished to add a layer of ruching to hide the deficiencies of her décolletage!"

Lady Camford flushed red, and a hand unconsciously lifted to finger the fabric at her bosom.

"Of course, the modiste, she refuses this insult to her art," Carlotta concluded, with an arch look that almost provoked Fiona into outright laughter.

"And Aunt Fiona obtained an exquisite gown. Does she not look breathtaking?" The expression that accompanied Nigel's observation was far too warm, and Fiona wondered if she was going to have to deny yet another proposal of marriage from Alec's nephew.

"I would love to continue this discussion of female fashion, Lady Camford," Fiona said. "But I see James Mill over in the corner. He was a good friend of my father's."

"I would be delighted to meet him if you would be kind enough to introduce me, Lady Denby." The Earl took advantage of Lady Camford's momentary paralysis to extract his arm from her grasp. "During my illness, there was little to do but read, and I am now in a position to bring some of his ideas on reform into the public forum.

He crooked his arm in invitation and Fiona accepted his offer of escort.

"*Touché*, Lady Denby!" he murmured. "Remind me never to cross swords with you in a verbal duel of wits."

"I was all politeness."

"All the more reason to admire your skill, especially considering that she was the one who threw down the gauntlet," he commented. "Lillian was rendered speechless. Certainly an event worth celebrating."

While they crossed the room, whispers rose around them like an autumn wind. Fiona could only hope that the rumors and speculation would serve to draw the rats from the woodwork.

"Your nephew is looking daggers my way," the Earl commented.

"Nigel has been extremely protective of me," Fiona explained. "He has even been kind enough as to offer marriage, more than once."

"From what I recall, that would be much to his advantage. Alec always said he was pockets-to-let, and relying on his sinecure to get by."

"Actually," Fiona said, "Nigel has become quite the eligible young man. Alec left him a substantial bequest."

"Why then do you refuse him?"

Fiona tried not to be offended. Given her reputation, Nigel would be considered a reasonable match. "You served on the Peninsula, milord, and were once a friend to my late husband. I would be a fool to believe you know nothing of the tales that were told about us." A matron in their path scurried away, lifting her skirt as if Fiona's proximity would sully it.

Fiona smiled at her graciously, knowing that it would needle the woman no end.

"I am a gambler's daughter, and my father taught me to always appraise the odds. Alec and I did well despite the hand we were dealt. I would not bet on that twice." She shook her head, as if it could clear the melancholy. "Besides, Nigel can do far better than his uncle's relict."

"But you forget, Lady Denby, that you are breathtaking."

He grinned at her, and once again, she felt a frisson of memory, a touch of heat that warmed her to the very core. It was most disturbing, for surely if she had seen that smile before, she would have never forgotten it.

. . .

Viscount Wellington leaned back against the seat cushions of the Camford carriage and sighed. "I do not know how many more of these evenings I can abide, supper at midnight, bed at dawn. How the Prince did prose on! It almost makes one long for the sound of cannon fire."

"It served." Stephan rubbed a soothing hand over his heavy-lidded eyes. "It appears she does not remember me."

"Not surprising, I've seen men who've taken a bullet who cannot recall the battle that laid them low."

Wellington said thoughtfully. "I sometimes wish we could make more of them forget. I suppose you will just have to jog her memory."

"I intend to call on her, sir."

"You ought to accustom yourself to calling me 'Arthur,'" Wellington admonished him with a frown. "And don't go too quickly, Stephan. Just follow the plan. You are far too wealthy to be a fortune hunter. You were a friend of Alec's, and you were ill to near death while the scandal stewed."

"How fortunate for the plan."

"Indeed," his former commanding officer asserted, with no suggestion that he had caught Stephan's sarcasm. "Our campaign's success rests on making it plain that it is marriage you're after, not dalliance."

"And if she has no desire for marriage?"

Wellington's expression pokered at the very notion. "Nonsense! You cannot fail to engage her interest. In the meanwhile, tantalize her with details of my schedule; tell her of planned military movements. Once she's taken the bait, we must keep her appetite whetted with just enough so she won't suspect anything amiss."

"I will be careful, sir—pray forgive me—Arthur." He twisted the carved ivory head of his cane. "How can I woo a woman that I ought to despise if, as you believe, she has chosen to conspire with Hades?"

"You must, Stephan. I understand your feelings, but lives are in the balance here. We now know that Hades was responsible for the debacle of the Convention of Cintra!" Even by the poor light of the carriage lamp, Stephan could see Wellington's face transforming into a mask of rage. "We could have finished the French after Vimeiro. Instead, we sent Junot and his army home to La Rochelle on our own ships. He disembarked with a mistress on each arm, his troops with their weapons in hand and stolen Portuguese gold in their pockets! Bonaparte must have busted his corset laughing at our folly!

Until the inquest, I could not fathom how this farcical agreement was perpetrated."

"I still find it difficult to credit that Lady Denby—"

"There is evidence," Wellington said stiffly. "Thank Heaven we were able to keep it hidden from the public eye, or else there would have been even more hell to pay. Made us into a laughingstock, nearly ruined our Spanish alliance, and almost destroyed me." His glowering expression had made many a subaltern cower.

"Surely someone else is better suited..."

The Viscount cut him short. "You are the *only* man for this task. She is a cunning woman, but given your history, she has no reason to believe that you are motivated by anything other than sympathy and friendship. With Alec's death, the group ceased its activities, but since Lady Denby's return to London, the cycle of blackmail for betrayal that was the hallmark of Hades has begun again."

"But why? From what you have told me, she is now a wealthy woman. Her father died in service of the Crown."

"She was orphaned, labeled a doxy, and discarded by those who should have shielded her. There was no inquiry into her father's murder." Wellington reminded him. Considering his previous anger, Stephan was surprised by the General's surprising tone of sympathy. "I do not defend her actions, but you must understand what you may face. If Hell hath no greater fury than a scorned female, how much more so is the wrath of a woman betrayed. If she has revived Hades, then the news that was announced this evening will make you utterly irresistible to her."

"And here I thought that you were relying on my handsome face and winning ways," Stephan commented with a self-deprecating laugh.

"Definite assets, those." Wellington's answering smile seemed a trifle forced. "However, she now knows that you have access to highly confidential information. That is the lure we are counting on. The hook is baited."

"And now I must worm my way into her affections?" Stephan was gratified to see a ghost of a grin before Wellington groaned at the pun, but his expression turned serious once more.

"Make no mistake, Stephan. Give her no reason to suspect your motives. Do not underestimate her."

"I will not, believe me. I have seen the measure of her mettle, and I have no intention of repeating Alec's error."

Despite his statement, he could not help but feel a deep sense of sadness. Although he had met her only briefly, he had carried Fiona with him as a cherished memory, a personification of beauty, valor, and duty. He had often wondered about what might have been if they had met again, if she had not been forced to marry Alec.

There were few things sadder than the words *might have been*.

. . .

Carlotta pulled the pins from her hair with a sigh, and slipped her knife into her palm before whirling to face the shadow that had appeared in her mirror.

"You are a lunatic!" she whispered, setting her weapon aside. "Someone will see you!"

"No one did," the man growled. "I have told you before that it is far too easy to get into this house, and I'll be out soon enough once you tell me what I need to know."

"You do realize that you are forcing me to betray my dearest friend." Carlotta sat on the bed and covered her face with her hands. "There has to be some other way to achieve our goals."

"You know my reasons," he said, seating himself beside her. "Now tell me everything that happened tonight, and I'll be gone. Who spoke to her and what was said?"

...

As Stephan was ushered into the stately home on Berkeley Square, it seemed that every available space in the drawing room was filled with a profusion of floral tributes. Nosegays and bouquets competed for the attention with their myriad colors and scents. Stephan was sure that the accompanying notes had been equally florid. The Foreign Secretary's first sally was a definite success. The Prince's invitation had given Lady Denby additional cachet, and the abundance of offerings was indicative of her social triumph.

Stephan saw that his own gift was placed apart from the others. The out-of- season red-and-gold sprays of autumn leaves contrasted boldly with the roses and hot-house blooms, making them seem dull and almost common. It appeared that he had distinguished himself as he had aimed to. The deceptive quality of his gift evoked a private sense of irony. Except upon close examination, the cunningly painted silk leaves were indistinguishable from the genuine article. He would soon see if Lady Denby was similarly false.

While he waited, the Stephan inspected the haven that had once been a second home to him. Other than the abundance of flowers, little had changed. The rich Turkish carpet still drew the eye with its patterns of blue, gold, and crimson. Alec's collection of jade and ivory figures watched mutely from their perches of carved teakwood. An array of puzzle boxes of various sizes and shapes challenged the unwary with their illusory straightforward appearance. The jade Kwan Yin, goddess of mercy, stood within her shrine, gazing at him with blind pity.

As always, the Chinese chessboard was disarranged,

a game in progress. He strode over and fingered an ivory warrior pawn, enjoying its familiar smooth, cool feel. The memories were almost tangible, and it seemed as if Alec would walk into the room at any second. Before the sadness overwhelmed him, Stephan focused his attention on the board. Both sides were nearly matched in the strength of their positions, but black had lost a bishop and king's pawn, and ivory, a knight.

The doors to the balcony were open, admitting breezes that carried the soft strains of music. Stephan stepped outside and saw Lady Denby, sitting in the garden below. An Indian patterned shawl adorned her shoulders, the bright colors relieving the severe black of her gown. At home, it would seem, she was still maintaining the fiction of mourning.

Sun glinted on the varnished wood of her guitar as she paused momentarily to tune a string. She hummed to herself until the note was right. Slowly, she began to pick out a song, her hands moving skillfully across the strings. The simple chords became complex, as her fingers embroidered the melody. A Portuguese *modinha*, Stephan had often heard the tune, but it always had seemed trite, sung with pretentious emotion. As she sang softly, he prayed that her servants would not find her too swiftly and interrupt.

Her voice was low and husky with emotion. She stumbled over some of the phrases as if they were painful, but the sheer, raw feeling of her delivery more than compensated for any deficiencies in her skills as a songstress. The strings cried of lost love, wasted emotion, unrequited passion. Although he did not understand every word, Stephan found himself swept away by the feelings that echoed his own, awash in despair, emptiness, betrayal.

The pretense of having his affections become engaged would be far easier than anticipated.

Too easy.

Since seeing her again at Carlton House, sleep had become increasingly elusive. His troubled dreams of a valiant, wounded waif had been transformed into nightmares, with the beautiful woman that Fiona had become at their center. In retrospect, he realized that he should not have been surprised by how deeply the news of her perfidy was distressing him. It was not just for Alec's sake that he mourned.

He had often wondered about her welfare. News in the field had been erratic, limited to occasional hearsay. He could make no inquiries of his own, since he had been warned to cease his usual correspondence with Alec.

Then came Busaca.

Until the Foreign Secretary had paid an unexpected personal visit to Brightlands in the spring, Stephan had been isolated in the country, recovering from his near-fatal flirtation with death. His own fight for survival had narrowed the scope of his life to how many steps he might take. With the help of Sergeant Hollins he had traveled many leagues.

From his bed to the door of his room, to force his foot to strengthen and heal.

From his room to the stair, into a house that echoed with emptiness due to the deaths of his parents.

From the manor to the estate office, where he struggled to shoulder his new responsibilities as the master of Brightlands, and then as the Earl of Camford.

The mission that the Foreign Secretary had proposed required Stephan to consider travel further afield. He had been meaning to go to London since unexpectedly inheriting the title. The solicitors for the Camford estate had long been urging Stephan to take matters directly in hand. When Richard had added a note with Wellington's own private plea, Stephan realized that there was little choice.

It was still painful to realize that Alec had been more

than a year dead and Stephan had not even known of it. Perhaps that was why it was so hard for him to come to grips with the rush of emotion that he had experienced upon seeing Fiona again. It was difficult to admit that he had thought of Lord Denby rarely and had imagined his wife all too frequently.

Stephan had finally acknowledged the truth. Since that night in Portugal, he had been struggling to contain his feelings for the woman Alec had been forced to wed. Even after their encounter at Carlton House, Stephan had managed to half-convince himself that those inappropriate longings were due to the fact that he owed her his life.

As her song plucked him back to the present, he recognized that those buried passions were rising to the surface once more. Although he could not afford to surrender to what he might have once felt, he could use the reality of those sentiments to maintain his charade.

While Fiona might have ample cause for her hatred, her motives did not matter. If she was a traitor, she had to be stopped.

The last notes faded into the morning air.

Below, a footman sonorously announced his arrival. When Lady Denby entered the room a few moments later, Stephan was studying the chess board.

"I apologize for the early hour." He bowed his greeting. "However, if this floral display is any indication, I doubt that I would have the opportunity for a private moment if I had waited until you normally receive visitors."

Lady Denby indicated a chair. "I must thank you for the lovely arrangement, milord. So unusual."

"Alec preferred beauty that transcended time." He gestured to the treasures that surrounded them, but his look deliberately included her in the tribute.

"My husband's collection was quite envied," Lady Denby stated briskly. "But he would have been the first to agree that even mankind's most exquisite fabrications are ephemeral." She lifted the figure of the Chinese goddess of mercy and caressed the jade before setting it gently in its place. "Love, loyalty, friendship, and honor are the most rare when they last." There was an underlying tone to her statement that verged on the accusatory, but before he could form a response, a servant entered with a cart of refreshments.

Fiona castigated herself. From the whispers that had swept Carlton House on the previous evening, it was clear that this man might have access to information of possible use. She could ill afford to drive him away. Even so, there was something profoundly unsettling about the strange feelings he roused within her. Daylight had not reduced the disturbing sense of familiarity. There was still a nebulous perception of ease in his presence, and worst of all, an inclination to trust him.

Fiona reminded herself that she still had Stephan Aubrey's letters to Alec. She had originally intended to return them, along with the legacy her late husband had bequeathed. It occurred to her now that it might be wise to read them first, to use Aubrey's own words to discover what manner of man the new Earl of Camford might be. In the meantime, she resolved to look upon him strictly as a resource to be cultivated.

"Would you like to join me?" she asked. "I am an early riser these days, and breakfast is some hours past."

As she busied herself with the mechanical ceremonies of hospitality, Fiona found herself puzzling over the nagging feeling of past acquaintance. Despite his familial relationship with George, she could see no resemblance. Even the color of Stephan Aubrey's hair differed from his cousins' inky locks. Blond waves swept back in a fashionable cut did little to soften the look of a man who had obviously seen and survived hardship. The new earl's face was narrow, with an aquiline bridge to his nose. A small scar marked his solid jaw and his build was muscular, but far too spare, no doubt due to his illness.

Certainly any connection to the late Earl of Camford would never have elicited the emotions that had almost overwhelmed her last night. His touch had made her feel sheltered and cared for once more.

Illusions, she reminded herself, *ephemeral and false*.

She had almost managed to convince herself that her unsettled feelings were nothing more than the result of finding a friendly face in hostile territory. Yet, now that she was back in his presence, she found herself viscerally drawn to this man, as if she had somehow known him in the past. Given her history, that was not necessarily a positive recommendation.

"Perhaps I should have written a paean to your beauty, the bright light of your *beaux yeux*?" he asked. "Unfortunately, my rhymes tend to be of the moon-and-June variety."

His self-mocking admission roused a rueful chuckle from her. "It is more the bright gleam of my sovereigns that inspires their eloquence, Lord Camford." Fiona was satisfied to see that her forthright sally had caused him a start. The display of bouquets garnered a dismissive gesture. "Almost two-thirds of these tributes are from men who are hopelessly attracted to my purse."

"At least I cannot be accused of being one of their number. George left me very comfortable, to say the least—the only kindness my cousin ever did me, and that, inadvertent," the Earl commented. "Still, I would not dismiss all those compliments as insincere, Lady Denby. A beautiful, rich wife is far superior to an ill-favored rich wife."

His frank retort was disarming, and Fiona found herself unsure as to what to reply. The silence stretched uncomfortably while she cast about for some topic to fill the wordless void. She lifted the jade queen from the chessboard beside her and moved it to the fore of the ivory bishop. Camford eased his chair toward the board, accepting the implicit challenge, and after a moment's survey, retreated to protect his exposed knight.

"A risky move," he stated. "Your rear flank is open to attack."

"I am rather a reckless player," Fiona admitted. "It bothered Alec no end. He could never determine what my next move would be."

"Alec was an excellent chessmaster."

Her guest castled the ivory king.

"That would have been Alec's next move," Fiona said. "His caution was both an asset and a problem. It made him predictable."

She moved her knight into an exposed position, directly in line of the white bishop. "One could almost always be certain that he would react in the same way to a given situation, never sacrificing a queen, castling at first option..."

Camford seized the knight. Fiona's pawn moved in the rear rank to take an ivory pawn, thereby exposing an open file. The ivory king retreated and was ultimately helpless before the jade queen.

"Checkmate!"

Her rook slid into final position and her opponent toppled his king in defeat.

"You play just as Alec did," she said. "One had only to bait the trap properly for him to step in."

"Alec taught me the game, so I suppose that our styles may be similar," Camford said. "I have learned a great deal though, since those days. Perhaps if we start the play from the beginning, the outcome would be different, Lady Denby."

Fiona eyed him sharply. Her years as her father's apprentice had taught her to be sensitive to every nuance. Was there an ironic cast to his voice? Or was this damnable fascination she was feeling affecting her judgement. His expression was bland, yet there was something extremely disquieting about the new Earl of Camford.

Mockery? A test of some kind?

She had never had such difficulty making such judgements before, or for that matter, putting a lid on the boiling kettle of her emotions.

A dangerous man.

Perhaps she had not yet reconciled the Stephan Aubrey that Alec had described and admired, with the flesh and blood man who stood beside her? Perhaps it was because of, not in spite of, her odd desire to be near him that Fiona felt a strange reluctance to vouchsafe him the use of her own first name, as she ought. It seemed almost as if the formality of her title was a shield.

Against what?

Was this sense of irritation that radiated from him merely Fiona's own perception of his pique at being bested on the board by a woman, or was it just her imagination?

"Then I invite you to return with the set for another match." Fiona attempted to smooth over the awkward moment, as she placed the chess pieces into their velvet-lined case. "The board is yours. I held on to your legacy in the hope that I could someday pass on Alec's gift to you. There are several other small items, also a minor bequest, but my man of business can give you the details..." Her voice trailed off. It was obvious that the Earl had ceased to listen. His gaze was directed at the portrait of Alec that hung in the center of the room.

Every time Fiona looked at the painting, she saw something new. Reynolds had painted an extraordinary portrait that caught Alec truly; the crook of his smile managed to convey a sense of his whimsy. Behind the world-weary pose had been a complex man that she had just begun to know before his death.

When had she begun to fall in love with her husband? It was hard to say. There had been no moment of epiphany, no burst of overwhelming passion. Her regard for Alec had grown unawares, nurtured by kindness and gentle affection. Despite its awkward beginnings, their relationship had matured within a brief time to a comfortable companionship, leavened with laughter, a shared sense of the ridiculous.

A feeling that she was, at last, safe.

FIVE

I waive the quantum o' the sin,
The hazard of concealing

      — ROBERT BURNS, EPISTLE TO A
                    YOUNG FRIEND

S tephan, too, was wandering in the past. Alec's
legacy had brought back memories of innocent
times, when a young man's greatest worries were
the fall of his neck linen and the fit of his waistcoat. The
room still retained the essence of the man in the portrait. Echoes and images of late-night conversations,
spirited arguments, hard-fought games of piquet and
chess seemed to abide all around him.

Yet, despite the memories lingering in this place, he
felt a growing sense of helplessness. He had agreed to
this farce convinced that he was on the side of the an-
gels. In no way had Stephan reckoned with the likeli-
hood that he still had strong feelings for a woman he
had known for no more than an hour or two. As he regarded Alec's portrait, Stephan realized that he had been
unwittingly violating the Ninth Commandment.

He had long coveted Alec's wife, thought of her,
longed for her in the night. In the intervening years,

Stephan had half-convinced himself that his imagination had supplied the stuff of fantasy, told himself that those desires were nothing more than the longings of a lonely soldier staring into a campfire, or the delusions of a man near death, half out of his mind with pain and laudanum.

Now, with Alec gone to the grave, Stephan could finally admit that he still wanted Fiona, despite what the Wellesleys suspected she might have done.

He wondered if she was aware that he was watching her. Emotions seemed to flit effortlessly across her face. Was the pose of the grieving widow entirely for his benefit? Had he been an unwary observer he would have been entirely convinced of her abiding sorrow. Or was this show of emotion all a sham, and had she wrought Alec's destruction, seeking some manner of revenge? She had turned away, as if to hide her naked grief, so he was unprepared when she suddenly came about to face him once more.

Fiona recoiled from the force of his look, almost as if he had dealt her a physical blow. He tried to banish the antipathy beneath a bland veneer, but it was too late.

A look of resignation replaced her initial angry expression.

"I should have realized." She kept her voice steady. "I'm sure that they delighted in acquainting you with my perfidy, the real *truth* of Alec's suicide. Do I presume correctly that you have heard the rumors?" Her head held proudly, her eyes met his demanding an honest reply.

"I had heard some tittle-tattle," Stephan admitted, even as he cursed himself for a fool. Because of his ineptitude at concealing his feelings, the game might be done before it was begun. He had one more gambit to try.

"Why then?" he asked her. "Why did Alec take his own life? He was a strong man, seemingly with everything to live for." Once more he watched for the panoply of her reactions to give him some guidance as to her inner state, but it was as if she had drawn a shutter to conceal her feelings. She observed him with all the cold scrutiny of a judge on the bench, weighing him.

Finally she said, "I think that you should be seated, Stephan Aubrey."

Obediently, he took a chair. She walked to the balcony door and closed it. Then, after checking the door of the drawing room, she stood before Alec's portrait, staring at it momentarily, as if conferring with his spirit before she spoke.

"You served in Portugal. I am certain that you have heard some of the rumors surrounding my marriage."

She had given Stephan the opening he sought.

"I know in certainty that you did not trick Alec into the parson's mousetrap," he told her. "You were victims of circumstance on that night. It angers me to think of what was done to you both."

She eyed him in patent puzzlement and suspicion, waiting in silence for him to elucidate.

"How much do you remember about that night, Lady Denby?"

"Why do you ask?" Her question held a wealth of suspicion.

"It was only yesterday evening I realized that you might not recollect the entirety of the events leading to Alec's offer of marriage. Seemingly, you had forgotten me, even though between the whisky and the pain, you managed to keep your wits about you for a surprisingly long time."

Fiona's eyes widened and her hand went to her mouth as she put her other on the arm of a chair, as if in sudden need of support.

She regarded Stephan warily as he rose and approached her, but she did not retreat. "If you had managed to erase those hours from your memory, I would not force them upon you again. But from the look on your face, I think you are beginning to remember."

She slid into the seat, closed her eyes and took a deep breath. When she opened them again, she gazed at him with a puzzled expression. "I know you."

"You do." He sat down beside her, and took her hand in his.

"I am aware that someone else cared for me that night." Fiona stated carefully, still unwilling to confirm or deny.

Her fingers were chilled, and he rubbed them gently as he spoke. "But for Alec's quick thinking, I would have been embroiled in the scandal, just as you were. You, yourself may provide the proof of my truth. May I?" He touched the hem of her shawl. At her nod, he rose and slipped it from her shoulders, setting it aside on his chair.

A puffed suggestion of a sleeve rose from her demure décolletage, the fabric concealing what he knew was beneath. Once again he silently asked and received permission. He felt the intake of her breath as he slowly slid the strip of silk aside.

"I was always concerned about how well the wound had healed. But I did not realize how painful it might have been for you until after I took a bullet myself. I was inspired by your courage on that night." Stephan kept the statement casual, as if he were remarking on the possibility of rain. He knew that he was not prevaricating at all. He truly had wondered about her.

Where she was.

If she had healed.

If Denby was treating his unwanted wife as more than an unpleasant consequence of a forced marriage of inconvenience.

He thought about her more often than he might have wished on many a sleepless night, especially after he had been wounded. "Remembering you helped me get through. Your courage inspired me. If a slip of a girl could bear it, then it would be absolutely shameful if I could not."

"Your face. I knew I had seen it somewhere," she whispered, touching a hand to the ridge of his cheek.

"I've prayed for you, wondered about you since that night." Wondered and dreamed. It was in his sleep that his desires had crossed the boundaries of propriety. Fiona had haunted his nights. "Feared for you. I've seen too many injuries like yours that ended in a lifetime of pain, or death."

She stilled completely, as he revealed the puckered traces of knitted skin. "It was you then?" she asked softly.

He nodded. "If I might?"

He moved a finger lightly over the first of the scars and felt her shiver beneath his touch. "My mother would have been proud of my stitchery I think." He traced the mark slowly. Stephan rose and went around behind her to look at the exit wound. Bending so close to her, he could feel her warmth, the tickle of a stray lock of hair upon his cheek, but despite the temptation to turn the touch into a more prolonged caress, he did not press nearer and take the chance that she would shy away from him.

Later, he promised silently, as he pressed a tender kiss to each of the scars, before sliding the sleeve into place. "Forgive me the liberty, but my mother always used to say that a kiss had the power to heal."

"I remember my mother used to say the same." Her voice trembled. "Are you a doctor then?"

"You're shaking." He took up her shawl and set it back on her shoulders, wrapping her like a child. "Almost every soldier learns to do what he can in the field. You take care of your mates and they take care of you." He seated himself beside her and grasped her hands once again, to clasp them between his palms. "If I know a bit more than most, it was because my family followed the drum when I was a lad. My father was a colonel under Howe. My mother did more than her share of healing, and made certain that I was handy with a needle and thread."

"It was you then?" There was astonishment in her whispered words, a look of wonder in her eyes as if she believed that he was the one who hung the moon and the stars. "You were the man who saved my life that night! It is you who carries me safely through my nightmares! That is why I was so confused. Alec refused to name you. To protect you, he said. So that I might answer truthfully if it ever came to questioning under oath."

"And he did protect me. Protected us both, in fact, but in different ways. I must acknowledge that you saved my hide as well. Were it not for your timely warning that night, the shot from the man in the square would likely have killed me." Reluctantly, he let her hands slip to her lap and rose, forcing himself to rise and step away. "I'm glad it healed so remarkably well. Perhaps it was the whisky?"

"My Da always maintained that MacLean's Gold is brewed with witchcraft." Fiona knew she was rambling, but she could not help herself. Since her return to London, the nightmares had returned, but now her phantom savior had a face.

She pulled the shawl tighter around her shoulders, as if it could somehow tether her back into reality. "Alec always told that part of the tale with no small degree of pique. You cannot purchase it anymore, although I hear rumors that it may be brewed yet again." She mimicked her late husband's indignant accents as she sank into a chair. "Two! Full, well-aged bottles of precious Gold, when a basin of water would have done the trick."

"That night was the last time that I saw Alec," her

guest said, with a sadness in his eyes that was clearly genuine.

How she could have forgotten the anxious voice urging her to hold steady through the cloud of pain and confusion? This man was the source of strength and safety that she had felt. Cradled in the shelter of his arms, he had carried her through the labyrinth of dark streets.

Now she knew why the vague memories of a gentle hand holding a cup to her lips, and the smell of whisky had always been coupled with the tang of bergamot, citrus and shaving soap. It was the scent he wore.

Fiona's failure to recollect the particulars of those hours had always troubled her deeply. The Bruce had trained her to remember the smallest of details. He had drummed it into her head that it was often the minutiae that provided the key to unlocking information that could be exploited. Yet, that nightmare in Portugal had remained shrouded in a haze, the horrors of particulars lost in the waking.

She choked with emotion and smiled weakly before she spoke. "Robard or Weston could not have done better, milord. I usually wear gowns or a paste that covers the scars, but as you see, the remnants of your handiwork are easy to conceal."

"As your tailor then, could you please call me Stephan?"

"Only if you address me as Fiona."

"Fiona, it is!"

How to begin? How to tell the man her husband had regarded as a son of the facts and accusations that had led to Alec's death?

Fiona was choosing her words when the sounds of laughter and a baby's babble wafted up the stairs.

Carlotta burst into the room and deposited Alejo in her lap. "We now know the reason for our boy weeping all the night. Behold, we have joy in the morning! The

little one has a brand-new tooth! Look and see for yourself." All at once, she noticed that there was someone
else in the room. "Lord Camford. *Perdon*. I interrupt."

"Not at all. I am glad to share such welcome news.
You have a lovely child, *señora*."

"Actually, little Alejandro is my cousin," Nigel
Brewster entered the room followed by Percy Strethan.
"The infant Lord Denby, son of my Uncle Alec."

"My apologies for intruding, Lady Denby," Percy
made his greetings. "I had the good fortune of meeting
Señora del Castillo and Mr. Brewster in the park on my
way to pay a call upon you. If I am intruding—"

"Not at all," Fiona said, embracing her son. Alejo
burbled joyfully, his smile wide, as if to display his
newest accomplishment. "Cook has prepared a tray of
her almond cakes, and as usual, she has supplied enough
to feed a regiment."

"Then we ought not to disappoint her," Carlotta
asserted stoutly. "Although it may not be fashionable to
admit it, I, for one, am starved. Expeditions to Hyde
Park with the little one always enhance the appetite."

"A woman who will admit to eating more than a
nibble!" Percy exclaimed in delight. "How very refreshing!"

"Alas, I cannot indulge in Cook's treats, and have
limited time for a comfortable coze," Nigel informed
them all. "Wellesley has a meeting scheduled at which I
must translate."

"Which Wellesley do we speak of?" Percy asked.
"Arthur Wellesley, the general, now also known as Vis-
count Wellington? Henry Wellesley, the ambassador to
the council of Spain? Or do you refer to Richard, the
Marquis Wellesley, also Earl of Mornington, who is the
Foreign Secretary?"

"It does get confusing, doesn't it?" Nigel remarked
with a sardonic smirk. "The Wellesley brothers do seem
to have their fingers in any number of government pies.

Like little Jack Horner of the children's doggerel, they always manage to pull out a prime plum for themselves."

"I must say, Nigel. You are looking especially elegant today. Does he not, Fiona?" There was a wicked look on Carlotta's face. "Is that a new pair of boots? Waring?"

"Hoby's, of course!" Nigel took insult at the mistake. "I wear no others! I have nearly two dozen pair, all of them his make."

"No wonder, then, that they all look like new," Fiona said, in an attempt to soothe his ruffled feathers.

Mollified, Nigel picked another biscuit from the plate. "So, since you asked me to be specific, it is the Foreign Secretary I must attend this afternoon. He meets *ex officio* with a delegation from Caracas. One of them, Simón Bolívar, who you met the other night, may be a connection of yours, Aunt Fiona? His late wife, Maria del Toro, was also a connection to your mother's family. No doubt you knew your Inicio relations."

"Unfortunately, we were estranged from mama's side of the family, so I would not have made their acquaintance." Fiona offered Alejo a bit of biscuit to chew on and hoped that the direction of the conversation would change.

It did not.

"I do not understand," Nigel said, with a puzzled look. "Considering the fuss that the Inicio family kicked up in Portugal, I had always thought that you were a valued daughter of the house."

"If he is unattached, Bolívar is quite a catch," Carlotta interjected. "Francisco told us that he is one of the wealthiest men in the Spanish colonies. I hear that Simón paid the expenses for the entire embassy to England. He is quite the handsome devil, is he not?"

Fiona looked down at Alejo and offered him another taste of the confection in an effort to hide her smile. Carlotta was playing at *matador*, waving her cape to see if Stephan's friend was interested in her, and at the same time, acting to divert the direction of Nigel's chatter.

"Why is he here?" Strethan inquired, a hint of irritation in his voice as he all but glared at Carlotta.

And the bull charges, Fiona observed inwardly. *So that was the way the wind was blowing,*

"That would seem to depend upon which member of the delegation you ask," Stephan observed. "At Carlton House, Bolívar seemed to be advocating for nothing less than independence, but the senior delegates are talking of loyalty to the Spanish king."

"Bolívar is wasting his time and money!" Nigel said angrily. "Dear Heaven! Preserve us all from revolutionary idiots! Castlereagh had prepared to send a force to Caracas under Wellington, and he was actually laying in supplies and arms. The plan was Miranda's, and given his disastrous history we ought all to be grateful that it was nipped in the bud."

Fiona was astonished to see the normally even-tempered young man in such a lather.

Nigel took a breath and looked at them all awkwardly. "Please, do forgive my outburst. I was overcome by the fear that I shall be spending my afternoons henceforth translating the mad maunderings of yet another Francisco de Miranda."

"Poor Nigel!" Fiona chuckled, and wrapped up some of the baked goods in a napkin. "A terrible fate indeed to be subjected to a day of diplomatic deliberations. Please take some almond cakes with you in case you have the need to fortify yourself for the ordeal."

"Perhaps I shall." Nigel was about to take up the bundle when he clapped a hand to his forehead. "I had almost forgotten why I wished to stop here on my way to Number One London." He reached into his pocket and held out a silver rattle to Alejo. "This once belonged to Uncle Alec, and then it was passed on to my mother, his sister, when I was an infant."

To Nigel's obvious dismay, Alejo grabbed at his cousin's sleeve, transferring a sticky mass of cookie to the elegant coat. Nigel pulled away, brushing at the crumbs in a futile attempt to clean that only embedded the mess farther into the fabric.

"Bad boy!" he chided. "Bad boy!"

"Ba," Alejo mimicked "Ba ba!" Alejo reached for the rattle and Nigel all but threw it into Fiona's lap.

"I am so sorry, Nigel," Fiona said, swallowing a giggle at her nephew's horrified expression. "I shall call Eldridge and your jacket will be cleaned in a trice."

"No need. I shall go home and leave this to my valet. Weston's work, y'know." Nigel applied the napkin like a bandage to a wound. With a basilisk eye, he glared at the baby.

Alejo grasped the toy and started to chew on the handle.

"Well, it seems that the boy finally knows what to do," Nigel declared with a sniff. "There is a portrait at Denby Chase of Alec as an infant, holding this very rattle. It is the very image of Alejo."

At the door, the young man paused before taking his leave. "Pay no heed to what people are saying, Aunt Fiona. Little Alejandro is Alec's son. You should have the picture from Denby Chase sent to you so that you may hang it for all to see."

Torn between tears and laughter, Fiona managed to hold back her fit of giggles until he was gone.

"I no longer wonder why England is perpetually at war," Carlotta remarked. "With men like Brewster at the diplomatic helm, I marvel that we are not at odds with every country on Earth."

"He meant no harm." Fiona struggled to regain her composure. "Even before Alec's death, Nigel was always attempting to defend me." She looked at Percy apologetically. "I am sorry, Mr. Strethan, but there is no need to pretend ignorance of the sordid circumstances of my marriage. You had mentioned the other evening that you were on the Peninsula at the time and even if you had not been, all of London is well aware of the tale."

She rose, her head held high in defiance. There would be no more cowering in the corner. "Although Alec was blameless and a victim of circumstance, the scandal destroyed my husband's career. If you choose to take your leave rather than remain under the roof of a woman that all of society deems to be a harlot, I will not blame you. Or you, Lord Camford."

"I was proud to name your husband as a friend, Lady Denby." Strethan said. "And as such, I always have questioned the veracity of those stories."

"As you should! To paraphrase Voltaire, the value of a good question far surpasses a multitude of answers." Carlotta declared. "Especially when they are the insinuations of the *ton*."

"She paraphrases Voltaire," Percy murmured in bemusement.

Stephan gave his friend a look that seemed a mixture of amusement and exasperation. "I think we can all agree that Alec was a victim of vindictive envy. He was a man of honor who would never have sullied his name in a union with someone unworthy. If I may have the pleasure of calling upon you and your friend again, I would be most grateful."

"You will both be truly welcome."

Fiona managed to hold her calm expression until the door closed behind them.

Alejo began to fuss.

"The little one knows his mother is upset," Carlotta took up the baby and began to pace the room, jouncing the boy gently as she quieted him. "You see, already you have two most gallant defenders."

"Look at me! I am close to weeping with relief. Da

would be furious with me, letting my emotions rule me like this." Fiona took a deep breath. "I don't know if I can do this, Carlotta."

"Pah! It is past time to let yourself weep, if you ask me! All these years, your father made you into his puppet, forcing you to hide who you are and what you feel." Carlotta waved a dismissive hand. "You have played the maid in the house of Napoleon himself. You have penetrated the prison where they hold the King of Spain and carried to him messages of hope. You have cheated the guillotine. Do you tell me now that you fear the wagging tongues of so-called polite society?"

"It does seem ridiculous, doesn't it?" Fiona sniffed.

"No, my dear friend, it does not," Carlotta said. "Your father taught you how to handle all manner of weapons, but as we learned last night, the salons and ballrooms of the *ton* require a more subtle form of combat."

SIX

On ev'ry hand it will allow'd be,
He's just – nae better than he should be

— ROBERT BURNS, A
DEDICATION TO GAVIN
HAMILTON

2 7 Grafton Street was a modest brick residence in a neighborhood comprised mostly of those who could claim more breeding than funds, and those of the ambitious sort who aspired to climb above the middling class. Well-born, but revolutionary in creed, perpetually in need of the ready, with two sons by his housekeeper wife, Sarah, who wore no ring on her finger, Francisco de Miranda defied any attempt at categorization.

The house contained but nine rooms. At least one of them was usually occupied by a rotating roster of revolutionaries and thinkers, schemers and dreamers.

Fiona deliberately dropped her reticule and bent, using the opportunity to take a look at the street behind her, but no one was there. Even so, she couldn't shake the feeling that she had been followed.

Leander, Francisco's older son, abandoned the hoop

he was rolling to see Fiona inside. "Mama is busy in the nursery," he informed her as he opened the door to the barely controlled bedlam that was the Miranda household. "Are you come to see Papa?" he asked.

At Fiona's nod, Leander took the lead, although she would not have required the boy's escort to find his father. "*Basta con mirar a Montesquieu!*" echoed through the hall.

"And why must we look at Montesquieu?" Fiona asked, as she entered the room Francisco called his Great Library. It was among the few of his statements that contained no trace of exaggeration. Shelves of books, maps, and pamphlets overflowed onto every available surface, and many had migrated to occupy another full room.

"Ah, Fiona! A pretty face to brighten the day of an old man!" he said, giving her an enthusiastic greeting. "You have met these gentlemen, eh? At Carlton House?"

"*Old*?" Fiona replied, with just the right hint of flirtatiousness. "Your namesake is barely out of leading strings, and little Leander has but seven years in his dish."

"See how she flatters me, *mes amigos*, a smart woman," Francisco declared.

"A smart man should be wary of smart women," Simón Bolívar remarked with a cynical smile. "I am forever being chased by them."

"Then they are obviously not as smart as you believe, *Señor* Bolívar," she answered pertly.

"Ah, she has your measure, boy." Francisco chortled, as the laughter died down.

Fiona noted how Bolívar stiffened at the use of *boy*. Nonetheless, he took her hand and bowed. "*Touché*, Lady Denby," he said, eying her with renewed interest. "You must call me Simón."

Fiona decided that it would do no harm to vouchsafe her given name to Bolívar. The members of the delegation were meeting with the Foreign Secretary on a frequent basis, and she had found in the past that useful information frequently came from the most unlikely of sources. Slowly, she was building a network, and with Carlotta's help, making contact with some of the Bruce's old founts of information. Those members of her father's league of Scotsmen who were not employed by her directly were on the listen. Even Nigel's lack of discretion could be useful, although pumping that well outright for facts might arouse suspicions in the wrong quarters.

As she assessed the company, Fiona decided against a direct approach. Francisco was a canny one. The Bruce had once categorized the perpetual revolutionary as a tomcat who had spent all of his nine lives, and was ever willing to borrow the lives of others. Miranda was one of the few who dealt in the shadows who could honestly say that they had bested her father in the trade of secrets.

She could ill afford him using her investigation as currency with Wellington and his brothers. Word in those circles could very well chase the one she was seeking deeper into hiding. Oblique tactics might also bypass the *quid pro quo* that Francisco would inevitably demand with a more candid request for his cooperation.

"So, Fiona, we are equally divided between us," Francisco said. "We discuss a constitution for Spain's former colonies. What say you on Montesquieu?"

"A trifle premature, are you not?" Fiona reminded him with a laugh. Knowing his adoration for the philosopher, she proceeded to add her arguments on the side of Montesquieu. Simón, too, apparently worshipped at the same intellectual altar.

Before she took her leave, Fiona had an invitation for a drive in Hyde Park and a promise for a dance at Almack's. As Carlotta had predicted, after her appearance at Carlton House, Fiona's voucher was approved with gratifying alacrity.

Francisco escorted her to the door, all but rubbing his hands with glee. "Perhaps I may add a new skill to the many in my life," he whispered. "When they write of me, they will say, liberator, general, philosopher, raconteur, and perhaps, they may soon add—matchmaker, eh? Bolívar swears he will never remarry, but he looks at you like a man under the spell of a *bruja*."

. . .

It was Percy's fault that Stephan arrived at Almack's later than he had expected. The man had been fussing at his toilette like a miss just let loose from the schoolroom. Percy had paid another call at Berkeley Square and learned that the formidable *Señora* del Castillo would likely be attending the assembly.

Richard's insistence that Stephan parade his limping self through Almack's seemed beyond ridiculous. Although his foot was just reaching the point of being fit to reliably walk upon, dancing was still out of the question. In the Foreign Secretary's estimation, Stephan's very presence at the *ton's* most notorious marriage market would be tantamount to a declaration of his interest in Lady Denby.

Nonetheless, as Percy hauled him into the assembly rooms and he saw the couples weaving their patterns across the floor, Stephan felt the aftermath of his wound all the more keenly. Percy eyed his friend in anticipation. "Going to give it a whirl? Why did you come with me, if you did not believe your leg was fit for duty? I know that there are few things you love more than a lively tune and treading a measure."

"Perhaps another evening." Stephan forced a smile. "What philosopher do you have in your pocket tonight? Perhaps I might turn a page or two while I sit."

"I have left Descartes on my desk," Percy said. "I, sir, am going to dance."

Stephan could barely contain his shock. His friend rarely left home without a read on his person. "Well then, the evening will not be without amusement. I will content myself with enjoying the music and watching the dancing bear."

Percy gave a harrumph of disbelief. "I doubt that is your reason for braving the gauntlet of scheming eligibles, Captain Wallflower. As for watching me shuffle around the floor with a bent back, I will have you know that for once, I have the promise of a waltz with a woman who can look me in the eye!"

"A brace of dancing bears then." Percy's glare elicited the first genuine laugh that Stephan had experienced in a long time. It felt good. He put up his palm in mock surrender. "A most graceful, elegant, and beautiful bear, at least the female of the pair."

Percy gave a curt nod at the tacit apology and scanned the floor.

"The fair *señora* should be easy to spot, unless she is absent or you are blind," Stephan remarked, eying the dense crowd of would-be dancers. "Is she coming alone?"

"Ah, so you finally admit that you attend for someone specific?" Percy arched a bushy brow. "Her, perhaps?" His friend nodded toward a spot where the matrons, misses, and chaperones sat to cast their lures into the sea of potential partners, hoping for a dance and perhaps something that might last beyond the music.

Stephan followed Percy's direction, but lacking his friend's elevated vantage point, only the milling crowd was visible. Then the cloud of people blocking his view parted to reveal Fiona, sitting in a pose of utter serenity, calm as the beautiful statue of Buddha that occupied a niche in Alec's garden.

Once again, she wore a gown that was elegant in its simplicity. The figured silk sarsenet of celestial blue was trimmed with a light wreath of artificial cornflowers, surmounted by a trimming composed of pearls. Stephan felt a strange sense of privilege, sharing the secret behind the subtly draped sleeve that was becoming her fashion hallmark. Her hair was not piled high this time, but arranged in a coil down her back, woven with a matching mixture of both pearls and flowers.

Empty chairs on either side of her indicated a disturbing cordon of scandal-borne contagion, emphasized by the fact that every other seat and place to stand in the vicinity was full. The question of Carlotta's location was soon answered when she arrived carrying two glasses. The two women sipped their ratafia with every appearance of the smiling tolerance that passed for enjoyment when partaking of Almack's insipid excuses for refreshment.

Stephan watched as Lord Soames ignored the implicit social quarantine and made his bows to Carlotta. Further observation made it clear that the man was requesting the favor of a dance, while pointedly ignoring Fiona's presence. Surrounding onlookers at the edge of the invisible stockade kept a guarded lookout. The *señora's* smile froze into frigid dismissal that sent Soames into a huffing retreat. Without words, it became clear that an insult to Lady Denby was a slight to *Señora* del Castillo.

Percy's jaw tightened at the implicit disrespect, and with a glance at Stephan, he readied himself.

"Prepare to charge, Captain." Without waiting for an acknowledgement, Strethan began his sortie. Stephan felt like a cannon being hauled behind a team of stampeding cavalry mules as he was towed along. They plowed through the crowd of couples taking their partners in preparation for the upcoming waltz.

"See, you *can* walk well enough if you try!" Percy murmured as they neared their objective.

"Actually, I'm not quite sure if my feet touched the ground," Stephan replied.

"I'm finding love can do that," the hulking man observed in all seriousness. Presenting himself before Carlotta, Percy made his bow.

Stephan looked mournfully at his walking stick and felt a twinge of true regret. It was almost frightening to realize how intensely he felt the desire to dance with Fiona. He closed his eyes for a moment, and imagined leading her across the floor, holding her close and inhaling the scents that subtly spiced her presence. He wanted to hold her in his arms once more, to move with her and against her in the admittedly sinful sensuality that was the waltz. As he bent to make his bow, Stephan glumly reconciled himself to reality.

"Would you be willing to sit through this dance with me?" he asked.

Fiona almost laughed. Stephan asked the question as if there were a surfeit of gentlemen queued up to squire her to the floor. Strangely, despite her recognition of their shared past, there was a part of her that would prefer to be alone. She wanted neither the pity nor the condescension that might come as he shared her isolation.

Fiona was also concerned about the consequences of her reputation if the Earl was publicly associated with her. If he valued his post, merely sitting with her might put him at risk. Still, despite all the reasons she had marshalled to send him to safer ground, there was something in Stephan's eyes that caused her to smile and nod her assent.

With a look of satisfaction, Carlotta took the elbow that Percy offered and they made their way to the floor leaving Fiona in uncomfortable silence. Until Alec, relationships had always been a means to a specific end.

Even flirtation was a ploy to beget information. Although she felt a strange bond with Stephan, the forging of friendships required skills that Fiona was finding difficult to master. Establishing trust was more of an effort than enduring loneliness.

In the Algarve of Portugal, she had seen a peculiar creature that could assume the coloration of its surroundings, turning from brown to green to reflect the scrublands of the Peninsula. The Bruce had taught her how to become a human form of that clever lizard, taking on whatever role he desired her to assume, mimicking all necessary mannerisms and characteristics. Fiona was able to impersonate easily, but not quite sure how to be herself. It was a risk to allow anyone to potentially exploit the vulnerability that was the basis of trust.

Even Carlotta did not quite understand that, except for those brief months with Alec, the Bruce's daughter had always been very much alone. There had never been anyone else who understood who she was, what she had been. With Alec, Fiona had discovered what it was to be in the company of a man who had come to genuinely respect her past, as well as her present needs, her desires, her truth. She had forgotten that the truth was a danger, both to herself and others.

Ultimately, her husband had paid the price for that lapse of memory.

Fiona turned to find Stephan regarding her with a thoughtful air. She fabricated a smile.

"You don't have to, you know," he told her, turning his attention to the dancers.

"Have to—what?"

"Smile, if you don't feel like it. Make conversation," he answered. "I've always wondered at that phrase, *make conversation*. What are the raw materials for useless inanities?"

She considered the question seriously. "I suppose that the substance from which we build that type of talk is largely superficiality, hence the popularity of the weather, one's health. But then there is the temptation to give the words substance, consequence."

"Which is the natural precursor to gossip and lies." Stephan nodded his head in understanding and Fiona felt inordinately pleased that he had followed the thread through the tangle of her thoughts. "They are doubtlessly talking about us."

"No," Fiona corrected him. "I say without vanity that it is me they speak of. They wonder how I have managed to lure you into the valley of death that my very presence causes in the midst of this social oasis. They speculate about what the nature of our relationship is, and what it may become. Then, when they exhaust the present and future, they will delve into my notorious past, my late husband, and how I lured him to ruin, and speculate whether or when I will do the same to you."

"Our presence provides a signal service then, providing both amusement for the vicious and relief for others, who, but for our convenience as a target, might be more defenseless subjects of their venom."

She felt the bubble of laughter bursting out of her, breaking through her carefully constructed guise of composure. "Thank you!" she said, simply, smiling as she gazed out onto the dance floor.

"For what?" he asked.

"A refreshing moment of honesty."

Stephan abruptly turned his gaze back to the dance floor. "Look at them. I have never seen Percy waltz with so much grace. Usually it seems as if he is moving a fragile broomstick across the floor and doing a bad job of cleaning at that."

"And Carlotta is always hunched over, as if trying to make herself small. Dancing among the Lilliputians." She sighed and he looked at her, a question in his eyes.

"Give you a penny for the thought."

Fiona debated with herself and decided that there was no harm in an honest answer. "I was just thinking how wonderful it is, to simply be yourself with somebody, not to have to pretend to be someone that they want you to be. For a brief time, I had that." She blinked away a tear. "I will not weep. I will never allow them to make me weep ever again."

Stephan felt guilty amazement as he watched her ruthlessly shut off her tears. With a few blinks and a sniff, the glint in her eyes disappeared, and she contemplated the view with every appearance of enjoyment. She smiled at him, laughed at his sallies, and joked with Percy when he returned Carlotta to her side and asked Fiona to take the floor with him.

But it was as if some veil had been lifted and Stephan could see the controlled pain behind the bravura performance. Was he the only one who could recognize the absence of joy in her steps? Pierce the surface and one could see the clockwork of a living automaton that smiled, impervious to the frowns and lascivious knowing looks as she moved between partners in the set.

"You see her." Carlotta looked at Stephan's expression curiously. "You see her truly." It was a statement, not a question. "Perhaps it is because you and I know the reality of her past."

Interesting. *Señora* del Castillo implied she was aware of Fiona's history. One more nugget to be examined. Despite her conversational lure, he answered with silence. The confidence that Fiona had given him would be held in trust—for now.

"Ah, you are that most unique of males! One who knows how to hold his tongue." Carlotta laughed. "Men say that women are gossips, but we do not hold a candle in comparison to the indiscretion of your gender."

His brow furrowed in a frown, as if he did not quite understand what she was saying.

"Wrinkles," Carlotta murmured. "It is not fair! On men they are thought distinguished."

Before Stephan could ask the meaning of her cryptic comment, they were interrupted.

"*Señora* del Castillo. Lord Camford."

Stephan immediately recognized Francisco de Miranda's protégé. "*Señor* Bolívar, I had not realized that your mission extended to the sacred halls of Almack's."

Bolívar shrugged as the music ended. "Sometimes it is easier to win hearts than to win minds. I believe both may help my cause. And the dance? It needs no translation," he said, smiling as Percy returned Fiona to her seat. "Fiona, have you a waltz available to share with me?"

"I believe the one that is about to begin might serve," she replied, as Bolívar offered an elbow to lead her to the floor.

Stephan was not jealous that the handsome *criollo* addressed her easily by her first name. He did not envy Bolívar as he moved with the music, displaying the strength and agility of a panther on the prowl. It was concern and not resentment that caused his fists to clench when the man brought Fiona somewhat closer than the bounds of strict propriety would dictate. Only gratitude for Fiona's obvious pleasure caused a tightening in Stephan's chest, and it was joy for her that he felt, when she smiled and laughed with an air that seemed genuine.

And when the waltz was finally finished and Bolívar walked with his partner to obtain orgeat and buttered bread, Stephan did not note the looks that the vivacious couple garnered from both men and women. Or hear the whispers that followed them. No, it was not the green-eyed monster eating at him from within.

As he watched Bolívar and Fiona take the floor again for a second dance, Stephan knew he was a liar.

. . .

"It was unfortunate that Mr. Bolívar had to cancel our outing together. It is a beautiful day for a drive, and I appreciate your offer to take me up in his place." Fiona said as Stephan handed her up to her seat in the carriage. "Are you certain that you wish to be seen with me out in the open?" she asked once again. "They have already begun to talk about your attention to me at Almack's earlier this week. It does you no credit."

Stephan concealed a satisfied smile. It had been simple to arrange for Bolívar to be busy this afternoon. All it required was a request to Richard, and a meeting with the Caracas delegation underwent a regrettable change in schedule.

"On the contrary," Stephan said. "I am publicly expressing my belief in your innocence."

Fiona fidgeted with her parasol as he took up the reins. "You are in a sensitive position. The Wellesleys—"

"I confess I am becoming heartily weary of the Wellesleys and their assumptions." Carefully he guided his team into traffic. "If Richard and Arthur wish to dismiss me, they may jolly well do so."

In truth, Stephan was wondering how to steer the best course. He had decided to do some investigating of his own over the past few days. Despite her close connection with Fiona, Wellington had nothing but praise for *Señora* del Castillo and her late husband. The pair had organized substantial opposition to Napoleon's invasion.

Stephan had also discovered the notable fact that Sir Harry Burrard and Sir Hew Dalrymple, who were most responsible for the execrable agreement of Cintra, had emerged from the inquest exonerated. Despite the fact that they had overridden Wellington, who had been most vociferous in his objections, there had been few consequences of any substance.

The more Stephan read of the public record, the angrier he became. It was more than likely that the bullet that had nearly killed him in Spain had been shot by a soldier serving with Junot's troops, perhaps even one of those who had been repatriated to France, with gun in hand, courtesy of the British Navy. There was a stench about the affair that made him believe that there was something rotten buried beneath the investigation. Stephan had no question in his mind. Alec would never have involved himself in such a scheme.

His conversations with the Foreign Secretary had been less than productive, beyond his repeated demands that, as equals in nobility, Stephan address him as Richard. Unfortunately, it seemed that being on first name terms had made Richard no less evasive. Stephan's attempts to dig deeper had been thwarted. Beyond removing Bolívar for the day, the only thing of value that Stephan had learned was the fact that not a morsel of the sensitive information that he had fed to Fiona thus far had been served back to the Wellesleys by their contacts.

Stephan's contemplation of that conundrum nearly caused him to miss Fiona's question.

"Can I assume that your willingness to be seen with me means also that you are willing to help me?" Fiona asked.

Her request sounded inner claxons of alarm. "If I can," he said cautiously.

"Around the time of my husband's death," she began, eyeing him closely. "Alec had become secretive, as if he feared to tell me what he was doing."

"Alec was never the kind of man who was an open book," Stephan prevaricated, hoping to draw her out.

"An understatement, if ever there was one."

Fiona's lips quirked in a grin that seemed both wry and sad. "But when I questioned him, he admitted that he had been looking into the matter of the Bruce's murder, spending time at Whitehall searching the records. But one particular piece of information was missing."

Stephan braced for her request, reminding himself of his purpose, his duty. Yet, he found himself hoping that Fiona was not nibbling at the hook.

"Alec had been seeking the notes he had taken and the record of your interview about the events of that night. He hoped that there was some clue that had been missed, because my memories were hazy." Fiona gave a sigh of regret. "But it appeared neither was to be found. I was wondering if you might locate it and copy it out for me."

Tension dissipated into a startling sense of relief. This was a favor he might fulfill without qualm. "How peculiar," Stephan recalled his arrival at headquarters that night in Portugal. "Both Arthur and Richard Wellesley insisted that I recount every moment, from my dinner with Lord Denby to my flight from his residence. We went over the details multiple times, parsing, adding, and correcting the record until they were certain it was complete."

For the first time since Alec's death, Fiona felt a spark of hope. She had grown increasingly certain that the deaths of both her husband and her father had some connection. "But you remember it all, don't you? Perhaps we can reconstruct the chain of events, you and I?" she asked. "It might be that there is some clue as to the identity of the stranger in the square."

"Perhaps," Stephan agreed. "But right now, let us simply enjoy the sunshine and each other's company. You do look lovely, you know."

She felt a wash of color suffusing her cheeks. "Madame Robard is a genius. When confronted with a sow's ear, she can make it so fashionable that accessories made of porcine parts become *de rigeur*."

There was puzzlement in his glance. "An odd comment from a beautiful woman."

How could she tell him that before Alec, personal compliments had seldom been a part of her existence? Even now, she still found it difficult to prevent herself from dissecting any accolades to find hidden meanings. "I could never have worn this before my life as Lady Denby." Fiona caressed the peach-colored silk skirt with obvious joy. "For months, my hands were rough as a washerwoman's in keeping with the roles I had to play. It's the little details that often betray you."

"Never a lady?" Stephan asked.

"Rarely." Fiona admitted, opening up the matching parasol and twirling it gleefully over her shoulder. The stripes blended in a dizzy display of color, the ribbons dancing with the motion. "I am being so very childish. I should stop," she told herself.

"Why?"

"Because I am not a child."

"I am beginning to believe you were never a child," Stephan said. She could see the sympathy in his gaze, spoiling the moment. She didn't want his pity.

"No," she said, snapping the sunshade shut with a sad sigh. "I don't think I ever was."

The mass of carriages and riders on Rotten Row at this hour rivaled the busiest streets in London. The members of the *ton* became a slowly moving panorama that was an exhibition and a drama, especially for those who knew the stories that lurked beneath the poses. *A herd of hypocrites, if ever there was one,* Fiona thought, as she imagined their petty slights glancing off of her, like the cuts of a dull knife.

Lord and Lady Marsden nodded at Stephan but studiously snubbed Fiona, even though the woman had charged well in exchange for her favors before she became her protector's wife.

Lord Soames seemingly conversed with his most recent light-o'-love's cleavage, while his wife sat nearby, a frigid smile upon her face.

There were many others present in the park who slighted Fiona, but were actively violating their vows, caught in the throes of an *affaire de coeur* or paying in coin for a semblance of passion. So many blind eyes were turned in the *ton*, it was a wonder that anyone could see at all.

But the most ironic by far was Henry Wellesley, who bestowed a smile upon Stephan, but ignored her.

It was most tempting to give way to a wicked impulse. There were any number of stories circulating about his wife Charlotte. Many wondered what could possibly have compelled a woman to abandon her husband and three children and become the subject of a Bill of Divorcement in Parliament. A beatific *I know it all* smile would scare the stiffness from his arrogant spine.

But Fiona would not give way and scratch that itch. There was already too much needless suffering, even among these who counted themselves far above the ordinary folk of the world. In the shadow existence that she had inhabited, there were those who would cut just for the cruel pleasure of watching someone bleed. She had vowed never to become one of them.

Instead, she focused her attention upon Lord Camford, admiring his competence with the ribbons as he wove them through the crowded lane. The hollows in his cheeks were gradually filling out, smoothing the planes of his face, and the sun had helped to warm away some of the grey cast that bespoke too much time indoors and abed.

More than any imagined or real sin that she might have committed, Fiona knew that envy was motivating many of the angry looks that she was receiving, resent-

ment that this man was sitting beside her. Although
Stephan made light of the opinions of his peers, he was
risking much with his friendship. It was a strange feeling
to have someone who cared enough to put themselves at
hazard.

"Lady Denby!" Francisco de Miranda grinned
broadly as he waved their carriage to a halt. "I hear that
you dance divinely. Young Bolívar could not stop
speaking of your charms." He eyed Fiona with masculine appreciation before turning his attention to
Stephan. "He was deeply disappointed to miss the opportunity to drive with you, but I see you have quickly
found another *caballero*. Most convenient that you were
available to take his place, milord." There was a gleam in
his look and distinct speculation in the older man's
tone.

"One *caballero's* loss is another's opportunity,"
Stephan said with a shrug and a look that admitted
nothing.

"Indeed, this is true in all things, for both people
and nations," Miranda pronounced. "It is nearly upon
this very spot I told your General Wellesley that England
would regret turning its back on Spain's former
colonies, and sending the troops I was promised to the
Peninsula. As I predicted, England's foolish choice is
Napoleon's opportunity."

"Former colonies?" Stephan questioned.

"Revolution has already begun. They will be free,
milord." Miranda raised his fist in a gesture that put
Fiona in mind of paintings that she had seen depicting
the prophets of old. There was fire in his voice, both a
vow and a prediction. "By my blood and in my lifetime,
they will be free."

Miranda bowed and was turning to go on his way
when one of Stephan's team suddenly reared. The carriage plunged forward, the crowd ahead of them scattering with shrieks of fear, as Stephan tried to regain

control. He pulled hard on the reins, deliberately causing them to veer off the path toward an incline. Fiona held on to her seat as a horseman burst through the trees, coming at them from Stephan's side of the carriage.

All she could see of the stranger was his hat, so low was he in the saddle.

"Jump when we slow," Stephan called above the racketing of the wheels. Fiona pulled her attention to the terrain as their ascent caused the carriage to lose speed.

"Now, Fiona! Jump!" Stephan urged.

Fiona obeyed, coming out of the fall in the rolling motion that the Bruce had forced her to practice with seemingly endless frequency. To her dismay, Stephan did not follow, but stayed with the carriage, as did the rider who rode parallel to the horse's head. His greatcoat billowed behind him as his hand grasped at the mare's noseband, pulling to help Stephan slow the team.

"Aunt Fiona! Aunt Fiona!" She heard Nigel's frantic call and got to her knees. "Are you hurt?" he asked, his voice fraught with anxiety as he reached her side. "Can you stand?" He helped her up and brushed the dirt and debris from her skirts. To her relief, she saw that the carriage had come to a halt at the top of the incline.

Nigel insisted on supporting her. When she finally reached Stephan, he was holding the horse's leads, trying to calm them down amidst a gathering crowd.

"Are you all right?" he asked.

She looked at her dress ruefully. "A few bruises and a ruined dress. It could have been far worse if not for—" She searched their surroundings. "Where did he go?"

"He was here just a moment ago. Must've gone to walk his horse." Stephan peered through the crowd. "Has anyone seen the bearded gentleman who saved the day? I would like to thank him."

But the hero did not return, and apparently no one

knew who he was. Fiona, too, was disappointed not to meet the horseman. Although she had not seen his face, there had been something oddly familiar about him.

"What could have caused the horse to start like that?" she asked.

Nigel pointed. "That would have done it." Blood was welling from a small wound in the mare's flank.

Seven

May coward shame distain his name,
The wretch that dares not die.

— Robert Burns,
Macpherson's Farewell

The team and carriage had been walked to Camford House so that the mare could be seen to. The wound was minor, but there was no question that the horse had been deliberately goaded.

It had taken some time to persuade him, but Nigel had finally agreed to return to his work at Apsley House, having been convinced that Fiona was truly uninjured.

"It must have happened while everyone was distracted by Francisco," Fiona said, eyeing Alejo as he crawled at their feet.

"But why?" Stephan asked in puzzlement. "No one saw it done. We were fortunate that no one was injured. What purpose could have been served by such a malicious act?"

"It was obviously a deed of impulse," Carlotta said thoughtfully, taking the role of hostess upon herself and offering them each a tot of brandy. "Jealousy perhaps?

You are considered a prime catch, milord, and there are those in the *ton* who think my friend less than worthy."

"Thank Heaven for that stranger. I wonder why he did not stay so that we could thank him?" Stephan asked. "I asked among the crowd, but no one could put a name to him."

"There are some heroes who do not seek acclaim," Carlotta observed. "What did he look like? Was he handsome?"

"My concentration was on the reins and avoiding injury," Stephan admitted. "I don't think the man even dismounted once the carriage came to a halt. He was all but plastered flat to his horse's back as he grabbed for the bridle."

"He was on Stephan's side of the carriage," Fiona explained when Carlotta looked to her in inquiry. "As a result, I saw few details. I was too busy hanging on for dear life, and when I was on the ground I could see little but his greatcoat flying out behind him. But there was something about him." She shook her head as if trying to recall that unknown feature.

"Beyond the fact that I got a glimpse of a heavy beard, I could not describe him," Stephan said. "I only know that we could both have been killed if not for his heroism."

Fiona gathered Alejo into her arms and held him close. She closed her eyes and Stephan knew that she was thinking of what might have been. Perhaps a change of subject would be in order?

"How long have you known Francisco de Miranda?" Stephan asked, before taking a sip of Fiona's excellent brandy.

"Now that I think upon it, Francisco has been one of the few constants in my life," Fiona said, a smile lighting her face. "Wherever there were interesting people and trouble brewing, you could be certain that Miranda was somewhere about."

"After today, I can see why even Wellington is wary of him."

"Francisco himself told me about it." Fiona sent him a look filled with mischief. "When Wellington relayed the news that there would be no British troops sent to Caracas, Miranda pulled a public fit right there in Hyde Park. Wellington walked on like a nanny giving distance to a naughty charge."

Carlotta added. "In St. Petersburg, Francisco was a regular fixture at Queen Catherine's table, and some say in her bed. It is a wonder that his head still adorns his shoulders, even though Robespierre wanted it gone. The fact that he breathes England's air bothers the Spanish Royalists to no end, and they would love to arrest him."

"Yet he is still here." Stephan commented.

"As are we, and for that we must be grateful," Fiona said, setting Alejo down and raising her own glass in a toast of thanks. "That is Francisco's secret, I think. He has this ability to live in the moment. For him there is no such thing as failure, only the success that will surely occur next time. There is much to be learned from his irrepressible nature."

"Irrepressible nature!" Carlotta echoed with a scowl. "*Irresponsible* more like! But it is too fine a day to waste speaking of that old silver fox. Is it not, Alejo?" She made a face as she questioned the baby.

"Wrinkles, Carlotta," Fiona warned.

"Our little man does not care if Aunt Carlotta looks like a raisin, does he?"

Stephan bent down on his knees beside the child. "Now this is very important, Alejo. You must now say, 'But Aunt Carlotta, you are so very beautiful. You are no raisin, but the youngest and finest of grapes.'"

"Teaching my son to be a flatterer are you?" Fiona commented, reaching out a hand to Alejo who had pulled himself up on Carlotta's chair.

"Ma ma..." The baby let go of the support, and all of the adults held their breath for a moment.

"That's right. Come to Mama," Fiona said encouragingly, holding out both hands.

Alejo gave a toothy grin, delighted at being the center of attention. He took two awkward steps before falling on his well -padded behind with a wail of dismay. Fiona swept him into her arms.

"Look at you, such a big boy," she praised.

"Well done, indeed! My mother used to say that the moment a boy starts walking is the time his mother should prepare herself to begin running," Stephan remarked, looking ruefully at his cane. "Until we run no more."

"Is the damage permanent then?" Carlotta asked.

"Hard to say. Yes or no depends upon the doctor and the day." Stephan said. "But according to my former batman, Hollins, all that is needed is time and exercise. I'm hoping that he is right. A month past, I could never have bent as I just did."

"Then take your inspiration from Alejo," Fiona said. "Day by day. Step by step. Sometimes, it is the only way to get through difficult times."

Alejo began to whimper and rub his eyes.

"Speaking of difficult times, I believe that our inspiration is in need of his bed," Fiona said.

"Allow me." Carlotta lifted the baby and soothed his way up the stairs babbling nonsense and endearments.

Fiona picked up his rattle from the floor.

"You are fortunate in your friend," Stephan observed, taking a seat close to her. "Not many ladies are willing to act as nursery maids."

"Carlotta is willing to do any task that I may need her to perform," Fiona explained. "She arrived in Denby Chase soon after Alec's death. I found that the Bruce had made provisions for my protection. There will always be someone watching out for me and mine."

There was a knock and a footman wheeled in a tea tray.

"Or more than one someone?" Stephan asked, glancing significantly as the servant exited.

Fiona cast him a look of amused curiosity. "Why did you suspect?"

"His eyes. Very inquisitive. A servant ought not to be seen to see too much."

"I will tell Eldridge that he is losing his touch," Fiona said, pouring the tea and adding his preferences. "Although to be fair, he was rarely called upon to be in service, as it were."

"Perfection from the first sip," Stephan said, setting his cup down. "You fixed it exactly right."

"My memory is usually excellent." Fiona took up her own tea and sipped. "That is why it irks me so, that I cannot remember the details of that night. It is as if there is something niggling at the back of my brain, something that I ought to remember. It's like one of Spilsbury's wooden puzzles that lock one part into the other."

"I had one of those when I was a boy. It belonged to my father." Stephan recollected. "We lost nearly half of the pieces when the bag came loose during a retreat."

"You had mentioned that your family followed the drum. Brothers or sisters?"

"A little sister, lost to a fever when she was but a tot," he said. "It was not an easy life."

"Few lives are, even though we might think them so," Fiona said, with a sad shake of her head. "A terrible thing it is, to lose a child. I know that Alejo is my reason for living now."

Who would care for the boy if it were proven that his mother had turned against her country? Stephan wondered.

Fiona was asking him a question. Stephan forced himself to focus on the here and now.

"So did you ever find the rest of your puzzle?"

"No," Stephan said, with a shake of the head. "Papa told me that I would just have to imagine those parts of the picture that had been lost."

"If only I could imagine those pieces," Fiona said, her expression thoughtful. "That was why I was hoping that you might be able to tell me about the sequence of events from your perspective. Even the smallest detail that you might think irrelevant might be of import."

So Stephan cast his mind back to conjure up the missing pieces of Fiona's puzzle. As Alec watched from his portrait, his enigmatic expression seemed to hide a surfeit of never-to-be-revealed secrets.

As she concentrated on his narrative, Fiona's face was a window with shutters wide open. The very telling of the tale seemed to dredge her feelings to the surface, and it was clear that her claim of forgetfulness was no deception. She listened intently to his every word, the expressions of suspense and surprise on her face seemed entirely unfeigned.

At her urging, Stephan tried to call upon the memories of every one of his senses, and he found that the very telling moved him, reminding him of the circumstances that bound the two of them. A welter of emotions that he could not fully understand entangled him once more, all the stronger because Fiona was no longer a mysterious unknown. Never before had he been able to forge this profound and rapid sense of connection with anyone. Although they had been together for less than two hours on that long-ago night, that bond they had forged had spanned the years.

Even as Stephan gave her the truth, he felt profoundly dishonest. There were parts of the experience that he kept to himself. How could he tell her that he still recalled every minute that he had held her in his arms? That she had often walked as a chimera through his nights over these years past? That her courage had inspired him to fight his way through battles, both without and within?

How could he tell her all these things, and in the end, betray her?

. . .

The bearded man waited in the shadowed corner of The Goose and Gander, nursing his beer. Although the tavern was crowded, no one dared to try for a place at his table, until the tall cove strode in the door and sat himself down.

"You're late," the man growled.

"Tired after your escapade this afternoon, are you, old man?" Carlotta pulled the brim of her hat down to better shade her face. "Need your sleep, do you?"

"I thought that he was going to drive her home and was ready to leave myself," he said, shaking his head. "It was a near thing."

Carlotta ceased her goading. "And a deliberate thing."

"I didn't see it," he said, when Carlotta finished repeating what she had heard. "All eyes were on Miranda, including mine, I'm shamed to admit."

"Do you think that he is in on it?" she asked after the waitress brought her tankard. "A distraction while the deed was done."

"Francisco de Miranda?" The man gave a lop-sided grin. "The man is to trouble like iron to a magnet."

Carlotta smothered her laugh. "Forgive a foolish question. With Francisco, anything is possible."

"I don't think so." All traces of humor vanished as he considered the possibilities. "Miranda was taken by surprise, else he wouldn't have been directly in the path of the carriage. He was scrambling out of their way, fast as anyone. No question though, she was the target. This investigation of hers has to stop. Get her back to Denby Chase."

Carlotta shook her head. "The only way she will back away is at gunpoint."

"It may become necessary." He took a last gulp of his beer and threw a coin on the table. "We may have no choice but to force her hand."

"There is one other way," Carlotta began.

"No," he said fiercely. "You swore an oath Carlotta del Castillo."

"The oath I swore was to honor the will of a dead man," she replied, before she rose and stalked out the door.

. . .

If Stephan had been a man of impulse, he would have kept riding on past Hyde Park corner, galloped full out beyond the toll gate, and not spared his steed until he was halfway to his home in Brightlands. Midsummer was almost upon them, and he imagined the fields, heavy with grain, waiting for the harvesters.

Prior to his soldiering days, he had worked with the reapers, swinging the scythe with wide, sweeping strokes as the wheaten world waved before him, beckoning. He was now a wealthy earl, able to afford all the hands he needed, but at the moment, he would gladly trade it all if he could turn the clock back to that simpler time.

The terse note Fiona had sent the previous evening to set up this early morning assignation rustled in his pocket.

After the incident in the park, I think that you deserve the truth. F

Did she mean to confess?

Perhaps there would be mercy if she were to turn on her confederates?

Stephan had spent a sleepless night wrestling with

the facts, reviewing them in his mind. Why hadn't Wellington and his brother mentioned that Alec had a son? What other material facts might they have omitted? It occurred to him that he had yet to see any of the evidence they had mentioned.

But with the implication that charges of treason had been in the works, the reason that Lord Denby had put a gun to his head rather than fight the accusations against him was abundantly clear. With a baby on the way, a verdict of treason would have cost no less than everything. His friend had been caught between two unthinkable choices.

The stony Scylla of a conviction of treason would have reduced his child's inheritance to shame and poverty, meaning the end of a title held since Norman times, and the property of his estate forfeited to the Crown.

The rocky Charybdis of vindication could only have been achieved with his wife dancing at the end of a hangman's noose.

Even if Alec's wife were guilty as sin, honor would never have allowed him to purchase his freedom with her life. Nonetheless, Stephan's duty was clear, regardless of any compromises his friend had made. It was vital to put an end to Hades once and for all.

Fiona was waiting for him at the gate, holding a restless roan in check. Her velvet habit, the green of new leaves, contrasted with the stallion's earth-colored coat. The horse reared impatiently. Rather than fight for control, she let the animal dance until he calmed. With easy grace, Fiona kept her seat, moving with her mount, putting Stephan in mind of a willow swaying with a strong wind.

As he approached, he searched for signs of the groom accompanying her. Apparently, Fiona detected the sweep of his gaze.

"I thought it best to come alone." Fiona told him.

"Thank you for meeting me when the milkmaids rise, but what I have to say requires privacy and I have no wish to have this conversation overheard or interrupted."

"What of your reputation?"

She gave a rueful shrug. "Alas, unlike Caesar's wife, there are few suspicions that have yet to fall upon me. However, being seen in a covert assignation with a notorious woman might enhance or ruin yours, depending on the observer." Her horse danced beneath her. "Would you mind if I give Robbie a bit of a run before he throws one of his fits?"

"My Echo is in need of some exercise as well," Stephan agreed, before urging his horse forward.

Fiona's stallion needed no other invitation. The two horses surged down the trail, their pace increasing as the fresh mounts spent their exuberance in a race through the empty park. To Stephan's surprise, his leg had improved to the point where riding was once again a pleasure.

Echo, true to her name, matched Robbie's pace, and they galloped side by side. The woman was an excellent rider, moving as one with the animal, with an ease that bespoke a wealth of experience in the saddle. When they reached the Serpentine, she slowed her horse to a trot, then a cooling walk.

Finally, she brought them to a halt in a small grove. Stephan noted that she had chosen the spot with care. Neither they nor their mounts could be easily seen, but they would quickly discern anyone else's approach. Stephan gingerly dismounted, and he was delighted to find that he felt no twinge as he found his feet. Nonetheless, he pulled his cane from its sheath in his saddle and headed for Fiona. Before he could move to assist her, she slid easily to the ground.

"I apologize for all the precautions, but I have lately

had the feeling that I am being observed," she said, scanning their surroundings.

Stephan inclined his head and said nothing, but decided it was more than likely that the Foreign Secretary had set someone on her tail.

The sunrise had promised fair weather. Now the clouds began to gather on the horizon as they walked together in silence. They hadn't gone far before she gestured to a fallen trunk and took a seat. He took his place beside her, waiting as she regarded him thoughtfully, as if she did not quite know how to begin.

"You are one of the few people who truly knows who I am," Fiona spoke hesitantly, as if feeling her way in the dark. "What I was."

This was the opening that Stephan had hoped for. One more step in gaining her confidence. "I found this among my things." Reaching into his pocket, Stephan unfolded the piece of oilcloth he had salvaged on that long-ago night, and smoothed it on the surface of the oak.

She picked it up by the corners and held up the fabric gingerly, almost as if she feared it could bite her. "Those bloody fingerprints. They're mine, aren't they?"

"You still don't remember?" he asked, watching the mercurial changes of her expression as she confronted this piece of her past.

"Now that I have put your face in my puzzle and you have provided some of the missing pieces, I fill in more of the blank spaces each day, in bits and snatches. But if I fail to solve that conundrum, I want someone to know the truth, someone who might have the power and connections to bring about justice."

With a deep breath, she stared down at the wrinkled bit of rag. "I will begin with the part I have never forgotten. The part I most wish to forget. An agent named Hendricks was to deliver the package to my father before sunset. But the moon had already risen when the

Bruce stumbled in through the door. He was bleeding, badly."

She regarded the cloth intently, her face clouding. There was a glint in her eye as she looked up at him again. "I remember now. I started to tend him, but he shoved this into my hands. It is his blood you see here."

Her demeanor grew stark as she pulled the moments from her memory. "I was dressed as a ragamuffin. We often did that to provide a distraction, a decoy, or a means for a hand-off to ensure delivery, in case the courier was followed."

Stephan found her casual explanation all the more chilling for its matter-of-course description of the life-and-death game that she had taken for granted.

"The Bruce had been wounded before, but this time —" she continued, shaking her head sadly, twisting the cloth in her hands. "This was different. He wouldn't even let me look at the gunshot. Every word was an effort. 'Betrayed...Hendricks' was all he could say. My last memory of my father is him on a bench, waiting in the dark with his pistol in hand, while I went out the back way."

She hugged her arms around herself, holding the fabric to her chest and rocking back and forth. "I should have stayed." Her words were both a sob and a whisper. "I should have stayed with him."

"You would likely have died as well." Stephan put a tentative hand over her shoulder. She moved closer, seeking comfort.

"Those are the worst," she whispered. "The doubts that plague you as you agonize over what you might have changed. But I'll never know what could have been, will I?" Fiona shook her head, and swallowed, wiping the tears with a swipe of her sleeve. She slid away from him and rose to her feet, looking around her as if trying to remind herself of the present. "I ran, hid the packet at the meet point—"

"In a midden pile," Stephan reminded her with a chuckle.

"Yes, I remember that." Her lips quirked for a moment before the pain of recall overtook her again. "Alec never came. But the man who was likely my father's killer did. He knew. The time. The place. He knew it all." Fiona shrugged her shoulders, as if trying to shed a burden that had become too heavy to bear. "You know the rest. Hendricks was found dead. Da was right. We were betrayed, and I failed him. Failed him, Hendricks, and Alec in the end. Failed us all."

The woman leaned against an oak, taking a sharp breath, as if the very air cut at her lungs. She folded the oilcloth carefully and looked at him. "If I may keep this?"

Stephan nodded. "Of course."

"Thank you." She tucked it carefully in the pocket hidden in her skirt. "If ever I need a reminder of why I must persevere. Of why I brought you here this morning. Your cousin offered me a post, you know. He said his son thought I was a prime piece. If I didn't die, George offered to keep me."

Stephan was surprised by the level of anger that filled him. If she had turned against England, the events of that night had given her ample reason. "It's abominable! The way you were treated—"

His indignation was a kind of gift. No one had ever been angry on her behalf. Even Alec had taken the way she was treated as a matter of course.

"Their behavior was in keeping with what they saw me to be," she said, with a dismissive wave of her hand. "I was a spy."

"You are a still a lady, and as such—"

"We both know that there are many kinds of *ladies*. There are the ladies with whom you enjoy an evening of sport, and the ladies you bring home to meet your mama. In the eyes of society, I was never considered to be one of the latter kind." It was only as she spoke that she realized her own bitterness, the feeling deep within that she was due more than she had been given. "Even my husband was astonished that I came to our marriage bed untouched."

Stephan's incredulous expression was not unexpected, but hurtful nonetheless.

"I don't ask you to believe me, nor do I reveal this to gain your respect or sympathy. I want to help you understand our situation after you left us that night." Fiona continued, trying to keep her tone calm and even, despite her internal rage at what had been done to them.

"Your cousin, Lord Camford, was delighted. One of his most able rivals was effectively ruined. When we finally returned to London in disgrace, there were few in diplomatic circles who would risk association with us. I must say, Alec quickly learned who his true friends were." Her faint smile felt like more of a grimace. "I thought Stephan Aubrey to be one of those who abandoned him. He kept your letters. The last one he received was dated prior to the night you saved me from dying in an alleyway."

"I was ordered to keep my distance."

"I realize that now." Fiona pulled a blade of grass and twisted it. "That was Alec to the core, protecting everyone but himself. And England above all. The Wellesley brothers knew that. They knew his worth, his talent, his intellect, his loyalty."

She looked deep into those sea-colored eyes, as if somehow she would will him to hear the truth of her words. He was working with these men, and might not be able to see that politics and appearance governed so much of their actions. "Although they dared not collaborate with Alec openly, lest they also be tainted by association, Richard, Arthur, and Henry Wellesley did not hesitate to use my husband and the remnants of the network he had created. There are still many of us out there, people who lived in the shadows for the sake of our country. People who ultimately reported to Lord Denby."

"You are saying that Alec was a spymaster?" Stephan shook his head in obvious disbelief.

Fiona studied him. "Why does this shock you, given the mission he asked you to undertake? Think upon that night, Stephan Aubrey."

Fiona realized that she was holding her breath waiting, and slowly inhaled.

"And if what you say is true?" Stephan asked, a chill in his voice. "Why do you tell me this now? What relevance could it possibly have?"

Anger?

Disbelief?

Perhaps a bit of both.

Still, she could not help but respond with a bite of her own. What right did this man have to disdain Alec, or any of them?

"I do not tell you this to impugn his reputation. I am proud of what he did, what we all did. What I am about to tell you requires you to understand all of the circumstances. I spent last night reading your letters to him."

He drew back, his eyes narrowing in dawning affront. She put a restraining hand on his shoulder.

"I apologize for any violations of your privacy, but I needed to know more about what manner of man you are."

"And what have you determined, Lady Denby?" he asked stiffly.

"It confirmed that which I had already assumed." She fixed her gaze upon him, once again willing him to believe her. "You are a man of honor, Stephan Aubrey. I understand why Alec was proud to name you a friend, why he chose to rely upon you for a mission of vital importance on that long-ago night, and why I am taking the risk of trusting you with what I am about to reveal. I ask for your word that what I am about to say remains between us, whether you choose to believe me or not."

Stephan inclined his head in a gesture of acceptance. "If I can honorably do so."

The piece of oilcloth in her pocket was an omen, a talisman bidding her to stake all on the throw of the dice. It would seem that she was still a gambler's daughter. It was time to lay the truth on the table and see if she had judged the odds correctly.

"Then I must rely on my judgement of your integrity, milord," Fiona said, "for I will need your help." She rose and took a deep breath, bracing herself to divulge the facts known only to a select few.

"My husband did not commit suicide because he believed that I was faithless. He had ample evidence that there had been no man before him. I was a loyal and true wife, and I had just told Alec that I was carrying his child. He was flying high with joy, like one of Blanchard's hot air balloons, floating on air at the prospect of an heir."

"Why, then?"

There was a wealth of inquiry in those two words.

Fiona fixed her eyes on his face. Before she spoke, she uttered a silent prayer that he would be receptive to the truth.

"Alec did not kill himself. He was murdered."

EIGHT

In durance vile here must I wake and
weep.

— ROBERT BURNS, EPISTLE
FROM ESOPUS TO MARIA

The silence lengthened. Stephan knew that Fiona was waiting for his response, but her words were so totally unexpected that he could not immediately formulate a reply. Finally, he chose to make his statement simple, to avoid any unwitting revelations about his covert mission.

"I ask again. Why?"

Fiona put a hand on her horse's neck, petting the animal as a child might smooth a beloved blanket for comfort, before seating herself on the fallen log once again.

"That is the answer I am seeking, the reason I have returned to London. That is why, I believe your horse was injured the other day. I have stirred the vipers' nest."

"Someone is trying to kill you?"

"Or prevent me from making further inquiry," she agreed with surprising calm. "Alec and I had reviewed our inventory of the events of that night gone wrong many times and concluded without question that the Bruce was correct. We were compromised."

Her fists clenched, reflecting the barely contained fury on her countenance. "Alec was disgraced and dismissed, making it impossible for him to investigate what had happened. Your cousin George likely believed that his Christmas box had come early." She reached into her pocket and pulled out the cloth that he had just given her, laying it out on her lap before folding it once more and returning it to her pocket. "Before we sailed back to England, Alec informed as many of our people as possible that our net had been jeopardized. With George at the helm, there was no one left in the field who would, or could, seek the truth, much less take care of our agents."

She took a deep breath and rose, her skirts swishing in the grass. Once again, she put a hand on her stallion's mane, and the animal nickered as if to encourage her. Fiona continued.

"Here in London, Alec encouraged me to take my place in the *ton* as his wife while my pregnancy was still a private matter. Society has a short memory when there is money and a title to induce forgetfulness. I realize now that it was likely a stratagem to keep me safe and out of the fray." Somehow holding back the tears that gleamed unshed, she soldiered on with her story. She bent and pulled up a clump of grass with her hands and tendered the shoots to her horse.

"But even before I learned that I was carrying our child, I realized that my husband was deeply troubled by his investigation. George had returned to England and was obstructing him at every turn." The woman stood silent for a moment, staring at the empty woodland path as if she were seeing another time and place. "One night, Nigel escorted me home from the opera. We found Alec's body."

Fiona paused, halting as she recollected the horror of

that night. She had seen death before, both violent and natural, but she would never forget any detail of that scene.

Those images would always be vivid in her mind. She still heard the screaming, the raw sound of her own voice as she denied the evidence of her eyes. There had been a scrawled note asking for her forgiveness, but saying nothing more.

"Nigel sent for your cousin, of course. After he arrived, George said that Alec was about to be taken up on charges of treason for his role in the Cintra affair. He gave me a choice: heat up the old scandal broth of my promiscuity and brand me as the doxy responsible for my husband's death, or blow up his reputation and our son's future with a charge of treason against a man who could no longer defend himself."

She turned her back upon her listener, unable to contain the wave of anger that engulfed her. Fiona wanted to scream, to throw something, to take the gun from her hidden pocket and fire it at the sky or better still, to fire it into one of the cold, calculating hearts that had condemned both her and her husband with no recourse. "Ultimately, I suspect that George was quite relieved that there would be no charges and no trial regarding my husband's alleged treachery in bringing about the betrayal at Cintra because there could be no evidence of our involvement. We had naught to do with that wretched travesty."

"A bad business that," Stephan murmured.

Even as the mundane observation annoyed, it also calmed her, recalling her to her purpose. Fiona forced herself to turn and face Stephan again. He had to believe her.

"A bad business indeed," she agreed. "They dosed me with laudanum and brandy and shipped me to the country with my husband's corpse. It was only later, when the fog of the drug diminished, that I could think clearly again. I realized the truth."

She stared into Stephan's eyes, as if she could somehow compel him to see what she had seen.

"Picture Alec's library. You knew it well. It has not changed. His desk is there." Waving her hands, pointing to locate the furnishings and objects, she tried to draw him into her vision. "The door is where I now stand."

She put a hand on his shoulder and pointed to a nearby rock. "We see Alec's body sprawled on the floor before us, by about the length of my horse."

So clear was the picture in her mind that she bent and touched the rock that stood in for Alec's skull, feeling the gorge rising as she recalled the distinctive odors. "There is a smell of blood, saltpeter, sulphur, urine," she whimpered the words softly. She shook her head, trying to clear it and forced herself to resume the narrative. "A bullet wound mars his skull."

Fiona could not help herself. She covered her mouth hastily and stumbled to a nearby tree, where she cast up the remnants of her breakfast. *Fool!* She castigated herself. *You have made yourself a hysterical female in appearance.* She felt a cool hand on her brow and a flask was pressed to her lips.

"Rinse, then drink," he urged her.

She obeyed, swishing the liquid in her mouth, ejecting it, then taking another swallow of brandy. He lifted her to her feet and his arms circled her. Overcome by despair, she leaned against his solid strength, hearing his heartbeat, fighting the tears that threatened. Fiona put her hand in her pocket, seeking her handkerchief and found the bloody oilcloth once again.

Her father's blood. Her blood. Alec's blood. Too much had been shed to give up now.

Fiona took a breath and edged out of the circle of his arms and forced herself to stand apart from him. He eyed her in surprise.

"It would seem you are forever fortifying me with a good stiff drink." She tried to smile, but she suspected it was more of a scowl. "I'm sorry. I am behaving like such a weakling."

"There is no weakness in a display of honest emotion." He took her hand in his, those blue eyes looking deeply into her soul. Fiona tried to look away, but he cupped her chin in his palm as he spoke. "It was the soldiers in my command who encountered death without a qualm who gave me pause. It takes considerable courage sometimes, to allow yourself to feel."

"I've been afraid to feel," she admitted, still battling against the threat of tears. "For a long time, I haven't allowed it, because I felt powerless. They had already buried Alec and would dearly have liked to bury me with him. I was pregnant, maligned, and utterly alone."

"You are not alone anymore," he said softly.

His words loosed the dam. She blinked helplessly, trying to stem the hot flow that streamed down her cheeks. He pulled her close.

Her body shook with the force of an internal storm. Stephan held her, letting the tempest batter against him as she shook and howled her pain. He could swear that these were not the calculated tears of a woman trying to swindle or sway. This was a flood of unabashed grief. When at last she looked up at him, her eyes were swollen and her pert nose was red.

"It is unlike me to be a rain cloud." Fiona mustered a weak smile. "Rarely do I allow myself the luxury of weeping. The Bruce always taught that deep emotion is like a sure tell at the card table, the quirk that informs your opponent of what cards you hold. You reveal a chink in the armor, and that vulnerability can be exploited by the enemy."

Once again, Stephan felt a stab of pity as he thought about a life lived on the razor's edge, where the revelation of honest emotion could be deadly. "My mother used to say that there was nothing like a good cry to cleanse the heart and spirit."

"No wonder I feel like I have been washed and wrung out to dry."

Still trembling, still clutching him, she was visibly trying to tamp down her emotions. *A tell*, indeed. His fingers swept at her cheeks, wiping the remnants of tears aside. Locks of curls had come loose from their moorings, and he tucked them gently back into place, reveling in their softness. Her breath came in sputtering gasps. There was no hiding the glitter of desperation in those eyes, and she was looking at him as if he was the harbor she was seeking. He wanted to be that shelter. He held her as the storm of her sorrow abated and another, different tempest engulfed them both.

He let himself kiss her. *Just for solace*, he told himself.

Fiona's lips were salted, but the taste was still sweet.

But this time, as he embraced her, Alec's shadow was gone, and with it, the sense of the covetous guilt that came with dreams of his friend's woman. Pulling her closer, Stephan allowed himself to feel the pent-up emotions that had plagued him since his world had turned topsy-turvy.

There was no way to determine when the burning anger kindled by her story turned into a need to protect, and from there flared to scorching passion. He was uncertain when the desire to comfort her was transformed into something deeper, but boundaries had been breached, and the invisible walls that had kept him from venturing into intimacy were falling.

He relished the lush feel of her body, savored the warmth and the sweet smell of flowering jasmine and cinnamon still scenting her skin. Her hair slipped against his cheek, a sensual reminder of that long-ago night, and he wished that he could pull it loose from its moorings, so he could lose himself in that softness.

She pressed herself closer, her arms twining around him.

As the kiss deepened into an invitation to something more, Stephan realized that he was coming perilously close to losing control of himself. There was one borderline that remained. Honor. Guilty or innocent, he was determined not to use her or treat her as a doxy. She deserved better than she had been given. It took every ounce of self-restraint that he possessed to step away from the brink and taking what she seemed willing to give, what he so badly wanted.

"Stephan?"

From her tone of puzzlement, he could tell that she, too, felt the uncanny sensation that seemed to draw them inexorably closer. Whether Fiona's sigh was one of relief or frustration, Stephan could not say. However, the depth of his own response had shaken him badly. Somehow she seemed to sense his unease, and her hand sought his. There was no need for words. Her light touch spoke volumes.

"I would not take advantage," he explained hoarsely.

"No," she agreed. "You did not, and you asked for nothing that I did not freely offer. Do you know how rare and precious that is to me? To be treated with respect?" She shook her head, looking at him with what could only be described as awe.

In the distance, he heard the sound of thunder and noticed that the skies were darkening with the threat of rain.

"Perhaps we ought to adjourn indoors."

She nodded. "I think that the rest of the story would do better if I showed you the scene rather than told you about it. Will you come home with me?"

He was about to help her mount when she put her hands upon his shoulders and regarded him with an expression that he was hard put to describe. "Thank you," she said. "Thank you for your kindness."

It was gratitude.

Her lips pressed against his cheek, and for a brief second, Stephan allowed himself to forget that he was deceiving a woman who had never allowed herself the comfort of a good cry.

A woman who deemed it a boon to be treated with respect.

A woman who claimed her husband had been murdered.

. . .

The first drops had begun to fall when they reached the mews behind Berkeley Square. Leaving their horses to the groom, Fiona and Stephan slipped into the house and made their way up the back stairs.

"Look at it now," Fiona said, pausing at the window to watch the downpour.

Thunder rattled the panes and lightning ripped through the darkened sky, illuminating the empty square.

"Just in time, it seems." Stephan said, setting his cane aside before taking out his handkerchief and wiping away a spatter of raindrops from her cheeks.

She took the linen from his hand and dabbed at the drops on his face, brushing aside the damp curls from his forehead. There was a question in his eyes as she moved closer and raised her lips to his. "Will you kiss me again?" she asked softly. "For courage this time, rather than comfort?"

His answer was a gentle touch of his lips upon hers. There was the simmering heat of desire, but no demand, as if he was giving her leave to guide him on this journey.

During her life as a spy, she had experienced more than a few hide-in-a-corner kind of kisses, to maintain her role, or satisfy her own curiosity. When she wed

Alec, his overtures had been gentle, almost tentative. Her husband had treated her like one of his fragile and delicate pieces of porcelain. Over time, it had seemed to her that there was something more than cautious regard growing between them, a tenderness which might have grown into more. Perhaps, if circumstance had allowed it to thrive, they might have achieved some semblance of passion.

But in the park, Stephan's embrace had caused her to realize that any such dreams had been self-deluding falsehoods. The tinder of her marriage to Alec might have sufficed someday to supply a measure of warmth. But with just a single kiss, Stephan Aubrey had ignited an all-consuming conflagration, a fire in her heart. His touch seared a pathway into an unknown realm of emotion that she had never imagined, much less explored.

Once again, Stephan's caress began as an offer of comfort and support, a butterfly touching upon a budding blossom. But as she drew him closer, he seemed to recognize that she was asking for a touch that was beyond mere reassurance. Stephan paused for a moment, those lapis eyes searching for permission.

Twining her arms tighter, she angled her lips to meet with his. He inhaled deeply in surprise, and his eyes grew darker, their focus intense, as if he was plumbing some unknown depth before he plunged them both into a soul-deep vastness. The hurricane of emotion that raged between them reflected the storm outside.

Fiona knew only that she wanted more, to press closer, to seek the union that joins bodies to spirits. Never before had she so resented the boundaries that her personal creed and sense of self-preservation demanded, but this new and strange longing pounded at the fortifications she had erected to protect herself.

Until Stephan kissed her, Fiona had never truly understood why otherwise sane women would risk everything for a man's embrace. But this was far more than mere desire. Although she had spoken the vows once before, the words *with my body I thee worship* suddenly had new meaning. Fiona wanted to give to him, to make him feel the same sudden sweet desire that flooded her, overwhelming every sense.

Including common sense, it seemed.

The sound of footsteps on the stairway from above brought reality to the fore, and she sighed before stepping back and leading him to the door.

"Alec's study," Stephan said, as if trying to remind them both of their objective.

Fiona nodded and pulled a housekeeper's ring from her pocket. Her hand trembled as she found the proper brass key and fit it into the lock.

"The day I returned to London, I came here to reassure myself of the facts," Fiona told him, as they peered into the shadowed chamber. "But I touched nothing, in the hope I could convince someone to see what I had seen. In fact, no one, other than myself, has been in this room since the night we found Alec's body. I had demanded that everything remain undisturbed. Due to what took place here, the servants were only too glad to leave it be. There are even those who say that Alec haunts it."

"As if he would ever be so vulgar." Stephan's wry comment dissolved some of her dread.

The dark study still exuded the stuffy smell of long disuse. Last time Fiona entered, she had feared that there would be other scents, the metallic tang of blood, the odor of spent powder and the other stenches of decay that had accompanied death on its visit that night. The reality of those smells had long dissipated, but they still lingered in her memory.

Fiona touched Stephan's hand for strength. With a gesture, she bade him to wait at the threshold. Taking a deep breath, Fiona drove herself toward the window and pulled the dust laden drapes aside. Rain still battered at the glass. The damp chill and clouded sky were signs of the waning of a summer that had already proven to be one of the coolest in memory. The weather mirrored her mood, and any lingering warmth from Stephan's embrace was gone. With growing dread, Fiona forced herself to face the interior of the room, afraid that she would falter, overcome by the horror of memory.

Instead, when she surveyed the scene in the gloom, Stephan stood waiting in the doorway, reminding her that this time, she was not alone. With that reassurance, anger quickly banished fear. Stalking to the fireplace, Fiona took up a flint and tinder to kindle the fire laid in the hearth. Using a spill, she set a branch of candles alight and placed it upon the desk.

"Last I stood here, I swore to Alec that I would find his killer," she told him.

He would believe her.

He had to.

As Fiona approached him, the clouds outside broke momentarily, illuminating her with shafts of sunlight. Her eyes seemed to blaze with wrath, and all that was needed was a fiery sword to complete the picture of an avenging angel. Dread touched him as he imagined the force of that fury turned upon him if she were ever to discover his duplicity.

Stephan looked past her at the familiar floor-to-ceiling shelves, filled with the wealth of rare volumes, souvenirs, and curios. Comfortable chairs flanked the fire. A cut-crystal decanter and glasses sat waiting on the tabletop of inlaid marble, ready to lubricate throats dry with late night conversation.

The room itself, disordered as if Alec had only briefly stepped away, forced Stephan to once again confront the reality that the friend who had once welcomed him here was now gone. His absence was the only reason that the woman who came to stand at his side was no longer beyond his touch. For a moment, he felt a twinge of guilt for his growing desire. Was it the force of that craving that was weighting his judgement, making him want to believe in her?

"You and I are now standing as Nigel and I stood that night." Fiona broke the silence, her words clipped and precise, her posture taut.

"The body was on the carpet before us." She moved forward, like a housekeeper he had seen once, who had guided a tour of the great house she served. "You have seen head wounds before?"

Stephan nodded, recalling a battlefield parade of bloody faces.

Fiona beckoned, gesturing him to come closer. On the carpet before them at their feet he could see the dried remnants of blood.

Alec's blood.

She bent, her fingers brushing the outline of the stains. "His head was here, with the point of entry facing upright in this direction." She gestured to the side of the carpet that bore the largest stains.

Fiona rose. This time, when she cupped his chin, there was nothing seductive about the touch. She moved his gaze much as she might move a telescope to a point that she wished to observe. "The overwhelming preponderance of bodily fluids are *immediate to the wound*. Almost all of the blood is on that one side of Alec's face and the carpet closely surrounding him. Look at it!"

"What are you trying to say, Fiona?" he asked gently. He knew she was not seeing the here and now.

"'Tis not what I say, but what I see, what you will see if you truly look carefully and think upon it. Try to view it yourself, Stephan, as if it is a play upon the stage." She was pleading, and then she composed herself once more.

"You say you've encountered head wounds?" she

began again. "You know they often bleed prodigiously. You've seen what a bullet does upon impact. Keep those memories in mind as we go on."

Fiona's look was encouraging, as if she were a teacher coaxing the correct answer from a student.

"If you were to describe the sequence of events that night leading to suicide, how would it go?"

Stephan swallowed, trying to clear the sudden lump from his throat. "From the way you say that you found him fallen, Alec must have been standing before the desk. He picked up the gun, held it to—" Stephan shook his head, unable to continue.

"He fired. The impact spattering blood and effluvia all about him before his body fell to the floor." Fiona's voice was soft with compassion as she concluded the scenario. "But look around where he fell. Do you see any signs of spattering anywhere other than the immediate vicinity where Alec lay? If he was standing when he fired, should there not be traces of blood on the desk? I could find no mark or splash that is above the level of my knee. The desk's top is completely clean. Look for yourself."

Stephan searched the desk and saw only a layer of dust, attesting to the fact that it had gone long undisturbed. He snatched the candelabra and looked all around, searching for what would have been the inevitable outcome of the impact of a ball to the head. But other than signs of dried blood on one leg of the desk and a nearby chair, there was nothing.

He looked at Fiona, his eyes blinking against an unfamiliar stinging sensation.

He had not wept since he was a child.

Stephan forced himself to follow where Fiona was leading.

"You are saying then, he was on the ground when he was shot?"

Hope blossomed, breaking through the shell of

pain. Still, it was demoralizing to realize how much she was depending on his acceptance of the evidence. If he refused to do so, she knew it would devastate her. She forced herself to go on. "When we entered the room, the gun was lying near Alec's right hand. His left hand was under his body. I ran to him and turned him to check for signs of life, even though I knew—I knew—" She shook her head, and pulled herself back again from the brink of breaking. If she failed...

She could not fail.

Carry on, girl, her father's voice demanded.

"The area beneath the body was clean. You can see that there was not a trace of blood on the floor under the body or on the front of his clothing that was beneath him."

"You could have overlooked—"

Fiona cut him off with a dismissive wave of the hand. "You forget that I am a trained observer. Alec was wearing a *white* shirt." She walked to a locked cabinet behind the desk and removed an elegant case.

She opened it to reveal a single pistol nestling in its velvet-lined hollow. A second pocket sat empty.

Stephan's eyes widened with recognition. "I remember when Alec had those delivered," he said, his voice hoarse with emotion. "Although we were in the middle of breaking our fast, nothing would do but a trip directly to Manton's to put them through their paces. They were made to his order, designed to fit his hand."

His lips thinned to a tight line, making it seem like he was forcing his words to emerge. "And you say that the wound was on the right side of his head? The pistol near his right hand? His left hand was beneath him?"

There was puzzlement in the staccato of his voice and something else—

Seething anger.

Fiona realized that she had been holding her breath. "Did you know that Alec was left-handed, then?"

A tight nod signified agreement before he spoke. "Alec often used his right in public. He was ambidextrous, and could write a fair copy right-handed. As happens with most children who tend to use the sinister side, he told me that he had been forced to employ his right, especially in public."

"When he was a boy, his tutor would tie the left behind his back," Fiona verified.

"That was why he was so delighted with those pistols," Stephan recalled. "Unlike most of the other weapons that one can buy in a shop, they were designed specifically for a left-handed man. He could hit the center of his target almost every time with that pair."

"Just so." Fiona picked up the remaining pistol. "This is the other half of the matched set, identical to the one that we found at Alec's side. George took it for evidence and it was never returned. Neither was the note that I know my husband did not write. So I have no way to prove it a forgery."

She transferred the weapon to her left hand in an attempt to demonstrate the point she was trying to illustrate. "My father taught me to shoot both right- and left-handed, but the right hand is natural to me," she explained.

Seating the base of the grip in her palm, she attempted to bring the barrel of the firearm around to the right side of her forehead. From that awkward, hopelessly contorted position, she could not even get the long barrel to align properly, much less keep the muzzle steady while she pointed and pulled the trigger. "Do you see now how impossible it would be? Notice that even the butt of the pistol seats badly. Fire it like this and it would jump right out of your hand. With the impact so close, the force of the recoil would have driven it anywhere, depending on how it was held."

"But not immediately near the hand that fired it?" Stephan asked, his face expressionless.

"No. Highly unlikely, to say the least." Her hand trembled as she handed him the firearm. "Your arms are longer. A man's grip would differ from mine. Try it."

Stephan made the attempt. Although the muzzle aligned, after a fashion, it took considerable effort to hold it steady and shoot. Even before attempting to pull the trigger with the pistol at his skull, he realized that suicide in such a manner was possible, but not extremely probable.

"Could he have done it right-handed?" Stephan asked still fighting the inevitable conclusion.

"Why? If Alec was seeking a quick, clean death, why would he not use his dominant hand," Alec's widow asked, her logic damnably flawless. "Especially if, as you say, the left was the hand he always shot with? There is no sign of spilled powder anywhere. Remarkably steady for a man contemplating ending his life, wouldn't you agree?"

"Once George was dead, why didn't you go to Wellesley with your suspicions?" Stephan asked, his growing frustration making his question curt and angry.

A look of patent disbelief preceded her answer. She spoke to him almost as if he was a child.

"Why would I have any confidence in their integrity, after their behavior in Portugal, where they allowed Camford to completely foil any investigation of my father's death?" she asked. "When the scandal erupted, the Wellesleys completely distanced themselves from my husband, even though they knew the truth of what happened. Alec's career was at an end, his attempts to seek answers were blocked. Ultimately, he did what he could to keep his agents safe, and they castigated him for it. The Convention of Cintra grieved my husband to no end. He fully believed he could have prevented it."

"Those of us in the field could scarcely believe the sheer stupidity of the agreement with Junot." Stephan shook his head, still trying to find a flaw in Fiona's reasoning.

"When George informed the Foreign Secretary that my husband could be the scapegoat to be sent off into the wilderness in penance for Cintra, I have no doubt that the cabal of Wellesley brothers danced with joy. And when that chosen sacrifice seemingly decided to throw himself off the cliff with all the blame attached, I am sure that they sighed with relief." Fiona's look pierced him with its hopelessness.

She put a hand on Stephan's shoulder. "I know that you work for them, but do you truly believe that Richard, Arthur, or Henry wish to see that powder keg of that debacle broached again?" she asked, hoarsely. "Especially since Viscount Wellington was nearly blown to bits by the scandal of Cintra."

"Let me help you," Stephan opened his arms and she walked into his embrace. "Tell me what I can do." Even as he offered his aid, he felt a twinge of guilt.

"I know there are records of what happened that night in Portugal," she said. "I truly believe that it all began with my father's murder. Alec was searching for those documents, and I think that his investigation stirred the hornets' nest. Find me those papers, and I think that we shall have our answers. But for now, this is the help I need most." She put her arms around him and looked up to gaze into the depths of his soul.

"You believe me," she whispered, those glorious eyes of hers gleaming with unshed tears and joy. "You believe me."

He wanted to. God help him. Stephan desperately wanted to. He kissed her lightly and stepped away, afraid of the invitation in her eyes and what he might do if he accepted.

Scanning the familiar room once more, he stared at the table that held the brandy decanter. Many an hour had been spent in those nearby chairs, evenings of conversation, chess, and cribbage. It was almost as if Alec had left and was just about to return. But there was something amiss.

Stephan moved closer. The liquor was gone. Over time, any remaining alcohol had evaporated. At the bottoms of the glasses there were still traces of residue.

"Yes, I believe you, Fiona," Stephan told her, the last of his doubts finally dismissed. "Alec did not take his own life, but there is one detail you missed."

Fiona tilted her head, waiting for an explanation.

"The decanter," Stephan pointed to the table. "The stopper is on the table, despite the fact that Alec always was ever meticulous about preserving every drop of his best." He held up the glasses.

"There are two. Alec likely knew his killer," Fiona whispered.

Stephan nodded. "Knew him well enough to share his finest brandy."

. . .

London was well into its early morning bustle as Stephan made his way home. His original intent after meeting with Fiona, had been to call upon Richard to discuss the latest developments. After Fiona's revelations, though, Stephan felt he needed time to think matters through.

He was not surprised to find that there was no one waiting to receive his horse. His household had been informed that he would be gone for most of the day. To his chagrin, Stephan had discovered that failing to apprise Hollins of his schedule led to storms in the kitchen.

After several instances of having his chef's offerings served exclusively as leavings to the staff, threats of notice had ensued. Given the superb qualities of the meals that his kitchen produced, Stephan had been more than willing to concede the details of his comings and goings in order to soothe his employee's need for proper appreciation of his culinary art.

As he led Echo into the stables, a startled groom dropped the leathers that he was cleaning.

"So sorry, milord." he gasped. "We was told you be out till nigh on evening, else there would ha' been someone out waitin' on you. Let me tell them in the kitchen."

"No need to trouble them," Stephan said with a smile as he handed over the reins. "I've just come to change clothes before taking breakfast with a friend."

He took the back gate from the mews and was starting up the stairs when he heard a noise in the study. Apparently, his orders must not have been properly relayed to the staff. The room was supposed to remain locked, with no one allowed to enter save him. George's papers were a muddle of unpaid bills, neglected estate business, correspondence and documents that should never have left Whitehall. It would take months to sort it all, and he had been slowly organizing the mess in terms of priority. The last thing he needed was someone deciding to *tidy up* his hard-won progress.

Upon entry he found, to his relief, that the piles of paper seemed undisturbed. The draperies remained closed. However, a lone candle burned on the inlaid side table, where a variety of what appeared to be jewelry cases were arrayed. The rustle of skirts in the corner of the room led him to the source of the disturbance that he had heard.

"Lillian, this is quite the surprise!"

With a startled intake of breath, his cousin's widow let go of the box in her hand.

"Allow me." Stephan retrieved the case and pulled the draperies open to the morning light. He sneezed at the cloud of dust.

"This is intolerable!" Lillian declared. "I must have a

word with the staff at once!" She made to leave the room, but Stephan stood between her and the door, blocking her way.

"Indeed, a word with the staff might be in order," Stephan said, recalling with growing suspicion the groom's consternation at his early return. "I shall attend to it myself. But first, let us discover what we have here before we call upon others to serve as witnesses."

Lillian stood stock still, obviously rooted by the threat implicit in his deceptively mild tones. Like a trapped rat in search of an avenue of escape, her gaze darted to and fro, then fixed fearfully on the case in his hand. She jumped as Stephan opened the clasp.

A diamond parure sparkled in the sunlight. "The Camford Wedding set. I was wondering where these had gotten to." He set it aside on the table and unfastened a similar box. "And the matching earrings."

Lillian found her voice. "They are hopelessly old-fashioned, aren't they? George gave them to me, and I refused to wear them."

"Well, if you now have come to regret the lost opportunity, I believe you have missed your chance," Stephan remarked, opening boxes randomly to reveal a variety of valuable pieces that had been in the family for generations.

"Those were given to me," Lillian moved forward, reaching for a diamond set.

Stephan gave her a look that had quelled many a subordinate in the ranks. The countess retracted her fingers, as if bitten.

"And you shall have any gifts that you received over the course of your marriage returned to your care, as was, no doubt, agreed upon in your settlements," he informed her in chill tones, as he shut the lids. "However, I shall sort through this. That which is part of the family legacy will remain in my keeping, for the next countess."

"If you have cast your eyes upon Denby's widow for

that role, there is much about that strumpet that you do not know." Lillian's countenance lit with malicious glee. "She was a spy, and you can easily guess the currency she used to pay for information."

"Do you know the penalty for revealing the identity of His Majesty's secret agents, Lillian? It is considered a form of treason." He moved toward her and she backed away, hand upon her breast in a gesture worthy of a theatrical heroine.

"I was trying to protect you, and the honor of our family," Lillian protested, only to be met with a look of menacing disdain. With her back to the wall, she quavered. "I would have said nothing, had I not known that you are in Richard's confidence."

Stephan realized that the woman could explode everything with her jealousy. "If either Richard or I hear any whispers about Lady Denby's previous activities for the Crown, we will assume that you are the source, Lillian," he warned. "Do you understand?"

"Of c-course," she stammered. Something flitted across her face, so quickly Stephan was not quite certain what he had seen, until she spoke again, her voice sure, seductively smooth as lush velvet. "For you, Stephan, I shall stay silent. All I am seeking is what belongs to me. But I was wrong not to ask you outright." She put a hand on his sleeve. "You ought to punish me. I have been a bad girl."

Stephan was about to shrug off her touch until he chanced to look beyond her at the open safe that had been hidden behind the paneling in the wall. The compartment was so cleverly concealed that he doubted it would have been found, but for Lillian's attempted pilfering. He manufactured a leering smirk.

"Yes, indeed," Stephan agreed, putting his hand upon hers. "You have been naughty. But before I punish you, show me how this opens and closes."

With new-found eagerness, Lillian demonstrated the closure in a carved rosette nearby.

"The keys, where did you find them?"

"George kept a set in his desk drawer," she said brightly. Stephan quickly found a ring and walked over to the safe. He removed another key from the lock, noting the pristine state of the keys on Lillian's ring in comparison to the ones in the desk.

He held the two rings up in unspoken question.

Lillian reddened. "George made me a set of my own." she said. "He didn't want to be bothered when I wanted a piece of jewelry to wear. You understand. We women dither so, making those choices."

Stephan's gaze swept the collection of boxes. "I can see that," he commented, unable to conceal the sarcasm as he locked the door and reset the disguising panel.

"I should not have done this without your consent. You truly ought to punish me." Lillian's voice grew husky as she moved closer. The excited glitter in her eyes roused both his disgust and caution. She attempted to pull him into her embrace, but he stepped aside and grasped the tasseled fabric cord to summon Hollins, before drawing the outer door open to public view. It seemed wise to have a witness and a chaperone.

"Remember the word *treason*, Countess. It would be a shame to stretch that lovely neck by way of a noose."

There was no telling what she might have replied in her patent fury, but the butler's arrival effectively silenced her. Hollins raised an eloquent eyebrow at Lady Camford's presence, as if to say, *How did she come to be here? I know I did not let her in.*

"It would seem that I no longer have to undertake the journey to Camford Keep." Under the circumstances, Stephan could not bring himself to feign a smile. "We must thank the countess for alerting us to the whereabouts of the missing family jewelry."

"I'm sorry for the delay, milord, but I was in the midst of checking the wine cellar."

Which the entire staff doubtless knew. "The wines will not suffer for waiting. If you would assist me in compiling a list of these treasures so that we may compare it to the reckoning the solicitor holds," Stephan said. "I am quite certain we can sort out that which properly belongs to the lady. My thanks, Lillian."

"Then, I shall be going." She said with a sniff. "My work here is done."

She reached for the reticule on the table, but Stephan picked it up first, noticing its unusual heft. He undid the bag and, to Lady Camford's open-mouthed dismay, emptied its contents. A few coins, a crumpled handkerchief, a card case, and a gold chain set in sapphires, with a matching bracelet and ear bobs, dropped to the table. "I believe I saw my Great-Grandmama wearing this very set in her portrait" He replaced the personal items and returned the reticule with a flourish. "We would not want you to have to inconvenience yourself to return these because you took them *by mistake*, would we? If there are any other family pieces, I expect them to be returned."

"There is an identical safe at the Keep, you might look there," Lillian suggested, her ire barely contained.

"Would you like me to call you a carriage or would you prefer to walk on this lovely day, since I have relieved you of some of your heavier burdens?" Stephan asked.

Lillian shook her head stiffly. "I believe I shall walk," she declared.

Stephan escorted her to the front door and watched her stalk away. Returning to the study, he heard a muffled noise and saw his butler nearly bent double before the hearth.

"Are you well Hollins?" Stephan rushed to the servant's side.

"Never better... milord." The man responded, pulling himself upright with noticeable effort, his hand rising to cover his mouth. But the gale of mirth could not be contained. "Forgive me...milord." Hollins gasped between gusts of laughter. "But...but...*relieved you of...some of your heavier burdens.* That was...that was...prime!"

"Wasn't it just? I have seen looters on the battlefield with more finesse." Stephan said, with a humorous quirk that quickly disappeared. "There may be yet another set of keys. Summon a locksmith and inform Barton that I wish to see the new groom immediately."

Stephan was unsurprised to find that his newest employee had not even bothered to unsaddle Echo before he made himself scarce.

NINE

But to see her was to love her,
Love but her, and love for ever.

— ROBERT BURN, AULD
LANG SYNE

Lady Melbourne congratulated herself as she greeted her most recently arrived guest. She had scored quite a coup, for she was the first hostess to receive the new Earl of Camford. It was an acquaintance that she vowed to cultivate. He was, after all, a neighbor, Camford House being but a few doors away from Melbourne House.

Moreover, she saw the newly made Lord Camford as a rising star. He was at Wellington's right hand, and a trusted confidante of the Foreign Secretary, definitely one of those select young men bound to grow in power and influence. A friendship with Camford would be a definite political asset.

Lady Soames was arriving, and the hostess could scarcely wait to see her rival's reaction when she realized that not only had Camford chosen to attend the Melbourne ball, but that rascal Francisco de Miranda had arrived with his handsome young protégé, Simón Bolívar.

The dashing, wealthy, Spanish colonial had caused the stones of the rumor mill to grind heavily since his appearance at Almack's, and the bread that had been made of that grist was rapidly rising.

His two dances with the notorious Lady Denby had quickly provided a yeasty chinwag that fermented as it spread throughout London. Although Lady Melbourne usually added a salutary measure of salt to all the rumors she consumed, their waltz at Almack's had set many a lady's fan aflutter to cool the heat they had produced. A variety of *toos* had been used to describe their tryst upon the floor, *too* close, *too* passionate, *too* lewd, among the many.

The new Lord Camford had provided the butter that was being spread liberally upon the loaf of delicious gossip. He had been depicted as a lone figure, sitting among the wallflowers, looking either woebegone or wrathful, or at times both, depending upon who had the telling of the tale. As for Lady Denby, until Camford's arrival, she and her companion had been described as isolated, yet proud as princesses among the peasants.

It was an attitude that Lady Melbourne could applaud. The gel had gumption, and apparently, the Prince's approval. Wellington was seemingly looking the other way and ignoring the talk as well. Quite the coup, since that man's big nose tended to notoriously invade the business of his minions. All in all, there seemed wisdom in cultivating the young widow, despite her unsavory reputation.

As for the stigma of Lord Denby's death, Lady Melbourne blamed the old fool for ending his life so dramatically. In her estimation, if his wife had been unfaithful, she had conducted herself with exemplary discretion. No one would have been the wiser if the man had simply kept quiet and lived with his horns. To Lady Melbourne's knowledge, which was considerable, no name had ever been linked to Lady Denby. Despite the earlier rumors that her husband had shuffled off this mortal coil believing that his wife's lover had sired a cuckoo for his nest, his nephew, Nigel Brewster, was declaring stoutly that the heir was the very image of his father.

The widow was already surrounded by a court of eager young swains, all vying for her attention. Dressed in a white samite and silver gown of Grecian style, she carried herself like a young goddess, seemingly oblivious of the fact that she was the object of whispers and curiosity. It would appear that others too, were considering the calculus of her discredit, and weighed her wealth and beauty against past disgrace, with the result that the past blemishes on her character were rapidly being blotted away.

The hoped-for drama had already begun. Lord Camford and Bolívar eyed each other like pugilists on the verge of a mill. Bolívar won the first round, escorting Lady Denby onto the floor. Lord Camford retired to his corner with a look that piqued Lady Melbourne's curiosity. There seemed something more intriguing there than mere jealousy.

As Fiona and Bolívar took their places, Stephan's good leg tapped impatient time to the music. Wellington had been so sure of the lure of the Camford wealth and title that he had not reckoned with the possibility of competition for the lady's favors. At least the pose of jealousy was easy to maintain since the reason for his pursuit of Fiona had changed from a sham to a reality.

Percy lumbered up to Stephan. "If looks were bullets, my friend, Bolívar would be riddled with holes," he joked.

"I did not realize that I was so obvious." The partners had come together in the figure of the dance. Bolívar wore the countenance of a man who had found the woman of his heart's desire and was determined to win her. Fiona was laughing, her eyes sparkling with some glorious brightness, as if she were lit from within.

But Percy was not listening. His attention was focused on Carlotta, who had just entered the ballroom wearing a gown of peony red.

"Who is that?" Percy growled, gesturing to the corner where she was conversing with a man in evening dress.

"And now whom are *you* slaying with your looks?" Stephan asked.

"Dunno, but he looks damnably familiar somehow, and she is standing very close, all but whispering in his ear." Percy rose, then shook his head. "No matter, he's abandoned the field. I shall now go and worship at my lady's feet."

"Nonsense, you lummox. Lady Melbourne would never allow you to clutter her ballroom in such a ridiculous fashion. Worship on your feet, man, like the rest of the pilgrims."

Fiona had elected to sit through the next dance in order to bear Stephan company.

"Have you ever seen anything more graceful?" Fiona asked softly.

To his relief, she was not speaking of the departing Bolívar. Her gaze was fixed upon Percy and Carlotta as they danced the waltz. Stephan could not help but smile as he watched the couple sweep across the floor. The two moved in a perfect accord of stately elegance, their steps in faultless harmony.

"Are you sorry that you are not dancing?" Stephan asked.

"Not at all." Fiona shook her head with a smile. "I am glad of the respite, especially in a room as hot as this."

"Lady Melbourne heard that Prinny might come, so she ordered all the windows shut in deference to him." Stephan was feeling considerable heat himself, less due to the closeness of the room than the proximity of the woman beside him. "Perhaps we could seek some cool air on the terrace?" he suggested, taking up his cane and offering his elbow.

The garden was lit with lanterns that swayed in the light breeze, casting shadows among the fountains and shrubbery. Because so many other couples had sought respite outdoors, they had to go far afield to find a solitary stone bench by the garden wall.

Stephan had spent a restless night, thinking or dreaming of Fiona. Near dawn, it had finally occurred to him that he might be able to honorably serve two masters at the same time. Cooperating with Fiona's investigation of her husband's murder would help him to gain her confidence, and thereby enhance the degree of intimacy and confidence that Wellington and his brother were seeking to create. Her innocence would be established. At the same time, solving the puzzle of Alec's death might bring them closer to the true identity of Hades.

Still, he could not help but feel a sense of conflict. Her face was bathed in moonlight, hair shining, with a dark coil of velvet woven with ribbons of silver. He ached to let it loose, watch it cascade down her back and shoulders. There was a piece of him, though, that held back. That thinking, logical part wondered what would happen when she found out the truth. He could only hope that she would understand that he was doing no more than his duty.

Fiona hummed softly with the music, stopping herself to offer a self-conscious apology. "I must apologize, this was one of my mother's favorite tunes."

"It is I who ought to be seeking forgiveness," he countered. "Despite your polite denial, I know that I'm keeping you from the floor. Did your mother love to dance as much as you clearly do?"

"I believe she did, although opportunities were rare," Fiona recalled. The dingy apartment in Montmartre was clear in her mind. "I remember once, in Paris, playing this very piece for her, and Da came into the door. He swept her up into his arms and the two of them danced around the room. It was the last time I remember Da laughing out loud. She died soon after. Shot, trying to help a family escape Paris. She stayed behind, provided covering fire while they got away. She didn't."

His fingers found hers and his clasp provided surprising comfort.

"How old were you?" he asked.

"It was just before I turned twelve. Sometimes when he would hit the bottom of the bottle, he would say that Mama was his heart and he buried it with her." She shook her head, as if that could somehow banish the memory. "Maybe it was the truth, because there was a hardness about him, after."

A cruel thing to say to a child, Stephan thought. "Was that when you began to—" He trailed off into uncertainty.

Fiona eyed him with amusement. His curiosity was delightfully transparent. She had never fully realized how much effort was involved in trying to listen to the true meaning beneath people's words, never taking anything at face value. Fiona had not considered the possibility that honesty might be a powerful aphrodisiac.

She moved closer to him until they were almost shoulder to shoulder. Keeping her voice to close to a whisper, she answered the question he was obviously reluctant to ask.

"Other than carrying an occasional message, my parents had never allowed me to become a part of their work. After she died, Da tried to send me away, to a ladies' seminary in London."

"*Tried?*"

"Caught that, I see." There was girlish mischief in her look. "I ran away, and caught up with Da in Brussels."

Twelve. He did a swift calculation, counting back the years. Likely, it was about the time that his father had just sold out, or was near to doing so. Stephan pictured Fiona as a young girl, daring to journey alone across a continent riven by war. His expression must have betrayed his dismay. This time, it was her fingers that squeezed his and she topped their twined clasp with her left hand in a gesture of comfort.

"Never fear—I travelled as a boy, and you yourself know how convincing I can be. I took my old guitar and played for my supper and lodging. Didn't sing though." While Stephan quailed at the potential disaster, Fiona clearly deemed it a clever jest. "Although I had never actively participated in the game, I had spent a lifetime watching and learning. So, when I arrived in Paris to find my father gone, it was not too difficult to find his direction."

With a smirk of satisfaction, she added, "The very fact that I tracked Da down so easily convinced him that I could be an asset. Though he would threaten to send me back from time to time, my father also understood that, short of clapping me in irons, I would go where I pleased."

Her narrative halted abruptly. "Isn't it amazing how we always seem to want that which we imagine our parents have withheld from us because we are considered too young? Before Mama died, I was always longing to be a part of their adventures, to share in that special camaraderie that seemed to connect with what they did." Her rueful tone was coupled with a look of profound regret. "It took me a long time to realize that my parents' *joie de vivre* was not the excitement of living on the edge of the blade. A spy spends hours of boredom, relieved occasionally by moments of fear and terror. What I was longing for was what my parents shared. What my father lost."

As the silence lengthened, Fiona was stunned by what she had revealed to a man who was essentially a stranger, and yet, not so. Stephan Aubrey would likely be aghast at how much about him she had been able to glean from his letters. He had an eccentric sense of humor, a healthy cynicism that informed his political views, a hatred of war and its outcomes. Yet, he had been ready to lay down his life for a belief in the cause for which he fought.

To her surprise, Stephan smiled. "We have that in common, I think. Even though I spent my childhood dogging the War Horseman of the Apocalypse, I was always Army mad, longing to purchase a commission, to be like my father, the Colonel." He shook his head, as if he did not quite believe his own folly. "Even after he inherited Brightlands and sold out, I was forever trying to persuade him to help me buy my colors. We clashed quite frequently on the subject, and it was only after I threatened to join up as a common soldier that my father finally gave in." Stephan paused for a moment of reflection. "I realize now that he was trying to protect me."

"That is what parents do," she agreed, thinking of her son. "I know that there is nothing I would not do to shield Alejo from harm."

"I did not fully understand how much my mother guarded us as well, even as we followed the drum. It was only when I was on my own that I realized what it meant to have a home regardless of where you roam, a place of welcome and warmth, no matter what chaos surrounds you. I truly regret that I never told them that

I understood." Stephan's sigh was a match to his mournful look.

Apparently he, too, was able to discern her unspoken questions. There was a pause and the explanation came.

"They died of fever, while I was recovering from my wounds," Stephan recalled. "Took the both of them within a week of each other, although it didn't touch me."

Once again, their fingers engaged in a clasp of mutual comfort, as they quietly reflected on those they had lost. The music stopped momentarily, and there was the sound of strings being tuned before the opening strains of a waltz wafted through the night air.

"Did you promise Bolívar this dance?" Stephan asked.

"After his behavior at Almack's, I decided that I had no more waltzes on my card for him." Fiona shook her head in rueful recollection. "I have never before had a man attempt to seduce me on the dance floor. There is talk enough without provoking more."

"He is quite eligible, you know." Stephan's look was searching, as if trying to gauge her reaction.

"Are you trying to make a match for me, milord?" Fiona gave a mild sniffle of derision, secretly thrilled by the small sign of jealousy. "I have no desire to be wed to the revolution. And you might be wise to be wary of Mr. Bolívar as well. He was asking me some very pointed questions about Wellington's future plans insofar as the Spanish colonies are concerned. You should consider being less forthcoming in your conversations with him."

Stephan's look was decidedly peculiar as he raised her hand and kissed it. "Do you think that I am too candid in my discussion then?" he asked.

"Perhaps," she ventured, feeling decidedly uncomfortable, but now that the topic had reared its head, she chose to face it. "I know you have been a bit too open with me about some of the information that you encounter in your position, even though you know that I may be trusted."

"Ought I to trust you?" His tone was humorous, but there was something in his expression that she could not quite define.

"And if I were to say yes?" Fiona replied wryly. "Quite the conundrum, isn't it? My father's solution was to ultimately trust no one."

"And yours?" he asked.

Perhaps it was the poor lighting, but it seemed to her that there was more to the question he was asking. Something significant was left unsaid. "In some ways, I am more willing to take that risk than Da was." Fiona thought about her answer. "Trust is an effort for me, but if you have no faith in anyone, then you are always alone. I am tired of always being alone."

"You are not alone," Stephan whispered, pulling her close. Fiona nestled against his shoulder, reveling in the scent that was uniquely his, beginning to believe that this man cared for her despite the revelations about her scandalous past. When the embrace became a kiss, all of her doubts seemed to disappear, vanishing beneath the pressure of his lips against hers, brushed away by the gentle touch of his fingers sliding down the slope of her neck to caress her shoulders. Fiona twined her arms around him, her pulse racing as her body begged for more.

She felt almost bereft as he gently drew back, his eyes dark with passion. But there was something else in his expression that she could not quite read.

"If I don't stop now, I am in danger of losing all sense of decency," Stephan explained, rising to his feet and drawing her up to stand with him. "Will you dance with me, Fiona?" he asked. "It will be safer."

"But your leg?" she asked in confusion.

"Is far better than I expected," he replied. "I'm not

yet agile enough to negotiate a crowded floor. But with just the two of us here, I might manage to avoid treading on your toes."

She stepped into his arms and he began to hum along with the band, finding his rhythm awkwardly at first. But a stumble and an apology brought them to a complete halt.

"Perhaps we ought to go back to the ballroom?" Stephan offered.

"No, never give up too quickly," Fiona asserted firmly.

"Another of the Bruce's aphorisms?" There was a chuckle in the question.

"Mine," Fiona said with a smile. "Will you let me lead? I've played the lad often enough, and I'm easy to follow, I've been told."

"Hard to think of you as a lad anymore."

Fiona felt herself blushing at his look of frank male admiration.

"There are few women available on the march. I remember more than one impromptu dance where I was wearing the ribbon that designated me as the one to be led around the floor," he admitted with a nervous laugh. "Lead me, if you will." He opened his arms and surrendered to her guidance.

Slowly, she eased him into the beat of the steps. "One, two, three. One, two, three," she whispered, leaning in more closely than she ought. It was so that he could hear both her and the music more easily, she told herself. The scent of shaving soap and citrus teased at her nostrils. A momentary stumble brought his cheek to hers, and once more she felt the rough of new beard, the zephyr of his breath as he whispered along with her.

"One, two, three. One, two, three."

There was a look of profound joy upon his face as they turned about the garden in each other's arms, and when the music stopped, Stephan would not. He re-

garded her, a question in his eyes and Fiona nodded.
With a grin, Stephan began to hum another waltz. They
whirled into the dance, stepping together in perfect
time.

When she reluctantly finished the tune, he began
another.

...

The reality of Fiona in his arms was far better than
Stephan's dreams. Her gown swirled with motion,
wings to their flight. He responded to her lead instinc-
tively, letting her set the pace. Step and rhythm, they
moved in perfect tandem until it felt as if they were one
being moving in joyous time through the night.

Stephan was searching his mind for more music,
when he heard his name, hissed like an explosion from
one of those infernal steam engines.

"Stephan!"

After his size, Percy's conception of a whisper was
the second reason why he was almost useless when it
came to covert military operations.

Startled, Stephan found himself toppling, but Fiona
managed to keep him steady.

"What do you think you are doing?" Percy asked.

"Until you came to bother us, I believe I was dancing," he remarked, feeling profoundly annoyed at the
interruption.

"Do you realize how long the two of you have been
gone?" Carlotta came up behind them. "This was supposed to be Bolívar's dance."

Fiona's face was the picture of consternation.

"You regain your common sense a bit late!" Carlotta
said sarcastically. "He is searching for you quite indignantly. It has already been remarked that Lord Camford
is also absent, and you were last seen together. Fortunately, Lillian must have seen you both making your

way the way to the garden, since she is assiduously directing the search party everywhere else. If you are to be found disporting yourself scandalously, milord, Lillian wishes to be the one who is forcing you into an offer of marriage."

"Can we get them indoors separately?" Percy asked.

"Unlikely," Carlotta muttered, starting to fuss with Fiona's dress, adjusting the shoulders and smoothing the creases. "Too many people in there hunting the fox."

"Wellington will surely dismiss you!" Fiona said. "It is all my fault."

"You!" Percy pointed to Stephan. "Get on the ground. Roll in the dirt a bit."

"Why?"

"Do as I say, Stephan," Percy demanded. "Before I lay you out myself and actually do you the terrible injury you are about to feign. Clumsy oaf that you are, you tripped and knocked yourself unconscious. Poor Lady Denby. She feared to leave your side to seek help."

"It might serve." Carlotta looked at Percy appreciatively. "It is good you have a clever friend, milord. Now weep, Fiona, look overset and worried. That will help to explain why you are so flushed."

As Stephan watched from his place on the ground, tears began to stream down Fiona's cheeks. It gave him pause to realize how easily she could produce them at will.

Carlotta took up his cane and was about to place it at a distance from his prone body.

"Right-handed," Fiona prompted, and Carlotta moved it to his other side.

"One last touch," Carlotta declared. Pulling a knife from a hidden sheath in her gown, she cut herself on the finger, smearing the welling blood on Stephan's forehead.

"Perfection." Percy raised her finger and kissed it

worshipfully, just as a hubbub began to emerge from the ballroom.

"They are coming." Percy bent as if to examine him and jabbed him in the side, causing Stephan to moan. "Serves you right, you stupid nitwit," he hissed. "Unless you wish to repeat history and wed the lady, you will remain unconscious. You could do worse, I think, but she could do better. I will carry you out and convey you home. Lucky thing that you are but a few doors distant. Do *anything* other than moan convincingly, and 'pon my oath, I will make certain you are *truly* unconscious. Do you understand me?"

Stephan gave a brief nod and closed his eyes.

It was like listening to a farce in the dark. Mirth posed the greatest risk as Fiona played the role of weak, dithering female, undone by the sight of blood. He recognized Bolívar's voice and tried to keep from frowning as the colonial tried to comfort her.

Lillian entered the garden screaming, "Stephan! My dearest Stephan!" She would likely have bent to clasp him to her befrilled bosom had not Percy pointed out that the blood on the Earl's brow would smear her gown. Stephan barely managed to choke his laughter into a moan, with the proximity of his ribs to the toe of Percy's boot helping him keep his chortles contained.

The gathering crowd's mood had turned from a scandal hunt to fete, with Fiona being heralded as the heroine of the hour for the simple act of doing nothing whatsoever in the presence of blood and injury. From the sound of it, several ladies apparently swooned in sympathy at the sight of the prostrate earl, conveniently caught, no doubt, by their nearby beaux.

The stones at his back were growing increasingly uncomfortable when Stephan moaned again, this time with real pain. His presence finally remembered, Percy hefted his friend up none too gently, to be carried out the garden gate and bounced down the street to Camford House.

"I could've been truly a corpse by the time you got around to me," Stephan muttered.

"Keep your piehole shut or I swear, you might yet be waiting for winding sheets. Servants talk," Percy warned. "You can regain consciousness once I dump you in your bed. Idiot!"

Stephan wisely chose to remain silent.

TEN

There is no such uncertainty as a sure
thing.

— ROBERT BURNS

Fiona returned home to find Denby House in an uproar.

"I saw him, I tell you!" Dottie Eldridge was speaking in the clipped tones signifying the impending eruption of her temper as she cradled the howling baby. "There *was* someone in the nursery, hiding in the shadows. I grabbed little Alejo first thing and ran for help."

"You've been reading *The Castle of Otranto* again, Dottie?" the butler asked. "The window's locked from the inside and no sign of intrusion, and I've checked the house completely."

"I know what I saw, Adam Eldridge!" she retorted.

Fiona swept Alejo into her arms. "Report!" Her calm tone demanded discipline as she raised her voice over the tumult.

"There was someone in the nursery tonight, milady," Dottie declared, with a defiant look at Eldridge. "I got the young master to safety, but by the time His Nibs got the search up, there was no sign of him."

"Because there was no one there in the first place, milady," Eldridge said, in that annoying voice that men often used when they are trying to convince women that they are being hysterical.

Fiona kept her exasperation in check. "And you know as well as I do there are ways of getting in and out of places undetected. Did anyone think to check the garden, beneath the windows?"

"I was just about to—" Eldridge began.

"Attempt to convince Dottie that it was all her imagination!" Carlotta said, skewering him with a look. "I myself will check, while Fiona tries to calm the child down."

"Move his things into my room, Dottie," Fiona said, rocking Alejo gently in a soothing motion. "We will take no chances. Tell me exactly what happened."

"I was gone for but a few moments. When I returned, I sat down in the chair for a bit with my knitting. You know the feeling you get, when you become aware you're being watched?" Dottie began.

Fiona knew it quite well. She had been feeling it often of late.

"A rat, perhaps?" Eldridge interrupted. "London is worse than Paris ever was, I swear."

"So now we have moved from *nothing* to a rat." Dottie snorted with contempt. "I tell you there was someone there behind me. I felt it."

Fiona felt cold slither down her spine. If Dottie had felt the phantom watching at her back, he had been present long enough to harm her and Alejo both. Or if murder was not his objective, he could easily have subdued Dottie, taken the child, and been gone before any alarm was raised. *Nothing happened*, she told herself. *No harm was done. Perhaps she was just...*

Fiona looked at Dottie and knew that attributing it to imagination was an insult. There had been an intruder.

"I have faith in your instincts, Dottie. All of us who remain alive are here because we *trust our guts*, as Da used to say. When Carlotta returns, we will take a closer look together, you and I."

Dottie nodded, satisfied.

"Tomorrow, we will summon a locksmith," Fiona told Eldridge. "I want every lock on this house changed and every window on every story to be made secure."

"All three, milady?" Eldridge asked.

Fiona's look could have pierced armor. "Could you get in from a third story window, Eldridge?"

"Been awhile, but I suppose I could," the butler admitted.

"We will treat this as if there is no *suppose*. Anything any of us might have once done, can obviously still be done," Fiona declared, trying to conceal her growing disquiet. "We have become complacent, and as a result, we are vulnerable. From now, someone will be with Alejo at all times. If we have been made a target, we will be ready. Understood?"

"Aye, milady," Eldridge and Dottie agreed.

Carlotta returned, shaking her head. "Footprints. Leading to the mews. Our shadow is gone."

Dottie cast a told-you-so look at Eldridge.

"Sorry, Dottie, m'love," he said. "I shouldn't have doubted. It's like wee Fee—I mean—milady said, we've gotten too used to easy."

"All right then." Dottie kissed her husband on the cheek.

"Perhaps we should withdraw," Carlotta suggested, "return to Denby Chase. It might be the safer choice."

Fiona considered. "No. I ran away once. I will not run again! Even if I chose to retreat, whoever stalks us here could merely follow. Any suggestions as to how we might tighten our line of defense?"

"Best we call in the Cutlow brothers," Eldridge said. "They made the offer when I told them you were going a-hunting for your father's killer, milady, but I didn't think there was a need at the time."

"They can be credible footmen, the both of them. Done it often for the Bruce," Dottie agreed. "And if you need someone to secure the house, there's no one like a good cracksman to plug up the ratholes we might miss."

"Aye, and Jim Cutlow was one of the best burglars there is," Eldridge added. "They'll be glad to help. Seems to me that they're right bored these days, running that fancy victuals business of theirs."

"That 'fancy victuals business,' as you call it, is making us all a fortune, Adam," Dottie chuckled. "Best investment we ever made. But you're right, they'll come running for our wee Fee, begging your pardon, milady. A lot of your Da's Scotsmen have come back to roost here in England."

"Those that survived," Fiona added glumly.

"Don't be taking that upon your head now, wee Fee!" Eldridge put a comforting paw on her shoulder. "There's not a one of the Bruce's company that did not know the risks of what we did, and not a man Jack—or woman Jill," he added with a hasty nod to his wife and Carlotta, "who wasn't ready to die in the service of King and Country."

"And thanks to you, none of us have had to go begging to Whitehall for the crust of bread that they owe us." Dottie wiped a tear from her eye. "We're all well to do, every one of us. The Cutlows and their shop. Barnes and his Emporium on Bond Street. LaMer and his— aye, now there's an idea for us!" she exclaimed. "All of us should have weapons at hand. A visit to LaMer's shop might be in order. One of those new rifles he sells would be a sweet treat."

"A good spare blade wouldn't go amiss either," Eldridge admitted, a martial gleam lighting beneath his bushy brow. "You must know, milady, that any one of us would come running to stand by you and yours. If it's a fight we're facing, I say 'tis our enemies ought to tremble. Scots wha hae!"

"Wi' Wallace bled!" The women chorused in response.

For the first moment since walking in the door, Fiona allowed herself to breathe, and reminded herself that, this time, she was not facing her unknown foe alone.

The question remained: If the intruder was indeed an enemy, what had been his objective, and had it been achieved?

...

To lend credibility to their story, it had been decided that Stephan would spend some time recovering from his fictitious injury. With so many eyes, servants and masters alike, watching what might be cooking in their neighbors' pots, it would be foolish to be seen strolling abroad and giving the lie to last night's charade.

As a self-imposed penance, he elected to spend the morning going through the piles of paperwork. Only Hollins knew the truth, since he had insisted upon examining the limb to ascertain that all their hard-won progress had not truly been destroyed. Even so, his former batman delighted in keeping up the pretense, maintaining that Stephan had been driving himself too hard.

It was especially irksome to be forced to pretend that his leg had failed him again, when his recovery had progressed far better than hoped. At Busaca, doctors had told him that he would surely lose the leg. Then, while he healed, their prognostications had declared that he would never walk upon it again. Hollins, bless him, had remained steadfast in his belief that time and steady exercise would heal, and the result was nothing short of a miracle.

Even the prospect of a day chained to George's desk could not diminish the broad grin that lit his face.

Last night, he had danced!

Those minutes in the garden with Fiona had been magical. Even being carried home like a sack of barley couldn't spoil the memory of holding her close and moving to the music that they themselves had made.

Stephan opened the stout lock that had been placed on the door to George's study. His ebullient mood faded slightly as he faced the reality of those piles of paperwork. Although he had worked for days, he had made precious little headway in sorting through the months of accumulation.

Yet he dared not leave the task to anyone else, mostly because of the dispatches or sensitive documents that should never have left the office of the Foreign Secretary. He had gleaned most of them from the heap and placed them under lock and key, in anticipation of handing them back to Richard. It was those missives that prevented Stephan from turning the whole lot into the hands of a competent manager.

More frequently, Stephan found letters asking permission to make repairs, buy livestock, clear and cultivate new acreage—petitions that he was in no position to evaluate. Most disturbing of all were the carefully couched missives informing him of unrest on the Camford estates, due to poor harvests and the state of disrepair of the tenant cottages. George had been an indifferent landlord, content to leave supervision of his holdings in the hands of others while pursuing his own pleasures in London.

Have I been any less negligent over the past year? Stephan wondered. Although he had never wished for the responsibilities of a title, he had been derelict, if the truth be told, preferring to focus on Brightlands what little energy he had recovered. In some ways, it was fortunate that the Wellesleys had all but forced him to come to London and take matters in hand.

A note from Mr. Forbush, the steward at Camford Keep, informed him of the capture of a pair of poachers, and required his agreement that the two be prosecuted, "to the fullest severity of the law, for poaching had become ryfe in the Home Wood. Others must be apprised of the dyre natur of the cryme."

Stephan grimaced as he read on. He would be damned if he would let two men be transported for trying to fill their empty pots with a few birds or hares. He knew that it would be far better if he visited the Keep himself; it was fairly close by. But until the Wellesleys' business was concluded, Stephan was forced to content himself with a note ordering the release of the poachers.

Hours later, it seemed that the paper mountain had not diminished one whit, even though the range of little mounds that surrounded it was slowly dwindling as he paid the massive debts that George and his wife owed to tradesmen. Stephan figured that he ought to pay them first, since they could least afford to wait.

The sound of the brass knocker at the door echoed through the house, and Stephan groaned at the prospect of having to hide away from hordes of company. Percy had warned him that visits from the curious were more than likely. Since the clock in the closed room was not being regularly wound, Stephan stretched back in his chair and checked the position of the sun. It was barely noon, he reckoned, far too early to pay a polite social call.

"Stephan, are you still at death's door?" The question echoed from the hall.

Stephan grinned. It was an impolite social call then. Sure enough, the door burst open and Percy entered, followed by an indignant Hollins.

"Milord, you had expected to spend the day at rest

from your ordeal," the batman-turned-butler reminded him.

"Looks like he's using papers for his blanket," Percy remarked.

Hollins sighed. "Does that mean you will be at home for company, milord?" he asked. "Shall I now inform Lady Camford that you are available for her visit?"

"Do not dare to threaten me with Lillian, Hollins or I shall dance a hornpipe for you on this foot of mine," Stephan said. "Which reminds me that I ought to take another look at the innards of that safe. There were a number of pieces that are not yet accounted for. Care to lend me a hand, Percy?"

Percy was duly impressed by the hidden vault, and voiced his indignation when Stephan informed him of Lady Camford's attempt at burglary.

"I must have caught her early on." Stephan held up some empty sacks that Lillian had obviously left behind. "These look new."

"Could've been cleaned out and you'd never have had a hint of it," Percy declared, as Stephan handed out an array of sacks and boxes containing jewelry and other valuables. "Like one of those treasure caves in Galland's Arabian tales. Wonder why she waited so long?"

Stephan had considered that, and arrived at some conclusions. "I was not expected to recover. After me, the next in the line of succession, I am told, lives somewhere in America. The longer the valuables stayed missing, the more likely that they would be presumed lost or stolen. In the meantime, they were stowed in a safe place known only to her."

"So when you remained uncomfortably alive and Lillian finally realized that she would not be able to turn you up sweet, housebreaking was her best choice," Percy added with a nod. "Sounds right to me."

Toward the back of the safe, Stephan found himself working by feel in the dark. It was only by accident that his hand strayed against a strongbox. "There's another locked box in here," he called as he dragged it into the light. He went upstairs to his own secure drawer and returned with both Lillian and George's sets of keys. It took several tries before they finally found the correct one to fit the lock.

Stephan sighed as he peered in beneath the lid. "Just what I required to make my life complete—more papers. I think I'll get us a lantern so we can thoroughly check Ali Baba's cave, else I might burn the place down with an unshielded candle. Now there's a solution, don't you think?"

But when Stephan returned with the light, his friend was uncharacteristically silent as he stared at a paper in his hand. There was no trace of Percy's usual bonhomie as he regarded Stephan. "Do you know what you have here?" Percy asked, shuffling rapidly through the pile.

"More unpaid bills?"

"Secret documents." Percy wore the expression that had sent many an enemy soldier into hasty retreat before a shot was fired. "Lists of agents and paid informers. Communications from the field, and dispatches, and a number of other things that ought never to see the light of day, much less my eyes."

"Richard will be at Apsley House with the Caracas Delegation," Stephan said, taking up a pen and scribbling a hasty note. "Take this to him, please."

"Yesterday, I was your stevedore. Today, your footman," Percy grumbled. "I'm moving up in the world, it seems."

"This is a serious matter, Percy."

"I know," Percy replied, taking the note in hand. "This reeks to high Heaven."

Stephan regarded the open safe in dismay. "It will have to be cleared out entirely to make certain that there is nothing else of this kind."

"Am I now demoted to chambermaid?" Percy huffed.

. . .

The hunched, wrinkled crone seated herself in the shadowed corner of the tavern. He noted that she had her back to the wall as she surreptitiously checked others who came in the door. Fortunately, he had arrived well before the meeting time and had already established his lookout. He took a gulp of his beer and looked up at his contact again. Just as he realized that she was gone, he felt the prick of a knife's point at his neck.

"No need for that, Carlotta," the stranger spoke softly in Spanish. "You win this round."

"Pah! Unlike you, old man, I usually play no games." Carlotta studiously spat at the edge of his boot, before withdrawing her blade and seating herself. "I just wished to demonstrate the fact that you have grown more and more careless. Fiona feels she is being followed. You walk in, bold as you please to Lady Melbourne's ball."

"I had an invitation, didn't I?" He waved her concern away dismissively. "And I was well disguised."

Carlotta rolled her eyes, but he ignored her. "It gave me an opportunity to assess all the players on the board before we remove anyone from play."

"And what was the necessity for your little visit the other night?" she asked, furiously. "Are you seeking to get yourself caught?"

"I got away." He grinned.

"Not clean. Dottie felt your presence," she said. "I tidied up after you, so that no one might see how you had entered."

"Maybe I didn't want it to be clean," he said, before taking another sip of his beer. "Complacency has its price."

Carlotta shrugged. "Don't play with me," she warned. "If it was your objective to frighten her back to the country, she will not be moved."

"It would have simplified matters. We cannot risk her getting closer to the truth yet. It's too dangerous, especially after she has roused the vipers from beneath their rocks."

"You underestimate her, as you did before." Carlotta gave a sigh of resignation. "Just remember, there is now a child involved. And I am still a less-than-willing tool."

"You are aware you have no choice." Green eyes pinned her in a glare.

"Which is why I am here, after all," she said grimly. "Nonetheless, I cannot pretend to like it."

"You know that I have no choice either."

"On the contrary—you do have other choices." Carlotta's stare was a rebuke. "You just refuse to take them."

He looked away first, any traces of affability vanishing as he swallowed the last of his beer. "Just do your part and all will be well."

"As it was the last time? Your blunder was a most memorable one." Carlotta said mockingly. "Just do not expect me to put the pieces back together this time. Now be on your way. I have an afternoon call to make and I have to go and change."

. . .

While Stephan waited for Percy's return, he continued to search the vault, but there were no more papers to be found. A crash from outside sent him rushing back in to the room, to find that the strongbox has slipped from its precarious perch to the carpet, scattering a snow of sheaves and pages.

It had occurred to him that this might be the evidence that they were seeking. Although it was difficult to imagine George in the roles of Hades, it was not outside the realm of possibility. Fiona would be vindicated.

Grumbling imprecations against his cousin and the foreign office, Stephan started to gather the fallen documents, and almost succeeded in avoiding the temptation to scan as he worked. But when a folio headed with Lord Denby's name came to hand, he could not resist. Leaving the rest of the papers on the floor, he seated himself and began to read.

Line by line, the facts matched Fiona's description without deviation.

Stephan read on, his suspicions growing.

Stephan dug through the pile of documents. Luckily, they had mostly been added to the pile by date. There among the most recent papers was a complete copy of the government inquest that followed the infamous Convention of Cintra. Unlike the version Stephan had reviewed, nothing had been redacted, and he sped rapidly through the unfamiliar passages, reading both the English and Spanish testimony.

Page after page, Stephan checked the file. Alec and Fiona had departed Portugal just before the arrival of the men who had snatched defeat from the jaws of Arthur Wellesley's victory at Vimeiro. Marshall Junot had waited until Sir Harry Burrard and Sir Hew Dalrymple had taken over Wellington's command before negotiating an armistice.

The timing contradicted any possibility that Lord Denby or his wife could have been involved.

Abruptly, Stephan recalled Lillian's comment about Fiona's past as a spy.

Lillian? Taking up the mantle of Hades after her husband's death? As unlikely as that seemed, she had access to the documents in the vault. The countess was seriously in debt.

His anger grew as he examined the rest of the papers. There was a significant gap of several months. Presumably it spanned the period when Alec had been a pariah. Then, entries began again, notations of the dates and times of Alec's visits to Whitehall. Clearly someone had been watching him, but there was seemingly no evidence in the file that would brand either Alec or his wife as a traitor.

Nothing.

Stephan looked up, unable to conceal his contempt as the Foreign Secretary walked into the room with Percy trailing behind him.

"Well done!" Richard exclaimed. "We have been searching for these missing documents for some time now. We knew that George had been in the habit of removing papers from the office, but not to this extent. Strethan here has volunteered to help me transport this trove. We will remove all of these to my office as soon as possible to sort it all out."

"It looks as if you will be playing both chambermaid and stevedore, my friend," Stephan said. "Unfortunately, the strongbox took a spill and the lid broke. Hollins can help you find some sacks left from the moving."

"Call me if I am needed." Percy glanced significantly toward the bags that Lillian had left, but said nothing. Only his raised eyebrow indicated awareness that something was amiss.

"Aye, I shall," Stephan said. "Richard and I have matters to discuss for the nonce."

Wellesley had already made his way to the box and was plucking up papers from the floor, clucking like an annoyed hen as he went. "You might have been more careful," he complained.

"I might say the same for you and your brothers, Richard," Stephan said, holding up the transcripts of the Cintra inquest.

"You are not authorized to read any of this," Richard said stiffly.

"I have already done so," Stephan was able to keep his voice surprisingly calm. "Have you? If you have, you know quite well that you and your brothers deliberately sent me on a wild goose chase, used me and Lady Denby both. Neither she nor Alec could possibly have been involved in the Cintra affair."

"She was a spy." Richard said.

"Who nearly died for England's sake." Stephan accused, throwing the transcript to the desk and crossing the room to confront Richard. "Whose father gave his life for our country. And if you are not honest with me, they will speak similarly of you at your funeral. Because I swear to you, sirrah, if you do not give me the truth now, you will name your seconds."

Richard sighed. "I have no wish to fight you."

"Honesty, then?"

"Aye, the truth," Richard agreed.

Stephan poured two glasses of whisky, gesturing his superior to a seat. The disconcerted politician gulped back the glass before refilling and seating himself.

"You are aware that George had always been trying to impugn Alec's integrity. Your cousin knew full well that he would have been assigned nothing more than a desk and a useless pile of papers to play with, were it not for his friendship with the Prince." Richard sighed and took another swallow. "My brothers and I had been studiously ignoring Camford and trying to minimize the damage done by his incompetence, until the fall of Lisbon." Richard sighed deeply and sipped. "Up until then, we were able to hide the fact that crucial information was being handed to the Bonapartists. We tried to keep the investigation quiet so as not to send our quarry into hiding. Then, fate and politics elevated George to the position that should have gone to Alec."

Richard shook his head. "Once he found out, George immediately began making noises that Denby was behind it. So a plan was devised to test Alec's loyalty once and for all. A plan that went terribly awry when Alec was injured and you took his place."

"But someone else knew of the rendezvous," Stephan posited. "George, of course?"

Richard gave a tight nod. "We were able to keep him ignorant until he somehow found out that Alec would not be at the dinner. Camford began to clamor about how Alec had insulted him by his absence. His wife had to pour him into the carriage that conveyed him home that night." Richard took another gulp and loosened his cravat. "So we know that George could not possibly have been the man sent to intercept you. He had no idea that the communiques that were passed on were fabricated, down to the imperial eagles. The information that they purportedly contained was vital, yet Alec neither opened nor delayed the contents, proving his innocence."

"But in the end, George had his way, Alec was utterly ruined, and the network that he had built over the years was dismantled to the detriment of our cause. Well done, Wellesley brothers!" Stephan lifted his glass in a mock toast.

"Denby has his share of the blame," the Foreign Secretary protested. "He would have weathered the scandal if he had not chosen to marry the—"

"Watch your tongue, Richard," Stephan rose. "Beware how you speak of Lord Denby's lady, because I have not yet decided to forego a dawn meeting."

"Is it because you might lose everything if George is proven a traitor?" Richard sneered.

"Interesting. That is the same threat of blackmail that George used to silence Lady Denby," Stephan remarked. "Has that now become standard procedure for your office?"

"What do you mean?" Richard asked, his face reddening.

"George threatened to reveal Alec as a traitor if she

contested the Banbury tale that he had concocted about her husband's death. She and her child would have been left destitute."

"Lord Denby was no traitor," Richard declared indignantly. "In fact, he had just met with me to let me know that he was close to unraveling the identity of George's confederates. I must say that I would not have believed that George had the wit to build an organization like Hades, but here we are," He shook his head, nodding at the piles of confidential materials. "Strangely, to the very end, Alec maintained that George was at best only a minor cog in the machine. I did note at the time, that Alec seemed somewhat despondent. I assumed, as did others, it was because of his wife's infidelities."

"When did those rumors begin?" Stephan asked. "Were there any before his supposed suicide?"

"More than a few men tried to storm that fortress," Richard said, Stephan's frigid expression causing him to raise his hands in a gesture of denial. "But I was not among them," The Foreign Secretary paused in thought. "Until Alec's death, I cannot recall hearing anything more than the usual lying braggadocio that plagues many pretty women. But if it was not a matter of the heart that caused him to take his own life, then why did he do it?"

Stephan recalled his promise to Fiona and tried to determine the path of honor. Clearly, the resurrection of Hades and the matter of Alec's death were connected. If they were to discover the identity of her husband's killer, Richard Wellesley had the resources at his disposal. Without his cooperation, they seemed to be at the end of the trail. As he broke the silence, Stephan watched Richard's reaction very carefully.

"Because it wasn't suicide, Wellesley. Alec was murdered."

"Murder?" The Foreign Minister rose, his stunned

expression seemingly unfeigned. "That makes more sense than what we had previously been led to believe," he said at last. "I had never thought Denby the type of man who would put sensibility above duty."

All at once, the door flew open.

"We can have it bagged in a trice," Percy announced as he charged into the room.

One look at Richard's thunderstruck visage and Percy performed a parade-perfect reverse and prepared to march out of the room. "Perhaps I ought to go down and join the other servants below stairs for a nice cuppa," he announced.

Richard sighed in resignation. "You might as well stay, Strethan," he called, before muttering, "at least this way, I can swear you to secrecy."

…

To his credit, Richard condescended to roll up his sleeves and helped to bag the pile of papers.

Stephan straightened a sheaf before binding it in twine and setting it with the others. "But I still do not comprehend why you believed that Fiona can possibly be behind Hades? What was the reason for this charade?"

Richard's stony look was a revelation.

"You never did believe it, did you?" Stephan questioned, as the stillness stretched on, confirming his damning conclusions. "This whole business with Cintra was mere faradiddle to lure me in to your scheme to woo Lady Denby. But why...?"

"Do you remember that tiger hunt in India, Stephan?" Percy asked, his normally amiable visage transforming into a glower.

The memory ignited a spark of rage as Stephan grasped his friend's meaning. "They staked out a goat and blooded it," he recalled, "then tied her kid nearby to bleat for its mama."

He glared daggers at Richard. "The man with the rifle waited in hiding until its distress caught the tiger's notice. You spent considerable time in India. As Governor-general, I recall." Stephan stalked across the room towards the Foreign Secretary. "You know how it goes, don't you? When the tiger took the poor beast, the hunter shot. I ought to wring you by the neck."

"Do you dare threaten me again, Lord Camford?" The Foreign Minister's attempt to intimidate was undermined by his slow backward progress toward the exit. "I will have you—"

"What? What will you and your brothers do to me, Wellesley?" Stephan asked as he advanced. "You have already made me into a liar. Now I understand why there was no sense of urgency, why you advised I go slowly. If you had asked me, I would have been willing to act as a lure for a killer and I am certain Lady Denby would have done the same. But you have risked the well-being and reputation of a woman for whom I have nothing but respect and admiration." *And love*, he added silently.

"Lady Denby's arrival in London coincided with an increase in the group's activity," Richard stated adamantly, as he reached the door, implying that it somehow proved his point. "A case can be made for her involvement."

"Politician's logic! You might want to read *A Treatise of Human Nature*. David Hume writes of the common error of improperly equating correlation with causation," Percy mused. "It is *you*, sir, who have roused the tiger to hunt human meat again. Hades stirs because *you* have staked Lady Denby as your sacrificial goat in the village square." Percy put out a paw, as if he meant to detain him. "I find myself vexed beyond words."

"I shall send someone for these papers shortly," Richard's last attempt to assert his authority was undercut by the decided squeak in his voice as he exited. "See to it that they are properly secured."

Percy redirected his ominous glare.

"And now, milord," Percy demanded. "What have *you* to say for yourself?"

ELEVEN

It's guid to be merrie and wise.
It's guid to be honest and true.

— ROBERT BURNS, HERE'S A
HEALTH TO THEM THAT'S AWA'

Jim Cutlow had already secured the last of the new locks and was standing at the door with his brother when Stephan and Percy arrived on Fiona's doorstep.

"I regret that milady is not accepting any callers today," Jim pronounced with the precise degree of upper-servant superciliousness.

From her vantage point on the stairway, Fiona applauded. "Perfect, Jim, that was excellent. However, you may practice denying entry on others. These are guests that are welcome at any time."

"Very good, milady," Jim bowed and took the gentlemen's hats.

"I am glad to see that you are fully recovered," Fiona said, sending a merry wink Stephan's way. She had expected that he might come to pay a call and had chosen one of her favorite new ensembles. The yellow lutestring fabric fell in soft folds from the waist, somehow contriving to give her the illusion of floating in the midst of a daffodil.

If Stephan chose to take her up in his phaeton, and there was still a hint of autumn chill in the air, Fiona had a Russian wrapping cloak of moleskin cloth. Lined with a contrast of pure white, it was trimmed with piping of the same yellow color. Completing the outfit was a cunning Parisian bonnet with a matching crepe band, wreath of white roses, and ostrich feather. Madame Robarde had provided a reticule, ornamented with white silk tassels, chamois leather shoes, and gloves. This morning, standing before the mirror, Fiona knew that she had never looked better.

After her marriage to Alec, Fiona's wardrobe had grown well beyond a few gowns and disguises, but she had always dressed simply to please herself. Oddly, she discovered that she was looking forward to Stephan's expression when he saw her in this new ensemble. It was a strange feeling, this sensation of deriving joy from someone else's pleasure as well as her own.

As Fiona came down the stairs to usher them into the drawing room, there was no sign of masculine approval. In fact, the grave expression on Stephan's face gave her pause. "Is all well with you?" she asked. "You were not actually hurt, were you?" She looked to Percy and found that his normally cheerful countenance was clouded as well.

"I see you have new footmen," Stephan said, clearly sending a message that she ought not to talk of their deception in front of the servants.

"Both are entirely trustworthy," Fiona assured him. "What is said in front of Jim and his brother will not go beyond this doorway. Nonetheless, we can retire to the drawing room, if you wish. I will have refreshments brought round."

"No need for that yet," came Stephan's brusque reply.

Once again, there was an apprehension in his expression that made Fiona feel uneasy.

Carlotta breezed into the entry. "All the new locks are in place," she declared, halting as she saw Percy. "So, Strethan, what do you think of Hume's treatises?" she asked playfully. "A soaring intellect."

"Such warm talk! For shame, Carlotta!" Fiona made a weak effort at a joke to relieve the tension. "You must not mind them—this is how the two of them conduct a flirtation. Some of their discussions of Plato put me to the blush."

But there was no answering smile from Stephan.

"You have installed new locks," Stephan observed. "And employed two new brawny footmen. Why?"

Fiona breathed an inward sigh of relief. Perhaps concern was the reason for the Stephan's strange behavior?

"You might as well tell them, Fiona," Carlotta said.

"Nothing happened," she prevaricated, as she pulled the door to the balcony closed, shivering slightly in growing disquiet. Percy remained unusually solemn, and the muted aspects of both men were profoundly disturbing. "It is becoming somewhat chill in the evening, don't you think, now that the leaves are beginning to turn?"

"Now that you have quite exhausted the weather, I shall say what you will not." Carlotta shook her head and announced dramatically. "We had an intruder the night of Lady Melbourne's ball."

"Was anyone harmed?" Stephan asked, aghast. "Has anything been taken?"

"As I said, nothing happened," Fiona said, trying to calm him. "We think that we may have interrupted the achievement of the burglar's true objective. Alec had many valuable objects in this house, which could fetch a pretty penny if they were to be sold. Hence, the new locks and new footmen."

"I believe Fiona is correct, if he had meant harm, he had ample opportunity to do so," Carlotta added.

The men erupted in a flood of questions that Fiona had already asked herself and been unable to answer.

Percy looked meaningfully at Stephan. "The tiger stalks, my friend. Do you still wish to keep your silence because you fear the consequences of truth? *To run away from trouble is a form of cowardice.*"

"Aristotle," Carlotta said softly.

"Correct, as usual. I have yet to stump you, *señora*." Percy's heart was in his eyes as he spoke. He turned upon Stephan and folded his hands across his chest in expectation. "There is no defense if you are ignorant of the enemy."

"And who said that?" Fiona asked.

"I believe that is a quote direct from Percy Strethan," Stephan said. "I have heard it often enough recently, and if the words belonged to someone else, he would doubtless have properly attributed it. He is an honest man."

Stephan had been avoiding looking directly at Fiona. Now, when his eyes met hers, there was sadness in those sea-dark depths, a pain in his expression that caused her to tense.

"When it comes to what I am about to reveal, I ask that you take my word for Percy's honesty. He had no part in this. I, however, have been less than candid." He regarded his friend with a bitter twist of the lips. "I no longer doubt your wisdom, my friend. If you would not mind escorting Carlotta from the room while I speak privately with Lady Denby?"

His use of her title gave Fiona pause.

Carlotta looked at her, silently questioning.

"The days when I required a *duenna* are long gone," Fiona said, mustering a weak smile. Her instincts were howling, telling her what was to come was beyond bad. "I will call you if I need you."

Once the pair had departed, Stephan gestured her to a seat, but she shook her head as she warily regarded this man who had somehow become so very dear to her in the space of a few weeks.

No, she corrected herself, years.

He had saved her life. But for him, she had little doubt that she would have died in that back alley in Portugal. From his letters, she knew his innermost musings, had shared the horrors and triumphs of war, the sorrow of the deaths of friends and loved ones, his achievements as he rose through the ranks of the military.

Stephan Aubrey had kissed her as no man ever had, and touched the core of her soul. Up until this moment, she knew that she would gladly have gifted him with all that she might give. Lay down her life for him, if need be.

"I think that I would prefer to stand," she said, as fear struck her to the marrow.

"I have lied to you, Fiona," he began his confession, candidly setting forth his part in the Wellesley's scheme to set a trap for Hades.

With every word, she felt more and more the fool. Stephan Aubrey had been recruited to woo her. Knowing that he too, had been deceived into believing that she was working with Hades damned him all the more and made his courtship into a humiliating farce. He had thought her capable of complicity with her father's killer, violated her confidences.

She had always prided herself on her *savoir faire*, yet she had been as naïve as a schoolroom miss, allowing him to use the fragments of a vague memory to take advantage of her. The only saving grace was that she had not yielded her body to him, but the fact that she had surrendered her heart was painful enough.

"I love you, Fiona. I swear it," Lord Camford concluded, his expression clouded with pain and entreaty.

"Please believe that." When he was done, he looked at her, waiting for her reply.

In the silence that followed, she was sorely tempted to be persuaded that he was telling the truth. More than Fiona had ever wanted any other thing in her life, she wished to convince herself of the fact that his touch and his kisses had been the honest expressions of his innermost feelings.

But it was the very depth of that desperate yearning to trust him that caused her to step back. In her years as a spy, she had seen love feigned far too many times to credit Lord Camford's efforts to convince her. Fiona knew full well that the most powerful fabrications are the lies that come from within. His confession might very well be part of a deeper plan. If she chose to believe his integrity, he could employ her feelings to further entangle her in whatever web of schemes that he and the Wellesley brothers were weaving. She could not afford the price of indulging in delusions of love.

"Thank you for your honesty, Lord Camford," she told him, proud that she managed to keep her voice steady even though she was screaming inside, raw with rage and sorrow.

"I love you, Fiona. Please listen to me. I love you." Stephan's face was a mask of pain. Those cobalt eyes were glistening with unshed tears.

"An hour ago, I would have paid any price for those words," Fiona said softly. "Now I will ask you to get yourself out of my house, milord."

Fiona held her head high, watching as he turned and walked away. He looked back in a moment of mute appeal, but she stood tall, holding herself steady until she heard the echo of the front door closing. Keeping her roiling emotions in check, she went up to Alejo's room and scooped the playing baby from the floor, holding him close.

"Leave us for a moment, Dottie," Fiona asked. "And tell Carlotta that I will speak to her later."

From Dottie's reaction, it was clear that Fiona had not managed to conceal her reactions as completely as she had thought.

"There, there, lassie." The woman put a comforting arm on Fiona's shoulder. "We'll be waiting should you need us."

Fiona sat with her boy in the chair that Alec had ordered as soon as he had heard that she was *enceinte*. It had been delivered after his death. Carved of maple, it rocked in a steady rhythm as Fiona sang her mother's old lullaby about the moon to the only one who might ever truly love her.

It was only when Alejo swiped his hand against her cheek in childish curiosity that she realized that her face was wet with tears. Her son had never seen her cry.

. . .

Dressed in a day gown of indigo cotton, Carlotta stood out like a peacock among starlings, in a park filled with nannies and their charges. Alejo was nestled beside her, fast asleep after an hour of playing on the grass. The face of the man beside her was obscured, cast in shadow by the brim of his hat and a bushy beard in need of a trim.

"So Camford was working for the Foreign Secretary all along," Carlotta said. "Confessed it all to her. She was devastated."

"Thought there might be something of that kind afoot," he observed, shaking his head ruefully. His jaw clenched in anger. "It seemed a havey-cavey business to me from the start."

"I think he really does care for her." Carlotta shook her head sadly.

"She's far too trusting," he muttered. "Is she going back to Denby Chase?"

"To lick her wounds and cry? Are you mad?" Carlotta gave him an incredulous look. "What do you think? She's at Apsley House right now."

"Mercy Lord." He groaned. "Cat's among the pigeons for certain."

...

Stephan arrived at his meeting at Hyde Park Corner with considerable trepidation. Trying to postpone another confrontation, Stephan had sent a note round to inform the Foreign Minister that Fiona was now aware of the fraud that had been perpetrated upon her. Stephan was prepared to be cast into prison for the revelation of secret information, or at the very least, reprimanded.

When he was ushered in to Richard's office, he was surprised to find that the man was almost ebullient, seemingly delighted with the turn of events.

"Lord Camford, I absolutely cannot condone your choice to act in this unilateral fashion," Richard chided, very much in the fashion of a schoolmaster scolding an unruly pupil. "But I will not argue with excellent results. Lady Denby approached me yesterday and agreed to cooperate with us in bringing this matter to a close."

"Has she?" Stephan asked.

"We hit upon a most excellent plan. I had been contemplating a diplomatically acceptable means of hosting a gathering to bid farewell to the Caracas delegation. Lady Denby and I have decided to use this as our opportunity to set our trap. As my protégé, you will act as the host, since I cannot officially sponsor such a gathering myself. The Caracas Junta is essentially in rebellion against the Spanish Regency and therefore—"

Stephan decided to forestall what would doubtless

be a long lecture. "No need to explain the endless complications of the fiction that our government has spun to maintain Spanish legitimacy. But I am surprised that negotiations are ending so quickly."

"Oddly enough, despite Mr. Bolívar's eloquent speeches on behalf of independence, his delegation was clearly instructed to affirm its allegiance to the Spanish Crown and I know that because—" He handed over a document with the flourish of a stage conjuror. "Brewster just translated it for me. This was clearly never meant for our eyes, but it was tucked in among the papers I was given by the delegation. The fact that they are bumbling novices worked in our favor!"

Richard sniffed in amusement. "These are the private instructions that Mr. Bolívar and the delegation were given by the Caracas *Junta*. As you can see for yourself, the Crown does not truly have to worry about the Spanish colonies turning to Bonaparte. Nonetheless, hotheads like Bolívar and Miranda, who constantly prate of revolution, are still useful. When Spain's representatives convene in Cádiz, my brother Henry can use the threat of revolution to gain trade concessions for Britain."

"I would not be too certain of that," Stephan remarked, handing back the translation.

"Amateurs!" The Foreign Secretary's dismissive wave included Stephan himself. "I must admit that it is a pleasure dealing with Lady Denby. She knows her craft, and between the two of us, we have contrived a plan of action."

It was deflating to realize that Fiona had been actively communicating with the man who had forced this deception upon him. Stephan had written half a dozen notes to her, asking to speak to her, but the woman had not deemed them worthy of reply.

"Will she be attending this party I am hosting at Camford House?"

"She will be an integral part of this scheme. However, when we discussed Camford House, it was decided that it would not serve. For a delicate operation such as this one, we decided that a house party at Camford Keep would provide the best possible setting for our endeavor. Bolívar has fixed his departure for the twenty-second of September. So we will set the date for two weeks from tomorrow."

Stephan quelled his initial impulse to protest the hasty plan made without his participation. It occurred to him that an opportunity might be salvaged from this debacle.

"Unfortunately, it is my understanding that Camford Keep is presently in no condition for a gathering of anything other than field mice. If I am to meet your schedule, I will require help, preferably a woman's touch."

"A survey of the house and grounds might be in order as well." Richard rested his chin upon his fingers as he considered, his look hovering between thoughtful and amused. "As my brother Arthur has pointed out, knowledge of terrain can make the difference between victory and defeat. Lady Denby will see the sense in it, I believe. *She*, after all, has the wisdom of experience."

...

"This is absurd!" Fiona waved the Foreign Minister's missive like a flag bidding the troops to the charge. "I am to bring Camford Keep up to snuff in two weeks' time, and work in tandem with Lord Camford."

"*Querida*, if you would but set your temper aside and think upon it, this is far better than we originally planned," Carlotta declared, selecting a pastry from the sideboard. "It will give you an opportunity to set the stage as you wish for this comedy."

"Or tragedy," Fiona commented, as she set the note aside and spooned a bite of egg into Alejo's mouth.

Carlotta shrugged. "If you make it so. You know my opinion and I have no wish to repeat our argument."

"I have no quarrel with Percy Strethan. He is still welcome here, so long as he ceases his attempts to play the peacemaker."

"Stephan Aubrey risked much to tell you the truth. He loves you," Carlotta protested. "Any fool can see it."

"Then I suppose that it is fortunate that I am not any fool!" Alejo's face crumpled at her outburst, and Fiona picked him up to soothe him, moderating her tone as she continued her reply. "You were not the one who was lied to, Carlotta. It was not you who was the subject of a deliberate, cold-blooded seduction."

"Cold-blooded?" Carlotta gave a derisive snort. "I think not!" The woman regarded Fiona steadily, then shook her head and sighed. There was a surprisingly profound sadness in her eyes when she spoke again. "And you have never lied to someone who deserved truth, wee Fee? Like you, I have been guilty of many falsehoods and deceptions in my life, but did we not do so in the belief that it was always for a just cause? If you cannot bring yourself to forgive him, what hope is there for anyone who loves you, if ever they are in need of your compassion?"

. . .

As Stephan rode up the drive, he saw that Camford Keep had become a hive of activity. He took a minute to survey the house that he remembered vaguely from childhood. The one visit he could recall had ended with his father's angry vows *never to set a toe in that pile of stone* again, and his mother in tears.

Thankfully, no gargoyles loomed from the eaves,

and it appeared that the exterior, at least, had been spared from George's fit of Gothic reconstruction. Workers were everywhere. Stonemasons mended the stairs. Painters had ladders up on the peeling portico. The sound of saws and hammers echoed in the chill September breeze.

Rather than disturb the laborers, Stephan rode directly to the stables. In truth, he was hoping for the opportunity to sneak into the house and freshen up somewhat for his first encounter with Fiona since she had ejected him from her home on Berkeley Square. The road from London had been crowded and seemingly every passing vehicle and horseman had been accompanied by their own cloud of dust which they had obligingly shared with him.

As he made his way to the block and dismounted, Stephan heard Fiona's raised voice.

"Let them unload immediately, Mr. Forbush!"

He rounded the corner to find Lady Denby confronting a burly, angry man with arms like hams.

So this was George's steward.

Forbush gestured to a nearby laden wagon. "We always purchase our provender and equipment for the stables from Dibble. I demand that you send this back where it came from at once."

"I have seen some of the receipts from Dibble," Fiona replied. "I know quite well what you are paying for, and more important, what you have actually gotten for those exorbitant expenditures," she said. "I will not be responsible for feeding these animals buckets of certain colic because you're taking a bite of the billing."

"What are you implying?" Forbush's face reddened and he moved forward, threat implicit in his raised fist, but Fiona wouldn't budge an inch. "Who do you think you are, coming in here and giving orders as if you own the place? Now go back to London where you belong! His lordship will hear of this!"

"Indeed he will," Fiona said as Forbush put a hand on her shoulder. "And you will take your fingers off of my person, or you will regret it."

Stephan started forward, but Jim, the footman, had suddenly materialized beside him with a restraining hand.

"Let it be, milord," Jim said softly. "The man's been a boil on our behinds since we got here, and she's finally got an excuse to lance it."

"Will you really?" Forbush laughed, pulling her close.

It was over in a matter of seconds. Fiona moved opposite to Forbush's expectation, using his unstable footing and momentum to sweep him onto the ground before launching herself on top of the big man. He howled in pain as she incapacitated him, applying her knee where he was most sensitive, before rolling quickly to her feet and pulling a pistol from a concealed pocket and cocking it to fire with an ominous click.

"Is this the urgent matter that you referred to in your note?" Stephan asked, suppressing a laugh with limited success as he stepped forward. "*La mordida?*" Stephan asked, using the Spanish idiom for graft.

To his disappointment, there was no hint of humor or welcome in Fiona's nod of agreement. He was not surprised, but he had been hoping that her note bidding him to come to the Keep indicated that she might have relented somewhat.

"Who the hell are you?" Forbush grunted, trying to get to his knees. The steward eyed Stephan disdainfully, clearly mistaking his unkempt state for lack of consequence. "Whoever you are, you're a witness to this unwarranted assault and threat with a deadly weapon. I shall be summoning the magistrate."

"I believe that I *am* the magistrate," Stephan declared. "And your soon-to-be former employer."

"It's loaded," Fiona cautioned before she carefully

handed the pistol to Stephan's care. "I have taken the liberty of securing the estate ledgers. He and the skeleton staff you maintain here have been in collusion, gutting the place like a pig for the roasting. Speaking of which, your cook and housekeeper had already taken flight, along with a fair selection of the silver. Jim's brother is on their trail."

Stephan sighed. "I will send for my chef. If you would be so kind as to give me a list of any shortfalls, Hollins will cull Camford House for our needs and bring any necessary staff."

Fiona nodded brusquely. "If you will attend to this matter, Lord Camford, I still have much work to be done in the face of long neglect and malfeasance. Should you wish to review the evidence before remanding this man to trial for embezzlement, I will set the ledgers in the estate office. *Both* of them." She glared at Forbush, who turned pale as a ghost.

"Wha... How?" He sputtered.

"He is also cheating your tenants shamelessly." She dusted off her skirts and gave Forbush a look that had him hastily covering his privates. "I have also brought some of the late Lord Denby's personal items that are part of his legacy to you. I will set them on the desk along with the ledgers. It is well past time that we bring these matters to a close. If you have needs or questions, please apply to Mr. Strethan or *Señora* del Castillo, milord."

The message could not have been clearer. Milord was rightly judged guilty of careless disregard and would be well-advised to keep his distance.

As he made his way to the house, her words echoed in his ears.

It is well past time that we bring these matters to a close.

Despite his hopes, it appeared she was done with him.

Neither of them noticed the groom who slipped away quietly, a smile of grim satisfaction on his face.

. . .

Resolutions and the vast size of Camford Keep notwithstanding, Fiona was finding it difficult to avoid Stephan's company in the final days before the house party. Dinners had become a series of uncomfortable silences with Percy and Carlotta resorting to discussions of philosophical treatises as a form of both innocuous conversation and punishment to their respective friends.

During the balance of the day, Carlotta, Percy, and the household staff served as conduits to convey information between Fiona and Lord Camford. While the servants seemed almost amused, it was clear that everyone else was becoming impatient with the role of intermediary.

Fiona had an urgent question of bedroom placement when she realized that one of their possible suspects had a wife and a mistress who had both responded positively to their invitations. While they were each one aware of the existence of the other, it did not necessarily mean that they would be complaisant with the accommodations.

She came upon Carlotta ensconced amidst piles of linens trying to cull those which would not suit. "Carlotta, could you please speak—"

Before Fiona said another word, Carlotta exploded in a flare of annoyance. "Why do I feel as if I am dealing with my sisters in the schoolroom?" she asked. "For Heaven's sake, go ask him yourself!"

"I didn't know that you have sisters," Fiona said, hoping to distract her.

"Had," Carlotta corrected briskly, focusing far too intently upon the sheet in her lap. "My older sister was executed with her French nobleman husband. The younger was killed when Junot's forces overran our estate near Seville. With the Supreme Junta holding the city and being located so far from Madrid, my father had thought the family safe." Her voice shook with unsuppressed emotion. With some deep breaths, Carlotta forced herself to calm. "The Bruce saved my life and took me in. It was through him that Benito and I met. I owe your father a great debt of gratitude."

"I am sorry to rouse bad memories," Fiona said.

"There are many good memories, too," Carlotta said with a melancholy smile. "Even childish quarrels now have their poignant charm. Perhaps, since you lack siblings, you are unfamiliar with that most dire threat of sisterly retribution." Her voice rose in mock infantile shrewishness. *"I hate you, Carlotta, because you were mean to me and I will never talk to you ever, ever again until I die!"* She paused, as if looking into a window upon the past before she spoke again in a high-pitched whine. *"Elena, you will repeat to me what Roberto just said, because I am not speaking to him. Ah,"* Carlotta whispered. "I pray God that I will one day speak to Roberto again. Last word I had of him, my little brother fights with the *guerillas.*"

"This is more than a squabble between children, Carlotta," Fiona said. "It hurts so much, sometimes I cannot bear it."

"Because you will not allow it to heal," Carlotta admonished. "You pick constantly at the scab to look if it bleeds still. My Benito and I, sometimes we pecked at each other like fighting birds in the pit, but it eases my loss when I remember that my last words to him were assurances of my love."

"And if I let it heal between us only to have him wound me again?" Fiona asked woefully.

"To open yourself to love opens you also to hurt, wee Fee."

Fiona finally gave voice to the fear that had been

haunting her. "But what if Stephan doesn't truly love me?"

"Then you will know the truth. There will be hurt and you will heal, because you are strong." Carlotta put a comforting hand on Fiona's shoulder. "You will find a better love, because you will discern from experience what love should not be."

"Carlotta!" Percy's irritated bellow penetrated the closed door. "My friend the idiot has a question that he wishes me to convey to Lady Denby."

Carlotta rose, lifting her eyes heavenward, as if begging deliverance. "And what if Lord Camford truly does love you and you send him away?" Carlotta asked before drawing the door open. "Is that not the greater tragedy?"

. . .

Stephan had holed up in the estate office, trying to get some sense of the financial mess that his erstwhile steward had made of Camford Keep. He sat back in his chair, massaging the ache in his neck. This would be the last evening of effort to set the stage for the final curtain in this affair.

He knew he ought to be assisting. Yet he was reluctant to face Fiona's continuing silence, the blank look when she encountered him. The total absence of emotion seemed to deny his very existence and all that had passed between them.

Even so, despite the fact that she ignored him, Stephan wanted to be with her. All too soon she would be gone altogether. Once Hades was unmasked, it was likely that she would never wish to set eyes on him again.

The statue of Kwan Yin gazed upon him serenely as he regarded the puzzle box that Lord Denby had left to him as part of his legacy. The inlaid polished strips of

fine wood were beautiful and soothing to the eye, orna-
mental in and of themselves. At the same time, they
served as part of a cunningly devised pattern that created
a locking mechanism to open the hidden chamber
within. Any observer, unfamiliar with the art, would see
nothing more than a beautifully decorated block.

As Stephan recalled, there was only one large inner
compartment to this particular box. To reveal it required
twenty steps in a precisely ordered sequence of manipu-
lation. Alec had considered it relatively simple, a begin-
ner's puzzle. Some of the more complex boxes in his
collection contained multiple chambers, and required a
thousand movements or more to achieve solution.

He decided to apply himself to the puzzle for a bit
before going back to Forbush's ledgers. Certainly,
solving the mystery of the box would be far easier than
unraveling the multitude of tangles that now comprised
his life.

TWELVE

O wad some Pow'r the giftie gie us;
To see oursels as ithers see us!

— ROBERT BURNS, TO A
LOUSE

The hammering and hustle had long since ceased.
It was well past midnight when Stephan finally
closed the estate books. Fiona's discovery of
Forbush's private records had made the affair far less
complicated than it might have been. The steward had
meticulously recorded the dates and amounts of his take
from the estate, as well as his payments from his cohorts,
such as Dibble and a number of other suppliers of
goods.

Forbush had also noted the stolen capitol he had in-
vested in the expectation of return. Stephan sincerely
hoped that the thieving steward had chosen to place the
money wisely. Recovering the coin would mean that
Camford Keep could be restored more rapidly.

Despite the hour, Stephan doubted that he would
find sleep. He picked up his unsolved puzzle inheritance
with the intent of putting the time-wasting distraction

away, but in the late-night quiet he heard a faint rustle from within the box. He tucked it under his arm to carry to bed with him. At the very least, trying to get it open might provide a soporific. If not, it would be a temporary distraction from the dismal thoughts that occupied his mind.

The house was dark, and Stephan nodded to Jim who was making his rounds of the interior. Since the incursion in London, Fiona was taking no chances. Hollins and Eldridge had joined forces and become thick with the thieving Cutlows. Together, they had co-ordinated to create a blanket of security and surveillance throughout the Keep that would expand to include their guests once the party was underway.

There was no light shining beneath Fiona's bedroom door. It was to be hoped that she was finally getting some sleep. Although she had barely spoken a word directly to him since the incident with the steward, the shadows beneath her eyes and her frenetic activity worried him. They had all been running themselves ragged to prepare for the onslaught, but she had outpaced the lot of them.

As he passed the nearby room that was Alejo's nursery he heard a thin wail. Stephan stopped and waited for a moment, but the baby would not quiet. He gave a light tap and waited until Dottie opened the door cautiously, greeting him with a raised pistol. Some of the strain eased when she recognized him, but the drained look that seemed to be common to them all these past days still remained.

"He's teething again, poor mite," Dorothy explained, setting the weapon aside and picking up the crying child. "It's a shame, exhausted as she is, but she'll be waking up if she hears him, even if she's sleeping like the dead. She always does."

"Let me hold him for a few minutes." Stephan put the puzzle box aside on a nearby table.

Dorothy eyed him with a blend of doubt and hope.

"Back when my family followed the drum, I was always good with the little ones," Stephan said, taking Alejo in his arms. As if to prove the point, the baby's cries subsided to whimpers. "There, there, little man," he whispered softly, cradling him as he walked about the room. "My mother used to daub a little bit of whisky on my sister's gums. Just a small amount seemed to do the trick. In the winter, I recall, Mamma would dip a cloth in fresh snow and let Lucy suck on it. The cold would numb the pain."

"No snow likely in September, but we do have whisky," Dottie allowed.

"No snow," Stephan agreed, "But we did get a delivery of ices from Gunter's this afternoon."

"Aye, that might do it." Dottie grinned, nodding her grizzled head. "The little one loves sweets."

"You might want to chip a chunk off one of the blocks of ice we purchased as well," Stephan suggested. "We can chill a cloth to hold against his cheek if need be."

"You were for your bed," Dottie said. "I can take him down with me."

Stephan shook his head. "He's quiet for the moment and the halls are chilly. Let Lady Denby get some sleep. Take him out of this warm room and he'll howl for sure."

"God knows that's the truth. I won't be but two shakes of a lamb's tail. Lock up after me. Two short raps, a pause, and then another knock, it's me." Dottie nodded toward the gun. "Anything else, take that with you when you answer."

"I shall," Stephan promised. The woman slid out the door, her footfalls silent. Now that he knew the provenance of Fiona's staff of former spies, he understood why they all moved like ghosts. He shot the shiny new bolt home and went to the rocking chair.

"You see how we care for you, little man," Stephan whispered. "You are a precious one, aren't you?" Alec's son stared up at him. Nigel was correct. The boy was the very image of his father, and had seemed to grow even more so in the few weeks he had known him. "You have your papa's expressions, Alejo," he murmured softly, "the same condescending look when anyone speaks nonsense baby words to you. He never suffered fools gladly, your papa."

Alejo had stopped his sniveling and was regarding Stephan gravely. "Yes, that look exactly." Stephan smiled. "You are quite right, dear boy. I have been a fool. Even so, I hope one day your mother will let me see you again, so that I may tell you about your father. He was a good man. A brave one. But right now, your mama is very angry at me, with good reason, I fear."

Alejo waved his little arms, as if preparing for an outburst. Stephan offered his thumb and after a moment of fixed consideration, the baby wrapped his fingers around it and drew it to his mouth, tasting, then wrinkling his nose before letting it go. "Rejecting my humble offering? I can well understand your annoyance, but there will soon be better to be had," Stephan continued in a sing-song voice as the child began to settle once again. "While we wait, I shall explain it all to you, since your mama will not hear me."

"You see, I deceived her because I thought I was doing the right thing. I must warn you to be very careful about dishonesty with people you love, Alejo, because it hurts them." Wide grey eyes blinked, as if the baby actually listened to the words rather than the tone. "Someday, you will lie too, I suspect, but she will likely forgive you if you are truly sorry. You are her son and she loves you. Unfortunately, I had no such claim upon her affections."

In the silence that followed, Stephan tensed at the sense of being watched. He raised his head slowly, ready to grab for the weapon on the table. Fiona stood in the connecting doorway, looking at him with an inscrutable expression. Her nightrail of lace-trimmed lawn was covered by a matching wrapper, but the fine fabric outlined portions of her figure like a glove upon a hand.

"You may count on my forgiveness, Alejo," Fiona said quietly, carefully working the hammer of her lowered pistol to gently release it from its firing position. "But do not think to make a habit of telling me falsehoods, my boy."

Alejo turned to the sound of her voice, but to Stephan's surprise, he did not start to wail again.

"He seems well content," Fiona observed. "I heard crying followed by the sounds of the door and voices. Given the recent past, it seemed wise to make sure that all was well."

"We tried not to wake you." Stephan tucked the blanket tighter around Alejo against the draft from the other room.

"I wasn't asleep." Fiona closed the door behind her. "I'm having a hard time finding slumber lately. Too many thoughts."

"I understand all too well."

The hush lengthened as she regarded him. For a few brief seconds, Stephan thought he could discern fear in her eyes, confusion, but she looked away.

"Do you truly love me?" Fiona asked abruptly.

"She asks if I love her, Alejo!" Stephan modulated his disbelief. "Listen and learn, young man. I have told your mother that I loved her, but that was after my lie was discovered. Therein lies a lesson. Love is based on trust, and you cannot have trust without truth." He looked up at her and she met his earnest gaze. "In my defense though, the lies came from people I had faith in. As for the belated claim of love? In all honesty, I think I loved your mother from the moment I saw her. She is a valiant soul, with more courage than a regiment. She was willing to risk her life for your grandfather's sake and ruin herself for your father's honor. Your mama saved my life. But when I first started to realize that I loved her, she was already wed to your papa. As much as you may doubt it, given my recent behavior, I too have a sense of honor, Alejo."

For the first time since Stephan had laid the Foreign Secretary's plot before her, he saw Fiona smile. She drew a chair close and set her weapon aside before seating herself and addressing her child.

"I, too, have been thinking, Alejo. Lord Camford may tell you someday how fond your father was of the process of reason. But I must make you aware that it is often difficult to be rational when you are hurting. It took me some time to realize that the man who holds you so sweetly was placed in an untenable position. I will tell you this again someday, my son, because you too, could find yourself confused by conflicting versions of the truth, without the wherewithal to determine the right of it."

"What advice would you give the lad in such a situation?" Stephan asked.

"If you are uncertain of whom to believe, your grandfather would say, 'Follow your gut, boyo.'" Fiona reached over to gently pat the baby's tummy.

Stephan tentatively placed his hand on top of hers. "And what is your gut telling you, Fiona?"

"You risked a great deal for honesty. Richard, Arthur, and Henry Wellesley are three of the most powerful men in England, if not the world. In telling me the truth, you interfered in their plans. Your wealth and position notwithstanding, the brothers could easily have destroyed you. Logic says that no one but a man of honor would take that chance."

"And love? How should your son know when someone truly loves him?" Stephan tried to put all his hope in his words, make all his feelings plain upon his face.

"Alejo seems to have faith in what he feels about you, and if he could speak, I am sure that he would be saying, 'Trust your gut, Mama.'"

The baby burbled, as if in agreement.

"Out of the mouths of babes," Stephan said, his fingers tightening, he brought her hand to his lips.

"Indeed." They sat in the nighttime quiet, looking into each other's faces. For the first time, Stephan dared to hope for the future he saw in her eyes. After a few reluctant blinks, Alejo's lids fluttered closed and he began to snore away in infantile puffs.

Desire flared and Stephan met Fiona's deep sigh with a rueful smile and a negative shake of the head at the sleeping child. Fiona rose and went behind the chair to put her arms around him. A gentle kiss brushed the top of his head and he felt her leaning upon him. If he could have caused time to stand still at that precious moment, he would have done so. The contentment of her warm embrace and the quiet breathing of the child in his arms enveloped him in the prospect of a lifetime of love.

Two knocks were followed by a pause and then a third rap.

Fiona opened the door for Dottie who was carrying a bottle of whisky, a dish of Gunter's ice confections, and a chunk of ice in a glass.

"Well, now," she said, casting a weather eye upon the smiling adults and the sleeping baby.

"Why don't you get some rest," Fiona suggested. "Come back in an hour or two. Lord Camford and I have some things to discuss."

"Aye, I would guess so, seeing as how you've been saving up your words nigh on two weeks," the woman commented wryly, keeping her pitch low. "Be a shame to let this just melt away, wouldn't it? I'll leave the whisky for Alejo's gums, but in case the two of you are up for a nip, I've heard tell that a good Scots whisky doesn't do badly with a bit of ice." She set the bottle and glass on the table, but kept the dish of Gunter's sweets in hand as she headed for the door. "After all that trouble! Isn't that always the way of it? A lot of sound and fury signifying nothing, as the Bard put it."

As her wry scrutiny swept the two of them, it was clear that Dottie was not speaking of little Alejo.

. . .

Fiona had not realized how much the situation between Stephan and herself had affected everyone around them. The atmosphere had lightened considerably as they went over the final plan with the key members of the staff.

"You all know the areas that are your responsibilities." Fiona eyes swept the table as the former Scotsmen nodded in response. "By the end of this party, Hades will be unmasked and the Bruce's killer will be brought to justice. You all know what you need to do. Scots wha hae!"

"Wi' Wallace bled!"

The group was dispersing to their posts when Dottie approached Stephan and Fiona. "You left this in the room last night," she drew out the puzzle box from a basket of baby clothing. "Way too pretty to be knocked about if the little one gets to it."

Stephan favored Fiona with a boyish grin. "I'd been trying to find the solution last night and I had completely forgotten about it. There might be something inside."

Fiona shook it experimentally, listening, before nodding in agreement. "There is. Would you like me to get it open?" Fiona asked hesitantly. "I became fairly skilled at getting these solved quickly."

"I'll turn my back then," Stephan said. "I'd like to be able to give it a try myself."

He had barely turned away when Fiona tapped him lightly on the shoulder, presenting him with the open box.

Stephan looked inside and set it on the table with a frown.

"I'd forgotten how annoyed Alec would get when I could solve these so quickly," Fiona said. "It's what comes from a life associating with thieves and cracksmen."

"Never apologize for the amazing things that you can do." Stephan slipped the envelope from the box. "It is seeing this that pained me."

"Alec's handwriting," Fiona said, tracing the script lightly. "Your name is upon it. Not surprising, since he was very specific about which box was to be yours. I will leave you to open it."

"No. Please stay." Stephan touched her shoulder lightly. "We can read it together." They took seats again, side by side, and he broke the seal.

"It's dated the week before his death," Fiona observed, a catch in her voice.

"*My dear friend,*" Stephan read, spreading the folds with a crackle of paper. "*I recently received word that you are alive, but in a grave state. If ever you receive this letter, know that I rejoice in your survival. Sadly, I am no longer in this life, else you would not be reading this particular missive.*" Stephan scanned quietly for a moment, then reached for Fiona's hand. His grasp was reassuring, steadying, as she felt the sadness and pain of those words from beyond the grave.

"*I have just been informed by Fiona that I am to be a father. It gives me comfort to know that there may be a part of me which lives on. This glad news is the reason why I take the precaution of writing while she is away from home, so I do not steal any of that joy."* Stephan hesitated, but with a nod, she bade him to continue.

"With Richard Wellesley providing me access to information that has hitherto been closed to me, I have proceeded to investigate the murder of Fiona's father, only to discover that key documents have gone missing. The Foreign Secretary and I have come to believe that those events in Portugal are our key to unlocking the identity of Hades. This afternoon, I managed to locate my notes and your testimony and they are contained herein. It is my suspicion that the reason these, too, have not disappeared is that they were misfiled under the name prior alphabetically to yours." Stephan checked the interior of the box and found a sheaf of papers. Putting them aside he continued.

"I hesitate to put this before Fiona and thereby renew her grief in this most happy time, but I have come to value her insights. I suggest you seek her guidance and solicit the help of Wellesley and his brothers.

"I confide one other thing which I sincerely hope you will never read since I mean to rectify it at the earliest opportunity." Fiona braced herself, wondering what could possibly have caused her late husband to hesitate. She loosened her hold on Stephan's hand. Surely that tight a grip was painful to him. But he took her fingers in his palm.

"Tell her that I loved her dearly and wish only for her happiness.

Farewell dear friend,

Alec"

Fiona felt the tears streaming down her cheek as she mourned anew. "He never said...never..." she began, her voice breaking on a sob.

Stephan's eyes glistened and he swiped his eyes with his sleeve. "I add another lesson learned from Alec. I will say it again to make certain you know. I love you,

Fiona." He rose and lifted her, pulling her to weep in his arms until she could cry no more.

"I have wept more frequently in these past weeks then I have in my entire life." She looked up at him, trying to put aside the regret. "I have been numb for so long and you have caused me to feel."

"I am sorry—" he began.

Fiona put a hushing finger on his lips to forestall any further statement of regret. "If tears are the fee I must pay for joy, then I count it well worth the price."

"Will you marry me then, Fiona? I will be the best of husbands to you and the finest of fathers to your boy."

"I love you Stephan Aubrey, and I say yes."

"It seems that you are salting your kisses for me all too often lately."

This time, there was no babe in arms to come between them. Fiona reveled in his embrace, receiving the gift of his kiss and returning it with all of the elation that she felt. The barrier of lies that had lain between them was gone, and she would not have thought it possible, but Stephan's response was stronger, enhanced by the truth of their emotions.

"Where have you been—" Percy's indignant roar ceased as they broke apart guiltily.

"Congratulate us, Percy." Stephan's grin nearly stretched from ear to ear. "Fiona has agreed to marry me!"

"And here I thought she was a sensible woman!" Percy's smile belied the statement. "Well, we have all we need for a party, and now it would appear that we have a reason to celebrate in truth!"

. . .

The devilment of last-minute details was upon

them, so there was barely time for a brief review of Alec's legacy before the guests began to arrive. Nonetheless, both Stephan and Fiona were mulling the information, comparing their memories when they met in passing, but private conversation became increasingly difficult as Camford Keep came to resemble a busy coaching inn.

To add to the mayhem, word arrived from the village that Mr. Forbush had somehow escaped from his confinement. Although a hue and cry had been raised, the thieving steward had last been sighted by a passing coach. A man matching his description had been seen riding hard toward London on a stolen horse.

"He'll stay far away, if he knows what's good for him," Bob Cutlow declared. "There isn't a tenant or a villager hereabouts who wouldn't relish giving Forbush a pounding."

As Fiona bustled about, greeting guests and answering a seemingly unending stream of questions and concerns, she found herself recalling Stephan's narrative and with it snatches of the events that occurred in that shadowed square in Portugal. With that clarity came the vivid memory of those endless moments of fear and the sense of helplessness she felt as she had waited for Alec's arrival. Now that she knew that her terror and frantic flight had been in the service of a useless mission, the irony made those events all the more bitter to bear.

A trap set to vindicate an honest man had destroyed him. The dismantling of Alec's network had cost the lives of many agents, as well as English soldiers and their allies. Her father and Hendricks had died, protecting a worthless forgery.

Despite her moments of melancholy, contemplating a future with Stephan gave her a growing sense of happiness and hope that seemed to outweigh all the sorrow. A seemingly unflagging wellspring of cheer allowed her to move among the arrivals, ignoring insults both veiled and outright.

Richard had contrived to invite as many as possible of those individuals who were present in Portugal at the time of her father's murder. Once it had been noised abroad that the Foreign Secretary and his victorious general brother, Arthur, the Viscount Wellington, would be in attendance, very few declined. Even those who had been among the most vicious of Alec's enemies and Fiona's detractors had accepted the invitation.

As they had hoped, George's countess had condescended to join them. Her access to the safe at Camford House and knowledge of Fiona's identity made her a prime suspect. Nonetheless, her encounters with Stephan had seemingly not engendered any sense of caution or courtesy. Lillian did not even bother to conceal her contempt as she was handed from her carriage.

"Camford Keep has not changed," she remarked to all who would listen. "Still as unfashionable as ever. I suppose one could not expect anything else," she added airily.

There were many who lingered at the entry, hoping for a nasty exchange. They were somewhat disappointed when Carlotta was the one who chose to reply. "Indeed, that is true, Lillian. In that respect, the property did reflect its previous owner and his wife, badly managed and broken down with age."

. . .

"Camford, I must congratulate you on achieving the impossible," Richard commented, as he surrendered his horse to a groom. "When last I visited the Keep for a hunt, the place was in a shambles."

"Actually, it is Lady Denby who deserves all of the credit," Stephan declared, drawing Fiona forward, hoping for a private moment with the Foreign Secretary, but a familiar voice demanded their attention.

"Ah, Lady Denby, you look even more radiant than

usual!" Francisco de Miranda made a courtly bow, as the unofficial ambassadors from Caracas joined them. "And my thanks to you, Lord Camford, for graciously hosting this delightful farewell event."

The older man smiled broadly, putting a fatherly arm upon Bolívar's shoulder. "Has Richard told you that this will be a farewell for me as well? Simón has convinced me that it is well past time to return home to Caracas, and I shall be travelling with him. When I come back to England once more, it will be as a liberator of my people," he declared. "Ah, I see Lady Stanhope, I must tell her the news. Come along, gentlemen, and I will introduce you. A fascinating woman is Lady Hester."

Bolívar cast Fiona a smoldering look. "We must talk," he said softly, before following Miranda.

"I think that I need to have a few words with Miranda," Richard said in patent annoyance. "If he thinks to travel on a British Naval vessel with Bolívar, he cannot be noising it about like this." He hurried away.

"Like a mama goose and her gaggle of deluded geese."

Stephan turned as Nigel punctuated his contemptuous statement with a snicker.

"Bolívar's attic must be to let, if he thinks of letting that Jonah sail home with him," Nigel added, his expression the epitome of derision. "At least I will no longer have to translate his noxious revolutionary drivel, so there is cause for a celebration after all." He brightened considerably at the thought. "Speaking of celebration, where is my nephew? It will soon be his birthday, and I have brought a gift for him."

"I fear Alejo is a bit under the weather." Fiona kept to the story that they had devised. If the intruder in London was a potential threat to the little one, all had agreed that it would be best to keep him least in sight.

"Dirties his diapers as fast as we can wash them,"

Stephan added, as Nigel's face contorted in disgust. "Teething seems to have affected his bowels, poor fellow."

"Poor fellow," Nigel echoed. "Another time perhaps, when he feels more the thing. I think I shall go to my room and rest. The roads are exhausting."

Stephan managed to contain his laughter until Nigel was well away.

THIRTEEN

And let us mind,
Faint heart ne'er wan. A lady fair.

— ROBERT BURNS, TO DR.
BLACKLOCK

"You are having entirely too much fun goading the Foreign Secretary," Stephan whispered in Fiona's ear as they watched the intricate dance of politics and power that was taking place before them. "Did you really tell him that the expenses for this party will be sent to his office?"

"That was the agreement, unless you wish it otherwise," Fiona said, pursing her lips as if trying to contain her mirth.

"No wonder he is looking like he has swallowed a lemon." Stephan laughed, and the release of honest joy felt divine. Fiona had agreed to be his wife.

"As I think of it now, I should have added the bill for this gown," Fiona added.

"Whoever pays for it, it was worth every penny," Stephan said, admiring the way that the sea-foam green crepe accentuated the color of her eyes. Her hair was dressed in ringlets in front that highlighted her amused grin. The wreath of silver silk leaves at the shoulders and the hem moved in the light.

It was a dress made for dancing and motion. Unfortunately, he had agreed to conceal the fact that his leg was entirely recovered. Although it meant that he could not dance publicly with Fiona, the lack of ability gave him the opportunity to better keep their suspects under observation. Stephan counted the fact that he did not have to partner any of his female guests as a blessing. If ever there was a true coven of witches, it was comprised of the politically scheming wives who were almost as bad as their husbands.

He and Fiona had withdrawn to a quiet corner to compare notes.

"I am learning to find happiness in the small pleasures of life," Fiona said, a look of sheer mischief lighting her face. "I am not certain what Richard expected. In truth, I warned him that this ploy might well fail. Espionage is not a Drury Lane drama, with heroes and villains discernable from almost the moment they walk onstage."

"You must admit that the rider was timed quite perfectly, showing up with those dispatches for Wellington just as we were about to go in for supper." Stephan said. "You did not deliberately cause him to miss his meal, did you?"

Fiona's wicked smile was an answer. "I thought it a trifle over-dramatic myself. But Wellington did quite well with his lines."

"Lillian must be aware of the safe in the library, but now others are as well. So we wait. Are you ready to stir the pot once more? This news should make the countess all the more willing to take a risk."

As the music came to an end, Stephan took Fiona's hand and found that it was cold. He held it between his palms and drew her to her feet. "Ladies and gentlemen, I have an announcement to make," he began. "I hope that you will wish Lady Denby and myself happy. She has agreed to make me the happiest of men and become my wife."

Richard regarded them, seemingly nonplussed. This had not been part of the plan. He mustered a smile, nodding his approval. "Won't pay for the breach of promise suit, Camford," he murmured as he went forward to shake Stephan's hand.

"We must have a toast!" Nigel declared. "To the happy couple, and to little Alejo who will now have a papa again."

The wine and wishes, both insincere and well-meant, flowed into the wee hours. The country folk were on the verge of waking for their morning chores before their betters finally settled into their beds.

. . .

"Do not dare to move," the whisper snaked through Fiona's dream. In the moments between nightmares and waking, there was no mistaking the reality of the point of a knife against her throat. Fiona blinked in the moonlit room, rapidly coming to the realization that it was Nigel who held the blade.

"I have already used this once to penetrate a horse's hide. It will easily slice through you," he whispered.

Alec's nephew wore a smile that she had never seen before. The fatuous façade of amiability was gone, replaced with the confident satisfaction of a hand well played.

"You will don your robe and come with me. You will act as if naught is amiss," he ordered softly. "I came through the window and no one is watching your door. I doubt we shall encounter anyone on the servant's stair at this hour. If we do, we are on our way for a late-night snack." She considered grabbing for the pistol in his other hand, but he was watching her too carefully. "Do not think to raise an alarm or run away, Fiona. I have a compatriot in the nursery who would not hesitate to dispatch your brat if there is any sign that things have gone awry."

Likely, he was lying, but she could not take the chance. "As you say," she agreed in a murmur, keeping her head rigid. Nigel removed the blade but kept his aim fixed as he backed away from the bed. The moonlight glistened on his boots and suddenly the fog of memory lifted.

She recognized those shiny boots that had stepped through her dreams—boots that she now knew had been fashioned by Hoby for a man who spoke English and understood Spanish and Portuguese. The Bruce was right, as usual—it was the question that they had failed to ask that would have supplied the answer. Why had the killer failed to chase her, when he knew she had the packet?

"Alec was the real target that night," she said softly.

His grin was sly. "Figured it out, did you? I had no desire to take on both the Bruce and Alec at once." A wave of the pistol directed her out of bed. "I would gladly tell you all, but my compatriot is on the lookout for my signal and if we are not on our way soon, your son will suffer for it. That would be a shame indeed since I would much prefer to keep the brat alive. As guardian to the young baron, there is much I could do with the entailed property. No sudden moves."

As Alec's closest relative, her son would be in his cousin's custody. One more reason to survive. Or make certain Nigel died with her.

Keeping her focus on her captor, Fiona's mind worked frantically as she set her blankets aside.

Weapons.

It was almost as if he read her mind. "The moonlight through silk is quite revealing. I suppose that sheath contains a knife. Remove it." Fiona tried to keep

herself from shivering as his eyes explored her body.
"You should have agreed to marry *me*, Fiona. I might
not have had to kill you so soon. Unfortunately, I
cannot allow you to wed Camford."

The sheath slipped to the carpeted floor with a muffled thud. Obedient to his waved instruction, Fiona
backed away carefully, open palms raised as he kicked it
out of reach. Hoping that her decision to wear one of
her Robard nightgowns would not prove fatal, Fiona
decided that it too could prove to be a weapon. "May I
pin up my hair? If I do not, anyone we might meet
might suspect something is amiss."

He nodded, still regarding her in salacious fixation.
Deliberately, Fiona angled her body to keep Nigel's
focus away from her hands, she anchored her braid carefully with a pair of Oriental hair sticks that LaMer had
fashioned for her. Fortunately due to the growing chill
of the evenings in the drafty manor, her warmest
evening robe was the one draped upon the chair. As she
drew it on, she stuck a fistful of hairpins into her
pocket. Ruefully, Fiona thought of the other weaponry
stashed in her room, but she dared not try for any of it,
not with Alejo potentially at risk.

"Put on your slippers, Aunt Fiona. You and I are
going for a lovely moonlight stroll."

She could only hope that someone would see her
being led away. In their efforts to uncover the traitor,
they had focused too narrowly upon the guests and the
interior of the house. A mistake. The best laid plans...

. . .

Stephan had chosen to take first watch. Fiona had
gotten precious little sleep in the days leading up to the
house party, and she was beyond exhaustion. He was
glad to give her an opportunity to rest, especially since it
was hours before the house finally became quiet.

Stephan found the surreptitious parade of invitees on their way to conduct their various affairs and assignations both sad and disturbing.

"Someone is in the library." Jim whispered.

"Inform the Foreign Secretary. And then wake Lady Denby."

. . .

Once they were out of sight of the house, Nigel had tied Fiona's hands before her. She hoped that the hairpins she had managed to drop along the way thus far would, at least, provide a trail to point out their direction. Until then, the best that she could do was play for time and hope for opportunity.

"Now that the pieces of the puzzle fit together, I finally can see the elegance of your planning," Fiona broke the silence, as she tried to keep working her hands free. If she could get Nigel to talk, it might cause him to slow his pace. "If Alec had been the one to keep the rendezvous that night, you would have gotten the dispatches, killed him, and inherited his fortune with no one the wiser."

Nigel drew to a halt and gave her a calculating look. "Are you seeking a confession?"

"You did say you would be glad to tell me all." Fiona gave a resigned shrug. "I am curious."

"You know what they say about curiosity and the cat." Nigel sneered. "Move along."

"You intend to kill this cat anyway," Fiona said with a sigh. "I doubt you will have the opportunity to tell anyone else."

"You're quite calm for a woman who is at her last prayers." He shook his head in puzzlement. As she had hoped, his desire to brag soon overcame him and he slowed his pace. "One day, Napoleon himself will read of my exploits, but I humor you as your last request."

He paused and turned her round to face him. "Hendricks was supposed to dispatch your father and deliver the packet and the password to me at the meeting point."

She was unable to contain her gasp of disbelief. Hendricks was a traitor. Nigel laughed, enjoying her consternation.

"Shocked you, didn't I?" he said, amusement in his voice. "When I reached our rendezvous that night, he told me that the Bruce had already handed off the packet."

She shook her head, amazed at her own foolishness. "My father was trying to warn me."

"Indeed. Hendricks wanted his money, said that you would, like as not, be meeting Lord Denby with the goods." Nigel laughed outright. "After that, I no longer needed him, did I? Ironic, isn't it? Hendricks was considered quite the hero after your garbled account."

They came to a fork on the overgrown pathway. Deliberately Fiona fell to the ground, tangling the stuff of her gown in a thorny patch of brush. Nigel pulled her up brutally, wrenching her shoulder. He was far stronger than he appeared, but as she hoped, in dragging her along she had managed to plow a furrow to indicate their direction. "Get up, I have no intention of carrying you as Aubrey did that night."

"You followed us?"

"Knew where you were headed. Once I evaluated the situation, it was a simple enough matter to gather up a few drunken fools. My dear uncle's reputation was shattered."

Again his derisive laughter hissed behind her. "It must have been a shock when Alec married me. You would have had to kill us both to inherit," she observed. "Things did not turn out quite as you planned."

He pushed her forward. "No, it will be far better all the way around. I will have control of your son's inheritance. George's ghost will eventually be damned as Hades by the evidence I planted in his safe after the *accident*." His amused emphasis on the word made it clear that he was the cause of their deaths. "Only fitting, since he leaked information like a sieve and I was forever translating crucial documents for him." Nigel guffawed. "When I *translated* the documents about *Uncle Alec's secret role* in the Convention of Cintra, George was in alt. Believed the Wellesleys were all in it against him. George was just waiting for the chance to bring it all down upon their heads."

"That's why George had to die, before he found out that you were feeding him lies." Fiona nodded. "And Lillian?" Fiona asked, determined to get as many details as she could. She would survive this. She had to.

"As indiscreet as her husband, but had no inkling of the potential value of the pillow talk she shared with me."

"A matched pair of idiots," she murmured. "So you killed your uncle, then went to meet me at the opera so we could discover the body together. Well played."

"Ah, Fiona. You understand the fine points of my art. I think I will regret your death."

At another juncture, she stumbled again, breaking a branch as she fell. Once again, Nigel pulled her to her feet. "Come along. You'll get a chance to rest, soon enough." There was mockery in his laughter. "Or maybe not. We have company expecting us, dear Aunt."

. . .

The safe was almost identical to the one at Camford House and it was open. Stephan stole into the room and heard the telltale snick of a hammer being cocked into position.

"Raise your hands where I can see them, dear boy," Miranda demanded quietly.

"If you shoot, Miranda, the whole house will come down upon your head," Stephan warned him.

"That is true," Miranda agreed, stepping to the fore, "and I would prefer not to kill you. Perhaps we can negotiate."

"Nonsense," Richard Wellesley entered the room. "Put the gun down, Miranda, or you and your young compatriots will end up in a British jail under charges of conspiracy and treason."

Miranda slowly set his gun down upon the table and poured himself a glass of brandy. "And what a debacle that would be, milord. Simón Bolívar, the wealthy, influential scion of a noble Spanish line, jailed along with other august, well-connected, ex-officio ambassadors on dubious charges? Or you might choose to characterize Bolívar as a young firebrand devotee of colonial freedom."

The old man's head angled in an attitude of mock consideration, before he smiled in blatant gloating. "No, no, that would not do either, would it?" Miranda asked the rhetorical question with a negative shake of the head. "It was *you* who brought him to England, Wellesley, on one of his Majesty's own vessels. You alienate the Spanish regency or you anger the colonials. Mayhap, even both? A diplomatic coup!" Gone was the façade of the hapless, jovial raconteur. Sharp eyes swept them both with the cold, shrewd regard of a born predator.

Stephan was reminded that the wily devil had matched wits and come out the winner with the likes of Czarina Catherine of Russia and Robespierre.

"If you confess fully, we might be able to spare you the harshest penalty of the law," the Foreign Secretary offered.

Miranda snickered and took a sip of brandy. "There will be no penalty of law. Because if anything so unpleasant were to happen to me, or I were to meet an untimely, unnatural death. I have compiled several batches of documents which will be delivered to the press."

"You dare to threaten me!" Richard blustered.

"Ah, you Wellesley boys are most amusing, especially since you have come to believe in your own invulnerability." There was a chilling menace in Miranda's semblance of a smile. "When your younger brother, Arthur, went back on his word to me I warned him that he would rue that day. Unlike you Wellesleys, Miranda keeps his word. Your Hades and I came to realize that we share a common purpose, if not a common cause."

"So you admit—"

"I admit that the longer that Spain remains in turmoil, the better the prospects for independence. Even now, revolution rocks the Americas like a series of earthquakes." With a show of unmitigated gall, Miranda played host, pouring and offering glasses. Stephan declined, but Richard clutched his and took a deep swallow.

"I admit that Hades' dedication to Bonaparte's cause was most convenient," Miranda commented, refreshing his own drink. "Even without intervention, Britain seems determined to blunder at every turn." He lifted his glass to Stephan. "According to Hades, your cousin George was a fool—a man who left secret Spanish documents on his desk, assuming because he could not read them, no one else could."

At that moment, Stephan set the final piece of the puzzle into place.

Nigel.

"So, you confess to treason!" Richard declared triumphantly. "I will not be influenced by your attempts at blackmail."

Miranda wagged a chiding finger. "Tsk, tsk, so ugly a word! Most surprising from a politician who knows that information is the very currency of diplomacy. To paraphrase Archimedes, secrets are the levers that can move worlds. Even seemingly insignificant confidences can assume disproportionate leverage. For instance, let us consider the matter of a divorce in the highest circles. How does your brother Henry?"

Richard's face reddened to the point of apoplexy. "You wouldn't."

"Wouldn't I?" Miranda asked. "The question is, would you?"

Jim burst into the library. "Milord, wee Fee is gone." He held up Fiona's sheathed dagger. "Found this on the floor."

"Check Brewster's room," Stephan ordered.

Miranda's smile of approval was a confirmation of Stephan's deductions. "I begin to think you are worthy of Fiona, despite the dubious intellect of your connections. And therein I believe I have yet another lever," Miranda said, picking up the dispatch case from the desk. "Worthless, I presume, yet Hades insisted that I retrieve it and deliver it to him tonight. I am almost certain that he intends to kill me, especially now since I will soon no longer be of use to him. You will not find Brewster, but I can."

"You knew Fiona as a child? Dandled her on your knee?" Stephan said, shaking his head in disbelief. "Yet you would bargain with her life?"

Miranda held out his cupped palms, miming a scale. "One life." he motioned dipping his right hand slightly. "The success of the revolution?" His left hand sank dramatically.

"However, unlike you Wellesleys, I am a man of honor." The old fox sighed. "Years ago, the Bruce saved me from the guillotine. The only thing he asked of me was my protection for his daughter if anything were to happen to him. For sake of that oath, I ask nothing more tonight than your guarantee of protection for mine, Richard. Let my family live in peace here in England. Allow me to leave with Bolívar, and I will deliver the traitor who has probably taken Lady Denby captive."

"I give you your family's safety and you may go, provided you will never set foot again on English soil," Richard countered. "But 'pon my oath, you will not leave this country on a British naval vessel, and those documents you hold will be destroyed." He gulped the rest of his drink in one swallow. "How do we know you will keep your word?"

Miranda stood and eyed the Foreign Secretary with a heat that could have melted stone.

But Stephan's own anger was on the boil. Every moment wasted in posturing increased Fiona's danger. "Lady Denby," he reminded them.

"Indeed," Miranda agreed. "We have a bargain. You have the oath of Francisco de Miranda upon it."

"I suppose that will have to do," Richard sighed.

. . .

In the dark of the woods, Fiona doubted that she would have seen the rude shack at all if not for the lantern in the doorway. She tried to tamp down her feelings of dread when Nigel dragged her through what passed for the door. The hovel might once have been fit for human habitation, but a long time had passed since anything other than animals and insects had made the place a home.

Although her hands were almost free, she made certain that Nigel still thought her fully bound. Other than the knives tucked into her hair ornaments, surprise was the best weapon that she had. Nigel shoved her inside and Fiona fell to her knees. Immediately, she rolled on her side to conceal the fact that her hands were now unbound.

"Who's flat on the ground now, milady?" Forbush growled at her.

"Just as I promised," Nigel said. "I'll head back to the Keep now. Wouldn't want to miss the fun when Lord Camford discovers you are missing."

"Just as you were on the spot when Alec's body was discovered."

"So very tragic. For all his much-vaunted intellect, my uncle always underestimated me. A few drops in his drink was all it took. Be comforted in the fact that he never felt the pain when I shot him, Fiona." His faux lugubrious tones transformed abruptly to artificial cheeriness. "But now I shall give the two of you some time to get reacquainted. Don't damage the merchandise too badly before I return, Forbush."

"Aye," Forbush agreed, rubbing his hands together eagerly. "There'll be plenty for us both."

As Nigel made his exit, Fiona edged toward the fireplace, deliberately keeping her eyes from the stout stick they were using as a poker.

"Nowhere to go, is there, milady?" Forbush sat down on a stool and eyed her with joyous malice. "Now you know what I felt."

"What I do know is that a man who has already killed to cover his bum has just admitted to an act of murder in front of you," Fiona kept her pitch low, getting a grip on the poker. "You did not become the steward of a large estate without having a good head on your shoulders, Mr. Forbush. I presume Nigel assisted your escape?"

"I'm not saying," Forbush said, his brow beetling in what Fiona hoped was thought.

"I'm warning you, I am about to scream now," Fiona said.

"Think there's anyone to hear you out here?" Forbush laughed raucously.

"Oh, I am quite sure that Nigel is lingering nearby, if only to make certain things are going as planned."

Fiona emitted an ear-piercing shriek. "PLEASE! DON'T! HAVE MERCY!"

Forbush jumped up, startled, toppling from the stool.

"Excellent touch. You must understand that my husband's nephew wants me dead, Mr. Forbush," Fiona explained, trying to hide her impatience. "Yet he wishes to be free to spend my son's inheritance. The only way that will be possible is if someone else is charged with my rape and murder. If I were placing a bet, I'd say Nigel will want no witnesses. The poor cull who will be accused won't be able to defend himself, because he will be found dead along with my battered body. Who might you think that Nigel has in mind to take the blame, Mr. Forbush?"

She tightened her grasp on the poker, ready to move, just in case he came to the wrong conclusions.

. . .

Stephan and Miranda met Percy out in the back garden.

"Jim and the others are checking the house," Percy said, "No sign of her. Nigel is gone."

They stilled as the glowing tip of a cigar ambled its way through the darkness.

"Are you looking for your fiancé?" Simón Bolívar smiled unpleasantly as he asked the question. "Because if you are seeking her, when last I saw her, she was walking in the garden with her nephew."

"When?" Stephan asked.

"A strange hour to be walking *en dishabille*. Wouldn't you say?" He looked disparagingly at Stephan's cane. "Do you intend to chase them down, milord?"

"When?" Stephan grabbed him by the neckcloth. "Answer me or you will be eating your linen."

"I demand satisfaction for this insult," Bolívar sputtered.

"Answer him, you insolent boy," Miranda demanded. "A life hangs in the balance. Explanations later. When and which direction?"

Bolívar eyed Miranda in surprise, like a pup who has received his first kick from his beloved master. "Half an hour," he answered sullenly and pointed.

"She came down the servant's stair." They all jumped as Carlotta materialized abruptly in the shadows. Clothed in black, her cheeks smeared in charcoal, she blended with the night until she threw back her hood. "She left pins to mark the way."

"*A chip off the old block,* as Spencer said," Miranda said approvingly.

"That was Milton, who said it," Carlotta contradicted him with an acid look. Percy nodded his agreement.

"Later, children, we will discuss this. We now may conclude that he is taking Fiona with him to the point of rendezvous." Miranda seemed to transform. The eager expression of a hound on the scent lit his eyes as he shed his jacket and handed it to Bolívar. Looping the dispatch case around his body, he added, "We must hurry. Now, I will show you the way." Miranda loped off into the night, sure-footed as a mountain goat. They followed, leaving an open-mouthed Bolívar holding his mentor's jacket.

. . .

The noises from the shack had diminished to occasional grunts and whimpers. Nigel cursed the need to keep watch on the path, but that old fool Miranda was due with the dispatches that had sent Wellington haring back to London.

Even so, Nigel was tempted to go back and partake

of the bounty, but it was far better that Forbush bear the brunt of Fiona's wrath and take a bit of the fight out of her. The steward's body would bear whatever wounds her fury would inflict. It would make the evidence all the more convincing.

Nigel plotted the aftermath. He would weep copious tears when the authorities found the sad remains and puzzled out the tragic tale of Lady Denby's kidnapping and death, after killing her assailant. As the sole surviving relative, he would take on the task of raising the poor lad and managing all of his lovely property. By the time Nigel had drained Alejo's estates dry, Napoleon would award him a title of his own, perhaps even a small country to rule, given the contributions of Hades to the cause.

There was a sound of weary shuffling on the pathway. Nigel moved into cover as Miranda emerged from the brush, wheezing like a worn concertina.

"Do you have the case?" Nigel asked, coming out into the open.

"Do you think me a fool?" Miranda sat heavily on a fallen tree trunk and groaned. "Let me see the color of your coin first, then you shall have the dispatches."

"You doubt me, old man? I am Hades." Nigel reached for the pistol in his pocket, but before he could draw it out, Miranda had his own pistol in hand.

"I doubt everyone, little boy, no matter what pompous name they might choose to style themselves with," Miranda retorted. "It is a good way to remain alive. Put the money on the ground and back away, or the dispatches stay where I have hidden them."

. . .

Percy was assigned to keep his eyes and ears on Miranda. Despite his assertions, they had mutually concluded that the only aspect of the revolutionary's character that they might fully depend upon was his tendency to act in his own self-interest.

Stephan and Carlotta circled behind to the structure that Miranda had found on the nearby neighboring property when he had gone to scout out the meeting point. According to the old man, the place was occupied, and from the description that he gave, Stephan guessed that he had located his missing steward.

Stephan tried to control his dread at the thought of Fiona, helpless in Forbush's hands. Light leaked through the gaps of the tumbledown walls, and Stephan put an eye to one of those holes, hoping to catch a glimpse of her whereabouts. His heart sank when he noted the traces of tumbled, broken furniture and hints of a recent struggle, but no sign of Fiona. All was quiet...too quiet.

He started at Carlotta's tap on his shoulder, and at her prompt, slid quietly to her vantage point through a gap near the door. Forbush was trussed up like a Christmas goose on the spit. Although seemingly unconscious he was gagged with the sash of Fiona's robe as well as bound. His lady had done a thorough job. Fiona, though, was out of sight.

All of a sudden, he heard Fiona's scream echoing into the night. Stephan burst into the room to find Fiona standing opposite him, a thin knife in one hand and a poker in the other. "Sorry to startle you," she whispered. "But one must keep up appearances."

Stephan held her at arm's length, wondering at the tale that might be inferred from the tattered night rail that showed through the gap at the front of her robe. He wiped a smear of blood from Fiona's cheek.

"Appearance is everything." Carlotta's concerned look belied her casual tones.

"Are you hurt in any way?" Stephan asked gently.

"His blood, not mine," Fiona said nodding towards the unconscious Forbush. "Other than a chill, a few bumps, assorted scratches, and sore feet, I am quite fit."

"Glad news indeed." Stephan hugged her close.

"Alejo?" she whispered. "Nigel said that a confederate had him hostage."

"Safe." Carlotta took up a defensive position. "Who would you say coined the term, 'a chip off the old block'?"

"I believe it was Milton," Fiona said.

"I knew it!" Carlotta gloated. "I knew it! Three ayes, one nay."

"She is insane," Stephan said.

"Been called worse things," Carlotta commented, glancing at a pocket watch. "It is about time. If you would scream again, please, and just tell Miranda that it is Milton."

Fiona covered Stephan's ears.

. . .

Nigel was startled by a shriek from behind him. Forbush was having entirely too much fun. He hoped that the brute would not use her up entirely.

"What is that?" Miranda asked.

"The reason I would like to complete our transaction quickly," Nigel said, with an apologetic bow.

"*Cherchez la femme*," Miranda frowned. "If we may get on with our exchange you can go back to your...amusements."

"I have half now," Nigel said grudgingly. He stepped forward slowly, placing a sack in the dirt and stepping back. "The rest will be yours when the papers are in my hands. I too am cautious."

Keeping both eye and hand steady, Miranda picked up the sack, peered within and shook it, before pouring it on the ground. "When last I visited the market, rocks are not legal tender. Sad, how you cannot trust anyone these days."

As Nigel fumbled for an explanation, another eldritch scream pierced the night.

"I agree, it was Milton, not Spencer," Fiona's voice declared.

"Children," Miranda declared with a sigh. "They delight in contradicting you."

Nigel was still wearing a confounded look when Miranda's shot hit him. All feelings were fading when he heard the whisper in his ear. "Even if you had not tried to cheat me, I could not afford to let you live, foolish boy. You could cause me far too much trouble." There was a clink of coins and then...

Nothing.

. . .

"You saw the gun in his pocket," Miranda protested. "Would you have preferred that it be *me* meeting my Maker?" The old man sighed. "On second thought, best not to ask questions when you might not appreciate the answer."

Stephan's expression grew thunderous, and Fiona felt him tightening his hold around her. Miranda's dry comments would have been laughable, but she could find no laughter within her. The man had betrayed the country that had sheltered him. He would be forever exiled.

"So I shall respond for you," Carlotta declared. "Yes, he knew that Wellesley wished to question Brewster. There is a saying among the guerilla fighters, *You don't take a leak in the well you might wish to drink from someday.* I would wager a candid talk with Brewster would have been a prodigious leak, eh *Tio*? Do you actually think to ever get help from England again after tonight's business?"

His sheepish shrug was not quite an admission. "When you have lived as long as I have, dear girl, you find that governments and powerful men rise and fall like the tides."

"I think Forbush is coming to," Percy said. "Glad if I don't have to carry him wherever we're going to put him. My back isn't what it used to be these days. Did you have to hit the man that hard?"

"I wouldn't have had to hit him at all, if he had been willing to listen to reason and keep his hands to himself," Fiona said, as Stephan hugged her closer. "Now he'll be lucky if he gets sent to Botany Bay."

"I'm sorry I missed it," Percy declared. "Fiona with the poker in one hand and the fatal hair pin at the ready."

"A chip off the old block." Miranda chuckled.

"Milton!" Fiona, Percy, and Carlotta chorused.

"Shall we head home?" Fiona asked. "I think the house party is done."

EPILOGUE

Stephan did not particularly care for the story that Richard Wellesley had fabricated as an explanation for the night's alarms and excursions. Nigel Brewster was lauded as a hero, who had gone out for a stroll with his aunt, and died defending her from Forbush's vengeful attack.

In reality, the sticky-fingered steward had been neatly removed from the board. Under another name, he would soon be in a prison hulk on his way to Botany Bay, and he deemed himself lucky not to be dancing at the end of a hangman's noose. According to the Foreign Minister's fiction, the villain had fled the scene of his dastardly deed and was wanted for murder, assault, and theft.

That news of a murderer on the loose did have the salubrious effect of keeping most of the guests at Camford Keep from lingering. Only Lillian had remained, until Stephan surrendered and increased her monthly allowance.

"Got the last of it. Hid the loot in her lingerie," Bob Cutlow declared, having divested the former Lady Camford's luggage of some of the more valuable pieces that she had attempted to pilfer. "It got me to thinking that maybe Barnes' Emporium ought to consider a line on the side. Garments for the bood-wore."

"If you can get Madame Robard to design it, count me in as a partner," Fiona said, looking at Stephan questioningly as an afterthought.

"It is your money, Fee, and Alejo's," Stephan said. "And so it will remain. As we agreed, the settlements will keep it that way. However, if you would allow me, I would be glad to invest in my own manner." He cast his fiancée a look that put her to blush.

"Should have let her have this one," Fiona commented, picking up a Dresden Shepherdess as an attempt to distract the grinning Bob Cutlow.

"Feel free to throw it at me when we have our first argument as husband and wife," Stephan offered as Bob departed the room. "But to do that, we have to be married." He pulled a folded paper from his pocket. "I have a special license in hand. Unless you were hoping for the usual banns, and St. George's, and a dress that would take weeks to make? I do warn you though, if you choose the latter, I'm afraid that we might have to invite the Foreign Minister."

"How soon?" Fiona asked eagerly, throwing her arms around him. "We couldn't possibly do it before everyone leaves, can we?"

"Actually," Stephan led Fiona to the dining room. He delighted in her joy as she saw the array of familiar faces setting up a festive table.

"LaMer!" she hugged the wiry Frenchman. "Madame Robard!"

"You will come upstairs, while I put the final touches on the dress," the modiste commanded. "Your fiancé will send his carriage for the cleric, and we will just have time enough."

"Alejo will attend?"

"But of course!" Madame declared.

As Fiona mounted the stairs, Stephan cast the modiste an anxious look.

"It will be well, milord, never you fear. Carlotta and I, we have planned everything."

. . .

"You need to tell her! You can finally live again, William." Carlotta spoke softly as the man jounced a delighted Alejo on his knee. "Hades is eliminated. Wasn't that the goal you were seeking?"

"Aye, as long as Hades existed, not a one of us was safe," the Bruce admitted. "It was good luck that you were the one that found me."

"Hendricks was a shock."

"Aye, 'tis why I demanded your oath to keep my survival a secret and had you bury a box of rocks in my stead. There was not a man, who I could trust, including my own Scotsmen. I knew George dinna have the brains to be behind the plot. And when those rumors about my wee Fee started again, I knew something nasty was afoot."

"But you no longer have to fear driving Hades underground," Carlotta said.

"Nay, now that Nigel is well and truly underground." He chuckled.

"It's time to release me from my promise, William," Carlotta said softly. "Tell your daughter that you stayed in the shadows to keep her safe."

The Bruce went on as if he did not hear her. "Richard and I searched Brewster's property, and he is more than pleased with the information we found. As Fiona guessed, the peacock kept records of his exploits for Napoleon. I'm certain we can mop up most of the mess in short order." The baby gurgled and reached to pull at his beard. "Now, laddie, if you are aiming to do harm, go for the jugular."

"So what is it now that prevents your second rise from the dead, old man?" Carlotta demanded. "I know that you were close as you can come to Hell's gate and still have a heartbeat. I nursed you back to health. I helped you to stay hidden because of your fears. But now, when the threat is gone, you would simply disappear from your daughter's life without a word?"

"And it is grateful that I am for your care, Carlotta," he said. "But my girl has thought me dead for nigh on two years. Might it not be better that I remain so?"

"You say to me that you did it all for her sake," Carlotta said accusingly. "But I begin to wonder whom it might be that you truly wish to protect?"

"There are other enemies that still remain," He ran an impatient hand through his shaggy mane. "And even if there were not, Fiona can have a respectable life now. She will be a countess. With my reputation, I'm scarcely a credit to her. I'll go back to the Peninsula and she'll never know."

"A coward!" Carlotta snatched the boy from his grasp. "Your grandfather is a coward. He will hide in the stable at Denby Chase, trail your mother all over London, stop a runaway carriage, climb a wall so that he may sneak up to watch you sleep in the middle of the night. Skulk in the autumn chill to follow his daughter into danger."

"Took care of herself like a champion, didn't she?" he said proudly. "Didn't need me at all."

"But he doesn't have the nerve to tell her that he survived and lived in the shadows so that he might protect her."

"I didn't keep the boy's father from harm, did I?" the Bruce said mournfully.

"Do you think yourself God Almighty, William Douglass?" Carlotta asked. "And she won't be thanking me, for keeping the truth from her. But I think that you're a fool if you walk away from your daughter and grandson."

"As I said, I have enemies yet," he retorted. "She would never let me keep her safe, my Fee. I could not bear to lose her like I did her mother. She'll be coming back soon, I'm thinking. I'd best be gone."

"You'll be going nowhere," Fiona said, stepping into the room. She had heard more than enough, but she still could not quite believe the evidence of her ears and eyes. Battered and looking like a tinker, those green eyes stared at her with a blend of fear and hope. The Bruce was alive.

"No one is ever safe, Da," Fiona said, her voice quavering. "You always said that 'safety is but an illusion that we create for those we love.' We can only do our best to keep them from harm, and pray for the grace of each day. Isn't that what you have always told me?"

"Just like a child, to use your own words against you!" The Bruce rose and pointed an accusing finger at Carlotta. Alejo imitated his gesture. "You set me up."

"Remember when we spoke of forgiveness, Fiona?" Carlotta asked, her expression matching the plea in her words.

Stephan seemed to sense that Fiona was feeling less than steady on her feet. He helped her to a chair and held her hand. She took a deep breath and struggled to find the right words. "We were actually wondering who would be giving the bride away, Da, so your timing is excellent. Barnes has drawn up the settlements for a look-over, so you might be wanting to see to my interests there as well."

"I'm looking a fair mess, not fit for a wedding," he grumbled, swiping a tear from his eye. "Yon trellis has many a loose nail. And you ought to be asking the Cutlows about a lock or three around here. Might as well not have doors, given that ye have nothing to secure them. And if it's that rascal Barnes you speak of, who had the drawing up of those papers, then you'd best be the one having a close scan of the wee print, Aubrey, lest you be giving away everything down to your last bottle. Barnes can cut throats with those contracts of his."

"I'll see to it," Stephan promised. "And thank you for bringing that carriage to a halt. Neither one of us might be here if not for your help." Stephan offered his hand. "I believe the two of us might be of a size, if you wish to help yourself to my wardrobe for something suitable for a wedding."

"Aye, I might do that," the Bruce said, testing his future son-in-law's grip and finding it entirely satisfactory. "A wedding, eh?" He eyed his daughter. "Are you sure you want to marry this man, wee Fee?" he asked. "He's a bushel of tells, this one."

"Aye," Fiona said. "That's one of his charms. As long as the tells say he loves me, that's all I need."

Stephan cleared his throat. "So, not having known that there was a requirement for permission before, I might as well ask for it now. Milord, may I have the honor of wedding your daughter Fiona?"

The Bruce looked at his little girl. "Wee Fee'll lead you a merry dance lad. I'm warning you, so that you canna complain that ye dinna know and were deceived in her."

"I'm looking forward to it," Stephan said, as Alejo raised his arms. He swooped the boy into an embrace and pulled Fiona close. "I cannot wait for the dance to begin. *But to see her was to love her. Love but her and forever.*"

"The lad quotes Robbie Burns to me, does he?" Fiona's father declared in delight. "Aye, you may marry her then, and the good Lord help ye both!"

. . .

On the twenty-first day of September in the year

1810, the Earl of Camford married the widow of Lord Denby. Lady Fiona was given away by her father, the man once known as *the Bruce*. Percy Strethan stood with the groom and Carlotta del Castillo attended the bride. The ceremony was witnessed and celebrated by an assortment of dubious characters who assembled under the *nom de guerre* of the Scotsmen.

The bride wore a dress of blue jaconet, with stripes of white. A large, square lace veil topped a cap of white crepe lisse, drawn with ribbons of the same blue. The ensemble was lovingly designed by Madame Robard.

On the twenty-second of September, Simón Bolívar departed England on His Majesty's brig the Sapphire. However, Stephan Aubrey and his wife wagered that Richard Wellesley did not breathe easily until Francisco de Miranda began his own journey to Caracas, in early October.

THE END

HISTORICAL NOTE

Writing historically based novels often results in delightful side trips into history. This book started as one of those journeys. Mike Duncan and his Revolutions podcasts led me to the story of Francisco de Miranda (March 28, 1750 – July 14, 1816).

Francisco de Miranda was a fascinating figure whose role in the wars of Spanish Colonial Independence garnered him the title of the Precursor. His network of friends and correspondents included the likes of Jeremy Bentham, Johan von Goethe, Catherine the Great, Alexander Hamilton, James Mill, William Wilberforce, Lady Stanhope and many of the other prominent intellectual and political figures of his time.

When Napoleon's invasion of Spain prevented Britain from sending forces to Caracas, Wellington took Miranda for a walk in Hyde Park to break the news, in hope of mitigating his anger. The Iron Duke did indeed, walk on, as Miranda publicly vented his outrage. The liberation of his homeland from Spanish rule at any cost was his passion.

Any of this story's plots of political espionage by Miranda are of my own invention. However, in 1810 the Caracas delegation met with Foreign Secretary, Richard Wellesley in London. At age 61, Francisco de Miranda elected to return to Caracas with them, but, as in the story, he was inexplicably refused passage via the British Navy at the last minute. After re-joining Simón Bolívar, Miranda went on to play a pivotal role in the fight for South American Independence. For the rest of his tale, I highly recommend Mike Duncan's podcasts as a great jumping off point. *Revolutions* is a fascinating,

fun and always interesting way to learn about the up-
heavals that shaped the modern world.

Also by Rita Boucher

ABOUT THE AUTHOR

Rita Boucher is the author of seven novels, including Miss Gabriel's Gambit. If you'd like to send her a message, please feel free to write her c/o Oliver Heber Books @publisher@oliver-heberbooks.com